BACK NOW

BACK NOW

Glenn Oleksak

STATION
SQUARE
MEDIA

New York, New York

BACK NOW

Editorial: Write to Sell Your Book, LLC
Cover and Interior Design: Karen Hudson
Production Management: Janet Spencer King

Printed in the United States of America for Worldwide Distribution.
ISBN: 978-0-9970178-4-7

Electronic editions:
Mobi ISBN: 978-0-9970178-5-4
Epub ISBN: 978-0-9970178-6-1

First Edition

10 9 8 7 6 5 4 3 2 1

Acknowledgements

I'd like to thank my mom and my friend Debbie for their
support throughout this project.
I'd also like to thank:
Diane O'Connell and the folks at Write To Sell Your Book.
Karen Hudson for her thoughtful cover and interior design.
Annie Nichol for copyediting.
Conor Mintzer for proofreading.
Brianna Flaherty for an early read and edit of the developing manuscript.

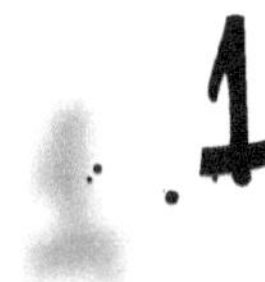

It was a fine day at George Washington Junior High School, weather-wise. Puffy cumulus clouds, prodded by a gentle breeze, drifted across the sky. In three more days we would be off for summer vacation and my nightmare freshman year in this hellhole would be over with.

Today was a once-a-year event called a "field day," which was kind of like an outdoor school Olympics. I stood off by myself, lost in my own world as I mentally soared through the clouds and gazed down from afar on activities that outcasts like me weren't included in.

A couple of the usual culprits who picked on me broke my little reverie as they surrounded me. One of their recent converts, a boy named Mark, I'd known for years from church and we used to be friends. Mark was climbing the social ladder, while I was in a downward spiral. The more ostracized I was by the other kids, the more Mark ignored me. My self-esteem was so low that I actually understood that it would hurt his reputation to be publicly associated with me, so I never greeted him any more if other kids were around. Such was my life.

But what really turned my former friend against me was a kid named Tyler, who targeted me as his bullying victim shortly after he moved into our neighborhood. Tyler and Mark quickly became friends and I was odd man out. At least in Mark's favor, when Tyler would pick on me after we got off of the school bus in the afternoon, Mark would sometimes say, "Leave him alone, Tyler."

But now it was Mark who began shoving me and trying to get me to fight him. Even though we were both fourteen, it was no contest; he'd become a strapping adolescent while I was still a skinny, prepubescent little boy.

I looked Mark in the eyes and pleaded, "Why are you doing this to me? I thought—"

Don't say it, my inner voice interrupted.

But it was too late.

"You thought *what?*" Mark taunted with a cruel face and squinty eyes, "You thought we were *friends?*"

Partially out of fright, but mostly to hide the tears that I would no longer be able to hold back, I bolted away at breakneck speed. Mark gave serious chase. Even though he was bigger and stronger than I was, I was quicker by far. No one could catch me—not even close—and I could have kicked ass if I'd been on track. But after the way my schoolmates (and the gym teachers) had treated me, I'd never help them win any championships. My inner voice would never let me off that easy, though, and would admonish me with, *"Well maybe if you were more of a team player, Mike..."*

As I blindly sprinted out into the playing fields, I accidentally crossed a competition where kids were running and jumping hurdles. I screwed up the whole race as kids crashed into me. While trying to just get out of their way, I fell backwards into one of the hurdles. A bar slammed me in the back and sent shock waves of pain up my spine.

Students and even teachers fired a barrage of insults at me as I stumbled away in agony. No one asked if I was OK.

"Thanks for screwing up the whole race, you little jerk," someone said.

"That kid's such a loser," I overheard a girl comment. "If I was him, I'd just kill myself, I swear. . ."

The outer edge of the playing fields sloped up to the woods and I defiantly limped towards the tree line. I was sure that at any moment one of the teachers would yell at me to stop, but no one did and I kept right on going. As upset as I was, I couldn't help but feel liberated by the fact that I'd just gotten away with walking off school grounds in the middle of a school day in full view of at least some authorities.

I continued deep enough into the woods to secure my escape and I paused. How had my life derailed so completely? Only a few years ago in grade school, I was a happy, athletic, well-liked kid. It wasn't *me* that had changed.

That's the problem, Mike. You didn't change.

'Well, I can't help if I'm. . .'

Still a ten-year-old inside?

I did a desultory shrug and sat on a log to sulk. In some ways, I had to admit that I was very immature. However, in other ways, I was years ahead not only of kids my age, but even many (most?) adults. I discovered this early on and I often manipulated adults with an ease that frightened me. But around adolescents, I was mature and immature in exactly all of the wrong ways.

The pulse of the world continued on around me: the shouts of the kids on the fields, the murmur of a nearby highway, the jets passing overhead on their approach to Newark Airport. All of this, it occurred to me in a strangely comforting manner, would continue on whether I was involved in it or not. I had one of those "I'm just a grain of sand in an endless universe" revelations that most of us have at one point or another. Most people would think that to do something, they need more money, or practice, or fame, or whatever. But my logic was convoluted:

"If I'm really nothing, then I can do . . . anything."

Then I heard the compelling call of a distant train horn, which invoked the lure of unknown, distant places. And that recalled a recurring dream that I'd been having for years.

In the dream, I'm about seven and my mom, dad, two older brothers, and I are going somewhere on a family car trip. We stop at an A&P supermarket for something and Dad goes in alone, leaving the rest of us in the sunbaked car to wait. I become obsessed with the railroad tracks that are in a deep tree-lined ditch on the other side of the highway. They run parallel to the road in this fashion for some distance and where the occasional road crosses the highway at a traffic light, it then continues on a bridge over the railroad tracks.

Even though I can't see the tracks from where we are, I get an inexplicable but urgent sense that another "me" is over there, "calling me in my head" and I *must* answer the call. I scamper over my brother (I always got stuck in the middle), tumble out of the car, and race across the highway towards my destiny. I can hear my mother yelling "Mike, Mike!" and then a more frantic "MICHAEL!" as I cross the first lanes. I ignore her as I pause on the grass center median for a break in traffic and then dash across into the woods.

I run down the embankment near an overhead bridge and look both ways down the tracks. In either direction, there is another overpass in the near distance. Frustratingly, the dream ends there and I wake up before anything actually happens.

It's not surprising that the dream involves railroad tracks, because I was fascinated with trains from an early age. I acquired illustrated children's books that identified the various types of freight cars and what their purposes were, cut-away illustrations that showed the inner workings of diesel locomotives, a book that described a day in the life of a railroad engineer, etc.

Whenever I reflected on the dream, the event and location seemed so real—more like an actual real-life memory than a dream.

"Memories" of places I've never been are not uncommon for me. When I was really little, I kept asking my mom about this particular train station and she kept insisting that I was never there. I'd describe how the nearby road went under the tracks past the "checkerboard" stuff. She'd frown and then smile kindly and say something to the effect of, "No, sweetie, we've never been there."

"Maybe Dad took a train into the city and we picked him up?"

"I'm sorry, honey, but your dad hasn't ridden a train since before we were married."

Well, me being Mike, I wouldn't let it go. "I was there! I was older then, but I remember. There's the checkerboard wall and the tunnel that you walk through with the little lights in the ceiling and…" I went on to describe the buildings and the town in detail.

Her eyes suddenly lit up with recognition and she cocked her head. "That sounds like the Ridgewood station, but you were never there. Maybe we've driven past it."

"No, we stood on the platform! Could we go there, please, please, please?"

So off we went to Ridgewood. As we rounded the last bend, I pointed and triumphantly said, "See—the checkerboard!" In a way that can only happen to a little kid who's been vindicated, my eyes filled with tears. It was actually black-and-white squares painted on the bridge abutments as a warning to motorists. The paint was faded and peeling. Modern, black-and-yellow-striped reflective signs had been installed over some of it. I went on to give Mom a tour of a station that I'd never been to. My "little tunnel lights" were actually small, round, glass skylights in a pedestrian underpass.

My first impulse is to say that something snapped inside of me on that fateful day in the woods behind the junior high school, but it would be better to say that something solidified. Never again would anyone get close enough to hurt me. From that moment on, I leaned inwards, trusting only in myself. The wall that I'd been building around my heart became an impenetrable fortress.

I retreated completely into my own private world of fantasy where anything seemed possible. My "inner voice" gradually took on a personality all its own, and I enjoyed having actual conversations with it. At times it could say something that would make me laugh out loud. But I could hide no secrets from my inner voice and it cut me no slack. As a result, it frequently made me face realities about myself that I preferred to suppress.

People picked on me less after I changed. Not because I was more popular or respected—quite the opposite. I think they sensed that, although I seemed harmless and vulnerable on the surface, I just—in some way that you couldn't quite put your finger on—might not be someone you should mess with. It feels awful to admit this, but I wasn't the kid who would meet you after school for a fistfight. No, I was a school psychologist's worst nightmare, the time-bomb kid who would take it and take it and then show up at school one day with a gun. Thank God I wasn't inclined to violence.

Although I debated it, I didn't run away from home that day back in the seventies. With the recurring dream fresh in my mind, I had a better plan: I vowed that no matter how long it took, I'd find the dream location. And then, well, who knew?

August, 2015

Although I stopped having the dream years ago, its impact never left me. Seeing as I'd always suspected that it was set in a real location, off and on throughout my adult years I've searched for it. During periods when I was depressed, the quest took center stage. When I was in a more positive frame of mind, it became more of a diversion, a part-time hobby.

I'd checked out dozens of spots over the years and all of them had turned out to be duds. Admittedly, I knew most were going to be duds before I even went there. Nevertheless, I hoped that they might be a close enough match for—I don't know—for whatever reason I was drawn there, I guess. But the setting was so unique and specific and New Jersey is such a small state that I pretty much exhausted all the possibilities.

Besides, the original dream was in the sixties, so the area could be unrecognizable by now. And what if the location wasn't even in New Jersey? We used to drive to Florida on vacation when I was a kid, so I could have seen something in another state that sparked the original dreams. Was I really going to broaden my search to the entire East Coast? Can you spell o-b-s-e-s-s-e-d?

Even so, the desire to find it never completely left me and one day I admitted to myself that I was ashamed to be suppressing something that had once seemed so big and important. Why not just give one last effort and settle this once and for all? What could I have to lose?

These days, I didn't have to look at street maps and drive all over the place to check out potential locations. Instead, I could sit home and sail through satellite images on Google Earth. I'd pick a highway and follow it from the air, or do the same thing with a railroad.

One August evening in 2015, I was sitting at my computer listening to Iron Maiden (my very favorite band) and idly re-searching an area of New Jersey that I thought was an unlikely candidate to be my dream location. The highway had what I took to be a meandering, tree-covered river that came close to it and paralleled it for a ways. Then I noticed an open area farther on where the "river" crossed a road. I froze for a few seconds—rivers don't cross roads.

"How could I have missed that before?"

I zoomed in on the crossing area and my pulse quickened: rails.

I slid the screen back to the highway. It looked like a perfect match.

I randomly looped the cursor around the screen as I stared at the image on my computer monitor and debated the possible outcomes of going there. The realistic adult one was that I'd go check it out, congratulate myself on finally finding it, and go home. The fantasy childish one was that if the location from the dream was real, another "me" could be waiting there. I fleetingly considered waiting a week or two before going to check it out. I tried to tell myself that I wanted to savor the suspense, but in reality I was avoiding the inevitable letdown if it turned out to be a dud.

It's not a dud, Mike, my inner voice chimed in.

I got all choked up as I nodded agreement.

Tomorrow is August 24. You should go.

Although August 24 is a significant date for me, I've never been sure why. It's not a holiday or my or anyone else's birthday that I know of. The only thing I could figure was that it was the date the dream was set in. On impulse, I'd already asked for the day off from work.

The events had already gained a flow of their own and my only reservation in jumping into the flow was the fear of disappointment.

I didn't need a map to get to the location and I didn't even bother finding out the name of the town because I could see how to get there just from the satellite image.

My voice cracked with emotion as I nodded and committed, "All right, I'll do it. Tomorrow morning, I'll drive out there."

Although I awoke early and excited the next morning to a clear August day, I didn't depart until mid-morning. You'd think that after finally finding a solid candidate, I would have left at the crack of dawn. I used the excuse that I "didn't want to drive out there in Monday morning rush hour traffic" as a reason to stall, but the truth was that I had this nagging feeling that I might not be coming back. I had no idea what circumstances might prevent my return ('Am I going to get into a horrible accident or something? Should I pack a bag to take with me?'), so I was a bit unnerved by this.

Actually, for the past few weeks I had this vague feeling that I'd be . . . I don't know, I'd say "going away for a while," but even that phrase doesn't adequately describe it.

For instance: my friend Howard had had a big, friendly, "happy idiot" Bernese mountain dog named Hoover. There was such a strong bond between that dog and me that Howie used to joke that Hoover thought I was one of his littermates.

One afternoon, while playing on the floor with the dog, I gave him a big hug and for some strange reason I said, "Oh Hoover, I'm sure gonna miss you."

My inner voice queried: *Why are you going to miss him? Are you going somewhere?*

'No.'

Oh. Do you think he's going somewhere?

'Gosh, I sure hope not.'

Okaaay . . .

A similar thing happened at the large retirement community where I worked as a groundskeeper. The leaf blower wouldn't start (as usual) and I was sweating and aggravated.

"Stupid piece of junk," I muttered as I backed off to kick it and then thought better of it. After all, it was a pricey retirement community and proper behavior was expected from the workers.

"Well, pretty soon it's not going to matter and I won't have to deal with any of this crap."

Why—are you planning on quitting?

'No.'

'*You think you're gonna get fired?*'

'Gosh, I sure hope not.'

And so it went.

So, on this August 24th morning I found myself wandering aimlessly around my apartment in the manner that I always did before a long trip: as though I was all packed, ahead of schedule, and waiting for the limo to come take me to the airport.

Finally I went out to my pickup truck and headed out into the usual New Jersey traffic. People were going to work, truckers were *at* work and here I was, driving off to a dreamed-up location.

'This is silly. I know I've done this before, but actually taking a day off and driving this far is . . . it's embarrassing.'

Mike, relax—no one knows what you're doing today.

'What if a cop pulls me over for something and asks me where I'm going? What could I possibly say?'

Forget about the "thought police," OK? Besides, this isn't the first time you've done this.

No, it certainly wasn't. But most times when I'd checked out a location, it was either a side trip when I was already in the area or one of several items on the day's agenda. Today was different and it seemed as though the outcome of this little jaunt was going to be a game-changer.

I pulled into a spot at the outer edge of a CVS Pharmacy parking lot, near the highway. The lot was ridiculously oversized, so the only other vehicle in the immediate vicinity was a silver Audi, which I supposed was parked way out here on an angle so as to prevent anyone from dinging it.

I shut off the engine and stepped out to survey the situation. I left the key in the ignition and the door open—as though I might need a quick getaway. The muted bonging from inside my truck counted off the seconds as I stood close by the front fender and took in the scene. Any residual doubts I had about its authenticity vanished. Although they'd tried to modernize the CVS Pharmacy building by covering the front with a metal veneer, it still had the original A&P-style peaked roof.

At some point this lot had been expanded because back in the sixties, where I'd just parked had been a grassy slope. The actual place where I started running from in the dream was much closer to the store. I briefly debated, but dismissed the idea of walking over to the approximate location and starting from there.

Countless times throughout the years, I'd fantasized about standing in this spot and my imaginary scenarios always had me dashing over to the bridge with reckless abandon. Yet here I was, seconds away from my goal, and the urge to get back in and drive home was almost as strong as the desire to venture over there. It didn't seem fair. I stiffly yanked the key from the ignition (if, for nothing else, to stop the bonging), closed and locked the door, and got moving.

As I crossed the highway at a traffic light, I felt as though everyone in the idling cars was staring at me and that they knew that I was up to something. There was no obvious destination along the section of road that I was heading for. To appease my paranoia, I slowly continued partway across the bridge over the tracks. Once the light changed and the traffic got rolling again, I did an about-face, jogged back to the intersection and ducked out of sight into a narrow strip of woods. I paused and peered down through the trees at an old rusty railroad track.

I glanced back through the interlacing tree branches. My truck basking in the hot August sunshine seemed to represent stability and reality. Compared to what, I had no idea. All I'd done was walk across a busy state highway in suburban New Jersey in broad daylight.

How long could my truck sit there before the cops investigated it and towed it away, I wondered. For that matter, how long before my family or friends filed a missing person report on me? They'd tie the vehicle to my last known location and search the area. Or maybe they'd think I'd been carjacked. They'd be devastated.

'Why am I even *thinking* these thoughts? Maybe I should come back another day.'

You've been searching all of these years, drove all this way. At least go down and take a peek or you know you'll regret it halfway home when you're too far away to turn around and come back. Then you'll chew on it all night and wind up doing this all over again tomorrow. Besides, what's the worst that could happen?

I didn't know, but there was something unsettling about this that I couldn't put my finger on. The fact that, on the surface, the scene itself seemed so harmless and benign unsettled me even more because there was nothing tangible to be afraid of.

Mike, go see whatever it is you came here to see. Finish this.

As I threaded my way down the embankment, I felt detached from the situation—as though I was slipping out of my body. A dirty, scruffy boy was sitting out of the rain under the nearby bridge. He looked indistinct—as though he was made out of mist. I was having trouble actually focusing on him. The closer I got to him, the more solid he appeared to be. I recognized him from somewhere long ago, but I couldn't remember where.

The boy got up, shook his long, dark hair out of his eyes, and started ascending towards me. I continued downward in a trance-like state, but a slip of my foot on the slick leaves brought me back.

When I'd crossed the highway a minute ago, everything was dry and the sun was out. It wasn't really the kind of day where it just . . . starts raining. Yet now, everything was soaked as though it had been raining for a while.

The hiss of traffic on the wet pavement behind me sounded as though it was echoing through a long, narrow metallic tunnel. And instead of being slightly above and in back of me as it should have been, it was all around me and directly in my face and way too close.

That weird noise is what started to push me over the edge. I wanted to hold my ears against it, but I sensed that doing so wouldn't matter. That last realization was the catalyst for an all-out panic and I swung around to bolt back up the hill. But I forced myself to stop in mid-turn.

'No! I'm going to do it! I'm just going to go down there and see what happens. I've been waiting for this moment all of my life.'

It was as difficult to take those next dozen or so steps as it would be to deliberately walk into a tomb that I knew—*knew*—was going to slam shut behind me and trap me forever.

And then it was over.

Just like that.

I felt whole and the world around me looked solid once again. The strange moment had passed and I was very much here, in the sloping woods leading down to the railroad tracks, in the rain, getting wet. And the boy was gone.

'Where the hell did he go? He couldn't have gotten past me. Did he go *through* me? Did we become one?'

I swung my head around and saw *myself* climbing the embankment towards the highway.

Absurd thoughts raced through my mind at lightning speed:

'Look, that's me! Is that what I look like? I mean, I *know* what I look like. But you never get to see yourself from someone else's eyes like this. Well, I guess you can see yourself in a mirror or in pictures or even movies, but this is different. How am I doing this?'

The image that I was watching now seemed as though *it* was made out of mist. I was too transfixed to even consider *why* I was watching myself walk away.

He/I turned at the top of the embankment and looked back down at me. "I'll see you around, kiddo," he/I said before vanishing from view over the crest.

I began scrambling up the embankment after him, intending to follow and see where he went.

He's gone. You're not going to see him crossing the highway.

I stopped and nodded. The moment had passed; any opportunity for interaction was lost.

'So, what just happened here? Did he steal my soul or something?'

Damned if I could figure it out. It flashed through my mind that if I never *did* figure out what just happened, this would create a worse obsession for me than the one over finding this place had been to begin with.

But no, something had physically changed because I'd definitely shrunk—and not by a few inches, either. More like a few feet, although I had no way to measure that. At home, I would notice the difference in the height of familiar objects such as doorknobs, shower faucets, etc. Here there was nothing to compare to, but I could tell anyways.

I gave myself a pat down. No keys, cell phone, wallet or even pocket change. "Hello?" I said out loud and my kid voice confirmed it. "We switched, we really did," I said softly. But why did I feel so much like . . . *myself?*

I shook my head. "I don't know if you're even *capable* of saying this in a dream . . . but this just *has* to be a dream."

A not-too-distant horn, and then the thrumming sound of a train approaching from the west broke my contemplations.

"That's funny, I assumed it was abandoned," I muttered as I glanced down towards the railway line.

My eyes widened. Five minutes ago, when I first looked down there, I'd seen only one weedy, rusty, abandoned-looking track with a rutted, muddy, all-terrain vehicle trail next to it. Now there were two sets of tracks, just as there were in the dream.

I drew in a loud breath of amazement and said, "I stepped into the dream."

The diesel engines slowly churned past, followed by a long freight train.

I pretty much knew what I'd see back up at the highway. In a way, I was hoping that I'd see something ridiculously absurd—such as a dinosaur eating my truck. Just to confirm that either this was just a dream, or someone had drugged me, or there was a gas leak down here, or chemical fumes and I'd been breathing them, or *something*.

The dry, sunny highway that I'd crossed five minutes ago had three paved lanes in each direction, divided by a narrow "jersey barrier" concrete wall that had gaps where the traffic lights were. Now it was only two concrete lanes in each direction, divided by a wide grass median with a few scattered old oak trees growing in it. Old cars and trucks rushed past on the wet pavement and "ka-chunked" over the joints in the concrete. The traffic lights were still there, and the CVS Pharmacy where I'd parked was now an A&P supermarket, just as it was in the dream.

I stood in the wet grass and gawked. It was as though every vehicle on the highway was going to or returning from an old car show, except that this was business as usual. I guessed that the newest-looking of the vehicles were from the sixties.

I noted that the exhaust from these passing vehicles smelled much stronger and more toxic than it had in 2015.

I retreated back under the bridge to collect my thoughts. The freight train was still rumbling past at about a fast walking speed and I had the crazy urge to jump onto it and head out on an adventure. But I was too frazzled to do that at this point. Besides, I didn't want to leave this area where we'd switched.

This body was famished. I knew there'd be a dumpster behind the A&P and I figured I'd wait until it got dark and then I'd go raid it. I'd worked in grocery stores (in the youth of my *other* life, I reminded myself) so I knew that at closing they threw stuff away that had been for sale only hours earlier.

A half-hour ago I could have stopped at a diner. Now I was waiting for nightfall to go dumpster-diving.

Half an hour ago, if you'd asked me to describe myself, I would have said I was a square peg in a world full of round holes. I'm not a "tough guy," yet in many ways I'm as tough as nails. I'm not a city slicker, a redneck, or even a suburbanite. Whether they are straight or gay, rich or poor, young or old, religious or atheist, I don't fit in with people.

I'm tolerated as an outcast among my co-workers at the large assisted-living complex where I work as a groundskeeper, although not truly disliked. Just not "one of the boys" I guess.

As I described earlier, school days had been a nightmare. If I had to come up with an adult scenario to equate with the torment I suffered in junior high school, it would be to be thrown into prison for a crime you didn't commit. My childhood experiences with kids had scarred me so deeply that it left me permanently intimidated by them. Even as an adult, I've avoided kids at all costs.

Although I graduated high school, I didn't go to the prom, my picture is not in the yearbook, and I didn't go to the graduation ceremony. My older brothers continued on to college and, although the opportunity was there for me to do so, I didn't bother.

I've always avoided parties, never been on a date (at least from my point of view) and I mostly only socialize with a few straight, male friends. I have nothing against women (or a few gay guys I've known) and I have, at times, hung out with them and even let them through my wall a little. The problem was that they weren't ten-year-olds looking for a buddy like I was—they were adults looking for relationships. At least I was always honest with them up front that I wasn't looking for love, kissing and I especially wasn't interested in sex. I made it as clear as possible that one can never get too close to Mike. If they kept pursuing me romantically, I eventually broke their hearts. I did. My inner voice accuses me of letting it get out of hand because I enjoy the extra attention and it refers to this as a "Mike Morrison hook and dump." This is not something I'm proud of, but it's a by-product of my nature that I have to own up to.

But aside from a few slips, I've kept my "wall" so well fortified that no one else had the chance to get too close to me, even if they tried. The mold is set in my head that once someone really gets to know me, they won't understand me. I picture myself as a layer cake, exposing the top, frosting-covered layer and forever hiding what's inside.

Although I can only judge by comparing my behavior to others, I would have to say that I've never had much of a sex drive. When your few friends are out on Saturday night being social and getting laid and you are alone in the woods at the edge of a swamp contentedly watching fireflies, you know that you are different. You also know that you're missing whatever it is that makes people invest so much time in having sex. The few times that I've tried it, I found it to be messy, smelly (I hate other people's scent being on me) and I wanted it to be over with as soon as it started. The amazing (or perhaps sad) thing is that I've always felt fortunate to be free of sexual desire.

And that is exactly the type of attitude that makes things worse. Once you cross the line from wanting to be more like everyone else to *embracing the fact that you are different*, you're on your way into your own little world. Take it from me.

But I took full advantage of it, Mike Morrison-style. I had adventures and experiences that no one else had, or would have bothered to pursue because they could never dream of the outcomes or open their minds to the possibilities. This adventure is a classic, although extreme, example of that.

And I did most of it alone, with no one in the entire world knowing where I was or what I was doing. I backpacked and camped far in the woods where the surly black bears ruled, ventured deep into long-forgotten underground iron mines and explored some insanely dangerous abandoned urban industrial sites. Sometimes I got injured and even got myself into a few real life-or-death situations that I had to rely solely on myself to get out of.

I used to be extremely anti-materialistic. I wouldn't possess any more than I could carry in a backpack—and I mean that quite literally. I wouldn't buy a car and I would only rent pre-furnished rooms so I didn't have to own furniture. Every friendship I made and every facet of my life had a kind of perforation in it, ready for me to tear it off and abandon it without a backwards glance. I lived like someone who was ready to cut and run at a moment's notice, like I was just waiting for that call . . .

But time can whittle your expectations down and I gradually pushed my obsession over finding the dream location to the back burner. Free to invest a little more in the life that I was actually living, I let myself acquire "stuff"—even a pickup truck and furniture (although I still rented an apartment). I made a few more friends after joining groups who were cleaning up rivers or fighting to preserve the woods that I loved so much. I was actually starting to live my life as though it was mine and it mattered and that *I* mattered, as though I actually planned on staying around for a while.

But, although I often felt like a crazy fool obsessed with something so vague that I didn't even know what I was searching for, I once again gave in to the fantasy. Speaking of which . . .

'You know,' I reasoned to my inner voice, 'I must still be at home sleeping. I bet I'll wake up and it will be this morning, before I ever drove out here.'

No, I don't think so, man. Dreams don't last this long, and they're never this well choreographed. You know how it is—in a dream, this could be New Jersey, but the Grand Canyon could be here.

'Yeah, but something like the Grand Canyon being in New Jersey seems normal in a dream. It's only after you wake up that it seems absurd.'

You're not going to just wake up from this at home and go back to your normal life, Mike.

'I know what happened! You see, I always *was* this kid but I fell down that hill and hit my head, and now I have amnesia.'

I don't remember falling down any hill.

After a few seconds, I shook my head and laughed.

The weather worked its way up to a downpour with occasional thunder and lightning, but it seemed that the storm had lost its real fury before it got here. The damn rain had the effect of making me feel even more trapped than I already felt.

My most immediate problem was that I was cold, wet, and starving. I wished I at least had my sleeping bag and tent from my other life. Even if I'd known this was going to happen, I couldn't have stashed that stuff ahead of time because it would exist far into the future. That realization made me feel kind of dizzy and by a sheer force of will, I fought a wave of fast-rising panic.

"All right, all right," I said in a pull-yourself-together tone. I glanced up towards the highway. Truth be told, I felt certain that this had been a one-time, one-way switch. But I deliberately tried to force a casual attitude, as though one can change an outcome merely by acting as though everything's okay.

"So now, how do I switch back?"

The rain had slackened to a drizzle again, so I nonchalantly crossed the highway while doggedly pretending that I was still the adult me. Once in the area where I'd parked, it was a bit more difficult to keep up the facade. They'd built a retaining wall and filled in when they'd expanded the lot in the future, so if not for the fact that I was back in the past, I would be standing underground right now.

'My truck is hovering about six feet above me where I left it in 2015.'

Unless the other you drove it away . . .

Well that just made me feel a *whole* lot better, as you can imagine.

'Once I figure out how I did this, I can—'

You didn't "do" it, Mike. It happened.

Like the door slamming shut on a tomb that I'd deliberately walked into.

The bridge was my only anchor at the moment, so I returned to it. The slope was much steeper down by the tracks than it was farther up and I got leaves and dirt in my sneakers as I did a controlled slide down the last fifty feet.

"Look at these cheap, crappy sneakers the kid was wearing," I bitched as I sat on the rail and dumped the crap out of my (his) sneakers. "But then, I bet they don't even make Reeboks or Nikes yet."

I waved my hand above the shiny wet rail just to make sure that I could see the reflection of my body on the rail.

But to an observer—say, someone walking the tracks—was I now a little kid or an adult that just *thought* he was a little kid? Or maybe they wouldn't see me at all because I only existed in my own imagination.

'Boy, I wish I knew what I was supposed to do now. If this was an adventure movie, right about now some person or fantasy creature would come along and tell me to "go on a quest to find a hidden idol to save humanity" or something corny like that.'

You're not a character in a movie or a book, Mike.

Maybe not, but I wasn't sure *what* my status was.

Where was the line between dream, fantasy, and reality? I didn't know anymore. Only thing I did know for sure was that it was sunny that day in the dream and it wasn't raining today before we switched, so I figured I got the short end of the stick on this deal.

"You'd think we could have at least found a nicer place to make this swap."

I realized that this was the first time that I'd even *thought* to question the scene selection. Why couldn't it have been somewhere nice, like a beach in Florida or something? Maybe in the original dream, or whatever it was, that kid sat under this bridge just calling any kid with his brain or something and I was the one who eventually answered the call. I'd always comforted myself by surmising that it was another "me" that had called me over. I'd never considered that it could have been a stranger. The concept gave me the chills and made me feel more trapped than I already felt.

I swung my head in expectation when I heard the crunch of the dry leaves up under the bridge being disturbed, but it was just a squirrel rooting around. Would the adult me *ever* come back? I didn't know. And here I was trapped in a kid's body, so I couldn't even freely roam about. I felt humiliated by the fact that I'd willfully gotten myself into this situation.

The murmur of traffic above on the highway—of normal people living normal, predictable lives—added to my growing despair. Those people lived in the real world and they'd go home to their quiet, warm, dry, well-lit homes and eat and watch TV. They knew better than to risk throwing everything away for some silly dream.

Just to be doing something so as to avoid a complete breakdown, I decided to walk to the next bridge, which was about a quarter-mile away.

You might want to wait 'till the rain stops. Getting sick will only make things worse.

"What do I care if it gets sick? This isn't even my body," I retorted rather loudly.

I tried to convince myself that this was an adventure and lots of people would kill just to be young again or to go back in time, but I couldn't get into it. Though as an adult I'd daydreamed about what might happen here today, I wasn't mentally prepared to tumble headfirst into this situation.

I slowly came to a halt as I reached the dispiriting conclusion that it didn't matter how far, or in which direction, I walked. Where was there to go?

'Man, this is nothing like I thought it would be. I mean—it looked so nice in the dream, with the misty sunlight streaming down through the trees . . .'

You're not a victim here. You chose this.

'I didn't know what I was getting myself into.'

Yes, you did.

'Well I didn't think it would actually . . . *happen.*'

Then why'd you drive all of the way out here?

Deep in the man-made railroad canyon darkened by the overhanging, dripping trees, I reached my meltdown point:

"Man, I shouldn't have *fucked* around like this!" I said in my new high-pitched voice. "I could have just gone to work today like a *normal* person and just kept this as a little fantasy to think about when the going got tough. But no, not me," I yelled as I picked up a handful of stones and threw them full force down the tracks. "No, no, I had to come here and . . . and . . . and—ya see? YA SEE?" I smacked myself in the head for emphasis. "This is what happens when you *mess* with reality, you asshole!"

I stood there with my hands clenched at my side and stewed for a few minutes.

Trying for levity, I said quietly, "Well, Mike, this is another fine mess you've gotten yourself into." But it wasn't working.

"I threw everything away for—" I reached down and pinched my ratty T-shirt between my thumbs and index fingers and pulled it away from my chest, "—this." I let the shirt drop back into place.

Oh, stop it. Last week you were complaining about how bad your life sucked.

That brought an embarrassed little smile to my lips and I took a deep, shaky breath and calmed myself down by imagining the absurdity of showing up at my best friend Alan's house as the new me and trying to explain everything. I had a whole little scenario going in my head with Alan quizzing me on stuff that only the real me would know the answers to. I smiled as I lost myself in the scenario and then my eyes widened with a great idea.

"Oh yeah, that's what I'll do! I'll find a pay phone and ask Alan to come and get me."

Um . . . except that Alan might not have been born yet.

I thought about that for a few seconds and, shaking my head, let out a half laugh, half cry.

Back under the bridge, I parked my butt on a rail to calm down. A train headlight appeared in the distance, but it was advancing so slowly that I had plenty of time to climb up into the shadows and watch it pass.

Three drab, smoky diesel locomotives led a long string of freight cars, which emitted loud, metal-on-metal groans and squeals as they clunked and swayed back and forth on tracks that behaved, quite frankly, as though they'd long since given up all hope and now only incidentally bore the weight of passing trains without collapsing. In one of the places where the rails were joined together with bolted bars, the wooden cross-ties lifted an inch or so before slamming back down into the mud under the weight of the wheels. To make matters worse, only half of the ties came up with the rail. The rest weren't attached anymore and they just stayed down. How many times could steel rails bend like that before they would break?

"Geez, no wonder they're going so slow," I commented quietly.

Both trains that I'd seen had used this same track. The other track was in even worse shape and it didn't look as though they used it at all.

Something down where the boy was originally sitting caught my eye and I investigated. Wedged in next to the retaining wall for the bridge supports was his (mine now, I supposed) canvas backpack.

I smiled as I picked it up. "Of course he'd have one of these."

All that was inside was a worn hooded sweatshirt and a tarnished, dented metal canteen. I dumped the water out with the intention of rinsing out the germs and saliva and refilling it. Then it dawned on me that it was *my* saliva now. I still felt more comfortable starting out fresh, though.

At least the rain had stopped. Although I didn't actually know how old I was, I did get a good-enough look at the kid sitting under the bridge before we switched to figure that I probably looked old enough to be walking around by the A&P across the highway alone. And now that I thought about it, doing it in daylight seemed like a better alternative to suspiciously sneaking around after dark.

'I'm just some kid from the neighborhood, out buying munchies, right?'

And there was always the possibility that this kid I'd switched with lived a five-minute walk from the bridge and someone might recognize me/him.

Either way, I wanted to get to a pay phone (I knew they'd still exist in whatever year I was in) and try to call my childhood home collect. I don't really know what I expected to get out of this. What the hell would I do when my mom answered? Ask to talk to myself? I guess I just wanted to confirm that the other me actually existed.

And who knew? Maybe I would switch back as I crossed the highway.

Don't get your hopes up.

I closed my eyes. 'Yeah, I know.'

And if you did switch back . . .

I sighed with resignation and rolled my eyes a little. 'I'd just drive back out here tomorrow.'

You wouldn't even wait that long. You'd try it again today. And what would your reaction be if it didn't work again?

Good question.

Under a cloudy sky, I again crossed the highway. My mood picked up as I left the depressing bridge and headed towards an open area with people around. People who, as I'd noted by their reactions at the traffic light, could indeed see me.

There were two ten-cent pay phones mounted to the brick wall in front of the A&P. Although I intended to call home "collect," I wasn't sure if I first needed to insert a dime and the instructions on the phones only further confused me.

I was going to intercept an older lady who was getting herself a cart and ask her for money, but at the last second I lost my nerve.

Instead, I opted to ask a young guy who was removing his grocer's apron as he exited the store.

"Could I borrow a dime to call my mother?"

I thought he'd be a pretty cool guy, but he screwed his face up as though I'd asked him for the world.

"'Borrow?' Are you going to pay me back?"

"I . . . well, no. Can I *have* a dime?"

He wordlessly dug change from his pocket, picked out a dime and dropped it into my outstretched hand.

"Thank you," I said and silently added, 'I hope I didn't break your bank.'

He nodded and headed to his car.

As I turned back to the phones, I caught a glimpse of my reflection in the store windows and I froze and stared. I was amazed that it hadn't occurred to me to look at my image first thing when I got here. How could I *not* have? But then, it's not really ingrained in one's mind to check a mirror every so often to—what— to confirm that you're still *you?* The kid from under the bridge stared back at me. It wasn't a great reflection, because I could see the store inside as well.

'See, that's how the kid and I looked under the bridge: sort of transparent. Hmmm, reflections . . .' I glanced across the highway.

Yeah, the whole thing under the bridge was just an elaborate magic trick done with mirrors, Mike. You figured it out. They couldn't get one over on you, could they?

'Well, I don't hear *you* coming up with any explanations here.'

I hesitated in front of the phone as I flipped the dime over and over between my fingers for a minute before it occurred to me to check the date on the coin:

1965.

'I was born in 1961, so assuming this dime is new, I would only be four years old now.'

I made a mental note to look into one of the newspaper vending boxes farther down the sidewalk for today's date as I slid the dime in the phone. I dialed zero, told the operator the number, my name and that I was calling collect. My dime dropped back into the change return slot and I pocketed it. I reached over and checked the change return slot on the adjacent phone for money as I nervously listened for my mom or dad to answer. When you used to call collect, you could hear the person you were calling talking to the operator.

"Hello?" answered someone who sort of sounded like my mom.

"I have a collect call for Barbara Morrison from a Mike Morrison," said the operator.

Silence on the other end. Whoever was there with my mom must have sensed something wrong with her, because all of the background chatter ceased. For a second, I thought she'd hung up.

"Hello?" asked the operator.

"Yes, hello," my mom said and cleared her throat. "The only Mike Morrison I know is sitting right here in front of me."

I hung up.

"That. Little. *Prick*," I seethed. "He took my pickup truck *and* my family!"

That "little prick" didn't take anything—he's you exactly where you should be in the sixties: at home, with your family. If you're going to accuse anyone of grand theft auto, it would be the adult you in 2015. I must say, it is touching that you thought of your pickup truck before your family.

I couldn't help but laugh at that. In an exaggerated redneck accent, I loudly said, "You can *take* my family, but *don't mess* with my pickup truck!" Another elderly lady, dressed all in grey and bundled up as though it was forty degrees out, heard me and gave me a cross look and that made me laugh even harder.

'So, I've got the original kid me living at home, the adult me in 2015 running around doing God only knows what and this me standing here in—what year is this, anyway?'

I dodged a few shoppers with carriages as I ran down to the newspaper boxes and peered through the foggy plastic at today's date on a newspaper: August 24, 1967.

'Is there any logical reason that the year changed but it's still the same day?'

The dream was set on August 24. For that reason, you left 2015 on that date. No big mystery there, Mike.

I rolled my eyes. 'So 1967 makes me—I mean him—what? Six years old right now? No, I *do* mean me because I'm . . . Boy, this is confusing.'

Think how your poor mom must feel. First her little kid runs away across a busy highway like a maniac and comes right back with no explanation for his actions. Then when they get home, someone (namely you) calls collect, claiming to be her kid!

I smiled. 'He—I mean I—only ran away in the dream, you dolt.'

I briefly considered going to the town I grew up in to spy on the six-year-old me or maybe even engage him in conversation. 'Nah, leave him out of this mess. Let him have his life in peace.' I huffed a laugh and added, "The little prick."

I sidled around back to do my dumpster diving. A small group of kids a few years older than the "new me" were back there bouncing balls into a huge puddle and against the back wall of the store about a hundred feet away. They all stopped and stared at me and I almost turned around and left. But did I really want to leave and come back later?

I ignored their stares and I hopped into the dumpster and hurriedly rooted through all kinds of wet crap as I searched for something edible. I spied some unopened loaves of bread. As I reached for them, I froze. A vehicle had pulled up alongside the dumpster.

"Oh man," I whispered, "I hope those kids didn't call the cops or something."
With what?

'Oh yeah, that's right. They don't have cell phones back . . . now.'

The phrase "back now" simply and accurately described my situation in this era and from that moment on, the phrase stuck.

I debated whether I should just stay hidden or hop out and run like a frightened alley cat. The door opened on the vehicle, and the squeaky, clunky sound said "old pickup truck."

It occurred to me that it might be someone illegally dumping something that would land on top of me. I grabbed my bread, stood up, and startled the crap out of a large, sixty-ish, heavyset, mostly bald man. He did indeed drive an old white rusty pickup truck.

"Sorry," I said. "My ball bounced in here. What are *you* doing?"

As he frowned at the previously neat box of old lettuce that I'd overturned, he explained that he was getting greens for his rabbits. He had a little ladder with him—to reach into the dumpster with, I supposed. Nice guy that I am, I piled the lettuce back in the box and hefted it up to him. Then I hopped out with my bread, but no ball.

He eyed up the bread and I shrugged and said, "Hey, the price is right! Bye now!"

I trotted away laughing, as the man and the kids gaped.

As I jogged back across the highway, the sky was clearing and a low sun was poking through. A cool dry breeze from the west swept my long hair across my face and I momentarily felt elated, as free as a bird.

I paused briefly before proceeding down the embankment, just in case that weird "switching" feeling returned. But I didn't really expect it to and it didn't. I'd already been back and forth across the highway several times, so if a switch was going to happen, it had already had ample chance to do so.

It was depressing under the trees and the bridge in the gathering gloom, so I figured I'd hop on the next train that came along. No sense hanging around here. I was certainly too young to stand by the highway hitchhiking. And where would I ask to be taken to anyway?

Besides, the thought of actually hopping a train—having no idea where it was going— was exciting. I mean, here I was in a new, young body, with no responsibilities or time limits. So, whether this was a dream or not, why not take it up a notch and go on a real adventure?

But which direction to go in? Either one had its drawbacks. To my left seemed to be eastbound (as it was on the parallel highway behind me) and would take me toward New York City. Riding into urban areas was a scary prospect. But then, the thought of catching a westbound and heading farther out into the country was also scary. The more people that were around, the less I'd draw attention.

"Wish I'd looked for mold on that bread when I was in the brighter light," I muttered before I drank water from a puddle along the tracks. "At least then when I got sick I'd know if it was the bread or the water. Oh, I should have bought a roll of toilet paper with my dime."

Actually, I should have stayed at the pay phone grubbing more dimes. Well, I wasn't going back there now. Kids my age should be home by now, not hanging around shopping centers. Or under bridges, for that matter, but at least I was hidden here. Whether this was a dream or not, I didn't want to spend it in a police station.

One side of me was itching to get out of here, but the other side was sort of attached to this place. But this bridge wasn't like a modern, interstate one with sloping concrete and a two-foot-wide flat area along the top under the girders where you could sleep and stay relatively clean and dry. These bridge abutments were just steeply cut out of the dirt and sandstone, so there were few smooth surfaces.

'Do interstates even exist yet?'

I sat on the tracks and watched the darkness fall. The raspy calls of katydids in the overhead trees were complemented by the soothing background music of so many crickets that they all blended into a pleasing "whirring" sound. My problems in 2015 seemed a million miles away and I was enjoying the fact that I was feeling so mellow. I did my best to banish all deep thoughts or worries that didn't involve my immediate future.

I wished I could take a shower. This body was dirty when I'd inherited it and now it also had that kind of oily sweat that you emit when you've been real nervous and emotional.

I heard a bunch of teenagers coming down the tracks. There was graffiti (painted with a brush instead of spray paint; how quaint) and broken beer bottles under the bridge. I didn't want to hide from the kids near the bridge and then be stuck there hidden if that was their destination, so I tiptoe-ran down the tracks a ways before ducking into the brush. They passed the bridge and continued on their way.

"Ah," I said, as I heard the sound of an eastbound train coming. "I think I hear my limousine out front."

It was probably about four o'clock in the morning. This was only the second train that had come by since the previous afternoon. No wonder they tore up one of the tracks at some point in the future. The katydids had gone to sleep, and only an occasional car or truck passed on the highway. I'd earlier let a westbound train slowly pass without trying to hop it. The prospect of small, country towns seemed scarier right now. Plus, it would be colder if I headed west. Even with the sweatshirt, I was already chilly.

I'd moved up by the highway because the lights from civilization were a comfort compared to the almost total darkness down by the tracks. But the possibility of being seen jumping onto a train in daylight was probably a bad idea—especially if you're a little kid—so I felt my way back down to the tracks to hop on the slow-moving eastbound.

I'd envisioned hopping into an empty boxcar that had an open door and I did see one. But after jogging alongside it for a hundred feet, I quickly determined that there was no chance of hefting my little body into it while it was moving. I almost—almost—gave it a try before common sense prevailed. Yes, yes, I know—they do it in the movies all of the time. Ever notice how there is always some convenient piece of rope or a handle or something to grab? Maybe even a ladder next to the door? Well, in the real world there was nothing to grab. There were ladders, but they were on the end corners of the car, not in the center near the door.

A car came rolling along that had frameworks and ladders on the end and I lunged for it. First, I pulled myself up a ways with my arms. Once I was stable and could do it without missing and falling under the train, I placed my feet and ascended the ladder. The open-topped car was loaded with what could only be coal. The ends of the car slanted outward over the wheels, obviously to facilitate the dumping of the coal through chutes that I'd seen in the bottom of the car. Railings and ladders went straight down from the top to floorless platforms on the ends of the car.

I tentatively sat on a two-foot-wide beam that went to the coupler, with the sloping floor of the coal compartment above me. I could look right down at the freight car wheels and the tracks. I didn't risk taking off my sneakers and dumping out the crap that I'd just picked up by sliding down the hill in the dark. If I dropped one, I'd never get it back. I couldn't dare fall asleep! And I knew that I would be visible in daylight if anyone was really looking.

After about an hour, my slow-moving train stopped completely. I hopped off and crept ahead to the open boxcar. After carefully listening and sniffing the air at the door in case it was occupied by some bum, I hoisted myself in and quietly probed the dark interior. Then something different about the boxcar registered: the door opening was wider before, wasn't it? I felt along the wall and confirmed that between when I'd run alongside before and now, the door had slid partway shut. I tried to push it back open but it wouldn't budge.

I hopped back off and as I searched the side of the tracks in the dark for something to jam into the door track to prevent it from moving, I stepped into an unseen flooded culvert and soaked my right sneaker and my jeans up to the knee. I finally found an old chunk of railroad tie and I wedged it in there good and tight.

The more I tried to suppress it, the more my imagination ran the scenario of the train stopping suddenly and the door slamming shut and trapping me in here.

Me yelling for help and banging on the walls until my voice was gone and my fists were bloody as the car sat unattended in a rail yard somewhere. Then the sun comes up and it begins to heat up . . . Me with my lips pressed tight against the crack where the boxcar door meets the wall, trying to suck in some precious, cool fresh air . . . I shuddered.

I'd just gotten my first incident-free lesson (well, second if you consider that I had the common sense not to risk getting my legs cut off by attempting to board a moving boxcar) on how *not* to get killed while riding freight trains. And I wasn't even out of Jersey yet. Even discounting getting caught or the dangerous characters I might run into out here, this train-riding was dangerous business.

We were stopped at what appeared to be many red signals up ahead. I hadn't even realized that there was another set of railroad tracks through a small patch of woods next to us until a train went flying past on it. A short time later, we got rolling again and picked up speed. Now this was more like it! I sat cross-legged at the open door (I still didn't trust the door enough to sit far from it) and watched the nighttime countryside pass by.

'This might sound weird, but I hope I'm not abducting myself.'

One can't "abduct" oneself, Mike.

Maybe not, but I knew nothing of this kid's previous life. My gut instinct told me that this body was previously unattached to anything or anyone. But still, it would be nice to know. I wasn't the type of person who could shirk off the guilt of some parents somewhere in 1967 getting grey hairs worrying about their lost little kid. So I'd need to find out whose body this was. But how to do it without just flat out walking into a police station?

5

A low, golden sun fought its way through early morning ground mist as my eastbound freight train groaned to a stop. My ears were ringing from the noise of riding in a boxcar, similar to the way they'd rung after a rock concert in my other adult life. I figured these "kid" ears were probably more sensitive. If I planned on making a habit out of this, I'd need earplugs.

The train was blocking what looked like a busy road up ahead of where I was riding. This wasn't working in my favor at all. I'd planned to get off at the first place the train stopped and go in search of some drinkable water and maybe even some food, seeing as I forgot to bring what was left of my bread when I hopped onto the train. My best bet was to sneak up to a hose spigot on the side of one of the nearby new-looking houses. But it was risky enough walking down the road and sneaking up to houses with traffic moving where people would only catch a glimpse. Did I really want all of these people staring at me as they sat there waiting?

And the backpack was a liability. In the world that I came from yesterday, almost every student you saw wore one. Kids even wore them to school just as fashion statements. Not so in this era that I was in now. In this day and age, it made me stand out even more as a runaway or something. I'd have to be careful.

Traffic was backing up pretty quickly. Could I just pick a house and walk up to it like I lived there and hope for the best as I ducked around to the side of it for water? Then what would I do? Jump back onto the train with everyone watching?

The tracks were up on an exposed embankment above a swamp, so I would be in plain view getting back on unless I walked quite a distance down along the train.

I peeked out of the door. Through the mist, I could see the distant headlight of a westbound train approaching on the other track. I hopped out of my boxcar and crossed over the train on a platform between the cars because I didn't want to be out walking on the side where the other train would be. I sidestepped down to the edge of the ditch along the tracks and took a piss in the weeds. How could I piss when I was so insanely thirsty?

Well, the people at the crossing on the other side of the train, if they were looking, just saw a little boy hop off about ten freight cars away. I could see them from up in the boxcar, which meant that they could have seen me. I crept up closer to the crossing. After stuffing myself with dry bread last night and only washing it down with a few sips of disgusting puddle water, I *had* to find something to drink.

Across the road at the railroad crossing was an old farmhouse. On the side lawn closest to the tracks, under the low-hanging branches of an ancient, gnarly tree, was an old water pump with a fairly new-looking metal water bucket under the spigot. This certainly seemed like a better option than the shallow, muddy, oily water in the ditch along the tracks (that I'd just pissed in, I reminded myself).

'Ah, screw it. Who cares what those people think? I don't actually exist any-ways.'

The lady in the first car in line repeatedly blew her horn at the train. This seemed fruitless because you couldn't really see either end of it from here. As I crossed the road ten feet in front of her bumper, she stared openly at me through her windshield. Her car looked brand new, but to me it was an antique. I'd have loved to walk up to her window and say, "Nice old car, did you restore it yourself?" just to see the baffled look on her face.

My sneakers got soaked in the dewy grass as I strode right into the yard and up to the pump like I lived there. That's the only way to do it if you're going to do it with people watching you. The folks on this side of the tracks hadn't seen me jump out of a boxcar, so I hoped that they would think that I was just some local kid who had been walking where he shouldn't be walking.

The bucket at the water pump was already full of clear water, but I was hesi-tant to drink it in case they had a dog that drank out of it. As that thought struck me, I whirled around fearfully. In my mind's eye, a huge, growling dog was charg-ing me from in back of the house. But there was just quiet lawn.

The pump squealed and clanked loudly as I cranked it, but it didn't produce a drop of water. The westbound train that I'd seen a few minutes ago roared past on the other track, so I didn't hear an old man and his dog approaching.

As opposed to the ferocious attack dog that I had been picturing, this was one of those friendly "happy idiot" chocolate Labradors. The owner looked like a classic picture-book old farmer, complete with denim coveralls.

"That pump hasn't worked in years," the old man said in a friendly manner. I glanced down at the full bucket. "Rainwater," he said, looking slightly amused. "And you don't want to drink that. The dog drinks out of there."

The man didn't seem the least bit perturbed that I was trespassing on his land. Even the *dog* didn't seem to care.

"Been out walking, have you?" the old man asked. "Where do you live?"

And I was dead in the water right there. I opened my mouth to speak, but I had no reply as I stood there blushing guiltily. He followed my glance over to the stopped train.

I told you to sneak up to a water spigot on the side of a house!

'Oh, shut the hell up,' I silently shot back.

He considered me in silence for a few more moments and then said, "Let's go in and get you some water. I bet you're hungry."

I didn't answer. I just looked up at the sky in thanks.

I hoped we'd go in the back, out of sight of the cars on the road. Not that it really mattered, seeing as I was walking into a house—perfectly acceptable behavior at *any* age. The people in the cars couldn't know that I was walking into a house with a total stranger. But I was in hyper-paranoia mode and I was glad when he headed for the back of the house. The other train had passed, and my train jerked into motion. I hesitated halfway to the door because my only way out of here was departing.

What're you gonna do, Mike? Leave this guy standing here, skip the water, run out to the road and hop onto the train in front of all these cars? Even without cell phones, someone would stop and call the cops and they'd be waiting for you at the next road crossing. Why not make it a complete *spectacle and grab the dog's water bucket as you run across the yard?*

I smiled at this last comment and then noticed that the old man was watching me closely.

"Out riding the rails, at *your* young age?"

He shook his head and headed for the kitchen door.

As I followed his bent frame into the house, I tried to banish the thought that in the era I came from yesterday, he and his dog would have been long dead. The screen door slammed loudly behind me before I could catch it and I was glad that he seemed not to notice.

"Have a seat," he said, with his back turned to me as he got me a glass of water.

I would have sat at the table on the side closest to the door so I could dash out of there if necessary, but there were newspapers and flower seed catalogs and crap piled there.

He gave me the water and I gulped it down without stopping for a breath.

"Could I have some more?" I asked as I held up the glass.

"Certainly."

I watched, perplexed, as he paused with the glass under the tap, then washed it and put it in the drying rack.

"Um . . . could I have another glass of water?" I asked again.

"Certainly."

He refilled my glass and eased himself into a chair at the table. The dog lay at his feet.

"So now young man, what's your name?" he asked.

'Good question,' I thought as I stifled a smile.

"Mike," I answered, using my old name.

I expected the old man to start admonishing me for "running away from home." Instead, he silently scrutinized me. I really wanted to start squirming, but I tried to look casual.

"Lived in this house all of my life," he began as he did me the favor of looking away and out the window. "My father built it and my wife and I brought up four kids in this house. Wife's gone five years now and my kids are scattered to the winds. They come by to see me from time to time, or vice versa. We still get along OK. We used to farm the land where all of those new homes are." He stopped and reflected. "Made a good bit of money selling the land, so my kids and grandkids will be well set up when I'm gone, I suppose. I'll stay here 'till I die. I kept the house and a few lots around it. Kids can sell it off if they want after I'm gone. I have a good life here. Miss my wife, but still have my friends. Friends and family are important."

'Oh, here it comes,' I thought, bracing myself for a lecture.

Instead, he asked, "Where'd you say you hiked here from?"

I thought we'd already determined that I'd just gotten off of a train. Maybe I was giving this guy too much credit. I had no qualms about lying, but I had no idea where I was. I couldn't make up the name of some local town and expect a guy that's lived here all of his life—even if he was borderline senile—to just think,

"Damn, I never heard of that town, and I thought I knew them all."

'What the *hell* is the name of that town with the bridge?' I silently asked myself.

Google Earth satellite image-ville?

'Oh yeah, that's it. How could I have forgotten?' I tried not to smile at my silliness.

The ticking of the kitchen clock seemed to draw attention to my silence. Finally, as he went to the counter, he said, "My youngest son spent quite a lot of time on the road before he finally settled down. Seemed to do him some good to get it out of his system while he was young . . ." As he opened a cabinet, he glanced my way and added, "Although he wasn't anywhere *near* as young as you are."

"I'm not really as young as I look," I said and smiled.

I somehow gave him a little scare and a shadow of wariness briefly crossed his eyes. The dog, which had appeared to be fast asleep, either picked up on his vibes or a change in his scent because it sat up and angled its greying snout at him in a questioning manner. The old man absently reached down and gave the dog a comforting rub behind the ears.

"Peanut butter and jelly sound good?"

"Just peanut butter," I answered.

As he set it before me, he told me that he always kept "the fixings for a kid's favorite sandwich" around for his grandkids. It had jelly, but starving beggars can't afford to be picky eaters and I gobbled it.

'I haven't had one of these since I was a little kid,' I thought and smiled at the irony of my statement.

I broke a lengthening silence by saying, "I, ah, I guess I'd better head home."

"Mmmm . . ." he grunted doubtfully. "Do you want some water to take with you?"

"Gosh, that'd be swell," I gushed, in what I hoped was boy-age-appropriate, sixties-style lingo. I handed him my canteen.

I glanced around at the kitchen, which had obviously been decorated by his late wife many years ago. There was a clear vase on the counter, which had dried stains on the inside of it from various water levels throughout the years. I absently wondered when that vase last held fresh-cut flowers.

I asked him if I could use his bathroom and he indicated where it was.

'The world needs more people like this guy,' I thought as I did my business.

What—the kind of people who would turn some little kid back out into the world on his own?

'I don't know *what* I meant, OK? Geez! *You're* me, and *you're* an adult, and *you've* got me out here on my own, don't ya? So there!'

That didn't even make any sense, but then neither does trying to win an argument with yourself.

You didn't even bother asking him his name.

I blushed at that and made a mental note to ask him.

On my way into the bathroom, as I'd unexpectedly caught a glimpse of my refection in the mirror, I got a little freaked out and quickly averted my eyes. From inside myself, I was still the same grown-up me. Just like, in my other adult life, from inside I'd always still kind of been the kid me. But as I met my eyes in the mirror, I confirmed that I was neither one—I was that boy from under the bridge.

As a child in my old life, my hair had been blondish-brown and wavy. Now it was dark and fairly straight. Whereas my eyes had been brown, these were green. Other than that and the fact that I'd worn glasses since first grade, we looked alike in a generic kid sort of way.

Although my face said I was too young to be on my own, my eyes said something different. I looked like a ten-year-old grown-up, if that makes any sense. A ten-year-old grown-up who didn't even exist.

At least your image reflects in mirrors.

'Doesn't that test only apply to vampires?'

And to little boys who don't exist.

I stared deep into my eyes. 'So, who *am* I?'

On the way out of the old man's kitchen door, I glanced at the calendar on the wall. It had a picture of an old covered bridge. August 1967. The number of the year didn't have the "shock value" that I would have expected it to have. I guess you live in the year you live in without stopping to dwell on the number. You note it on New Year's Eve, mistakenly write the old year a few times for the first few weeks, and then forget about it.

I kicked stray stones off of the ties as I ambled down the tracks. The old farmer had been growing increasingly uncomfortable with me there. Not in an unfriendly way, just in a "This kid scares me in a strange way because he seems not to be who he looks like he is, and I don't understand that, so I wish he'd just be gone" kind of way.

"Might as well get used to it, Mike," I muttered, as loneliness welled up in me.

Didn't you always brag in your other life that you "didn't need anyone" and that you "couldn't get lonely"?

'Whatever.'

I still couldn't believe that old guy hadn't called the cops and I kept a keen eye out. What would I have done if I were him? Probably I'd have called the cops. I know I certainly wouldn't have fed me and sent me on my way. If not for moral reasons, I'd at least be concerned for my own liability in aiding and abetting.

I followed the tracks for hours and miles. Any time a train approached, I retreated to the adjacent woods. All were going too fast to hop and none stopped.

Funny the little quirks we have that we never realize. In my old, adult body I wore glasses most of the time. In this kid one, I didn't. Yet several times since I switched, I caught myself reaching up to adjust glasses that weren't there to begin with. So had they *ever* needed adjusting, or was that just a compulsion? Who knows?

The countryside gave way to a run-down semi-urban area that I really didn't like the looks of. Even the limited wooded areas unnerved me because, mostly around firepits, the woods were littered with broken bottles, smashed beer cans, old cigarette packs, discarded bras, panties and guys underwear, the remnants of firecrackers, wet porno magazines, destroyed bicycles. One firepit had animal bones scattered about, as though some sort of satanic ritual had taken place there. It was obvious that the local teens hung out in these woods and this was their turf. I was worried about running into a gang of bored teenagers who had nothing better to do than hassle some strange little kid.

Up ahead, there appeared to be a major railroad junction or yard or something. I decided that it wasn't a good idea to walk any farther that way in daylight. After only one night, it was already set into my mind that I'd do my traveling at night when possible. Of course, I didn't know where I was traveling *to*, but I would do it at night. I now decided to head west, away from New York City.

So in my new style of walking along the tracks without actually *getting* anywhere that I'd perfected yesterday during my rant under the rainy bridge, I turned around and headed west away from town in search of a nicer area in which to wait for darkness.

I sat contentedly alongside a brook in the quiet woods. About fifty feet away, the brook gurgled under the railroad embankment through a large, beautifully-constructed stone arch. Clear afternoon sunlight slanted through the trees and illuminated the transparent, aqua-tinted glass insulators on the old telegraph poles that paralleled the tracks.

'Maybe I should walk all of the way back to that stupid bridge, and some grown-up me who's been searching for years will innocently show up not knowing what a nightmare he's getting himself into.' I chuckled at the memory of yesterday.

With your luck, it would be raining in 2015 when you switched back.

'Yeah, yeah, and I'd be all pissed off because now it's sunny in 1967 and I got screwed again!'

I laughed as I tossed a few pebbles into the brook.

'Going to be chilly tonight,' I thought as a breeze stirred the trees. 'Tonight when I ride, I'll stay on the train for more than a few hours, and when I wake up I won't be in Jersey anymore, baby. And when we pass that stupid bridge, I hope I'm *fast* asleep.'

Meaning that now you don't want to switch back?

I considered how anticlimactic it would be to just return to my old life after only one day in this adventure.

'No, no, I guess I don't,' I hesitantly admitted. 'I mean—if I could jump back and forth whenever I wanted to . . . But I certainly wouldn't switch back if it was going to be a one-shot deal and I could never come back here again.'

What if yesterday was a one-shot deal?

I shrugged. 'Too late now.'

A tingling sensation, not altogether unpleasant, ran up my spine as I considered completely abandoning my past life.

I passed the time watching the sunset while making a mental list of necessities for my backpack. At twilight, I decided to venture into town again.

I did my best to avoid detection, but a lot more people were outside in 1967—particularly kids. I got as close as I dared to the brightly lit junction or yard before I hid out in the brush and waited.

A train crept westbound towards me. As soon as the engines passed, I grabbed my backpack and started planning my move. I eyed up a brand-new-looking grey hopper car that would be easy to hop. It was similar to the coal car, but this type was covered on the top to keep plastic pellets, grain, or other granular stuff dry. I needed to get on and get hidden before the train went over the nearby road crossing, or the people in the waiting cars might spot me. The train picked up speed much faster than I would have expected it to and I hesitated. A little movie played in my head, showing myself grabbing the ladder, pulling myself up, missing the step, and falling under the wheels. I shuddered at the thought and sat back down, using my backpack as a cushion to keep my butt dry.

After about ten more cars, the train squealed to a halt. Back then, they still used cabooses and there wasn't one on this short train. After a few minutes, it slowly backed up the way it had come.

Across the tracks from me, a 1967 version of a SUV-looking vehicle pulled into a large dirt lot and I quickly dropped down on the ground in the weeds. I expected the driver to turn around, but they stopped facing the tracks with the headlights pointing right at me.

"Oh, for crying out loud, wouldn't you just know it," I complained softly. "What are the odds of that?"

I hadn't even had the chance to get in a comfortable position or a good spot because I'd figured that I'd only be down for a second or two as the lights swept past me.

'Did they see me here? How? They would have had to be watching with night-vision goggles, and they probably haven't even been invented yet. They *still* can't see me through the weeds and grass, can they?'

I figured it most likely was a railroad cop, watching for people doing exactly what I was doing. I knew that railroads employed their own police from my days of screwing around at the tracks with my friends as a kid in my other life. But it could have been someone sitting there drinking, or people making out or whatever.

At least a half hour passed. All the while, my dry clothes wicked moisture from the damp ground. Lying here all night shivering wasn't an option, so I shoved myself backwards through the weeds. The land behind me sloped down to a ten-foot-wide, water-filled, tree-and-brush-lined ditch. Once down by the water, I was in shadow and I could stand up.

I fought my way through stickers and over dead branches and small logs that would break unexpectedly underfoot. Everything was sharp, rotten, and the slanted ground was slippery and muddy. I fell a few times, muddying my hands and feeling thankful that nothing had poked my eye out.

"Oh, no," I whispered as I closed my eyes and let my shoulders and head slump in defeat. "My backpack! I had been sitting on it and I left it up by the tracks—right in the stupid *headlights*!"

I was already physically and emotionally drained and now I fought a panic attack. Not as though an immediate threat were near. Just overtired, nowhere-to-go, had-*way*-too-much-stimulation-in-the-past-day kind of panic.

I swatted a mosquito on my forehead with my filthy fingers and then tried to wipe the mud off with my sweatshirt sleeve.

'Do I *have* to fight my way back there through the stickers? Couldn't that stupid truck just leave? I—I *only* want to get out of here and go to sleep. That's *all* I'm asking for here. I haven't slept in—what?—almost two days? I just—I don't— I *just* want to find somewhere to crash.'

Being a little kid put huge stress on the situation. I couldn't merely sneak out to the road and walk along all innocent-like at night. The first cop that saw me would stop. And I would run from anyone else that might stop for a little kid in this area.

The train was pulling back out of the yard.

'All right, I've had enough laughs for one night. I'm out of here.'

I fought my way up to the tracks and scoped out the situation. The truck with the lights was still there. I ran back along the gravel road next to the tracks and grabbed my brightly illuminated backpack.

'Well, if they didn't see me before, they see me now.'

I was hoping that the train in front of whoever was in the truck would be so bright with their headlights on it that anything they could see on the other side of the tracks under the train would be dark by contrast.

But they saw me, all right. Either that or it was one hell of a coincidence, because the vehicle was instantly in motion. Between passing freight cars, I caught a glimpse of a spotlight mounted by the driver's window and some type of official insignia on the door. I continued on towards the railroad yard. Before getting to the brightly lit area, I veered off to the left, down towards the drainage ditch.

After catching my breath, I crept to the top to see what the cop was up to. He must have raced up to the crossing and driven around the front of the train, because now he was bouncing along on the dirt road on my side of the tracks. He halted back where he'd first spotted me and shined his spotlight on the train.

Despite how worn-out I was, I was tickled by the fact that a cop—a 1967 cop, no less—was searching for *me*. I allowed myself a congratulatory little smile.

What a fascinating and fun night this has been!

'Hey, don't say I never take you anywhere.'

The train rolled slowly on. I debated hopping on and hiding out of sight on the opposite side while I passed the cop. But I was afraid that my motion would catch his eye or he'd see me silhouetted against the railroad yard lights. And there was always the possibility that there were two cops, one on each side. The train stopped and backed up again, so it was a good thing I'd stayed put. I couldn't understand why it kept going back and forth, but I was too tired to care.

I didn't actually get out of there until, I would guess, the wee hours of the morning. The car I chose to ride was so new that you could still smell the paint. It was similar to the coal car from last night, with a platform on both ends. But these platforms had solid floors, so I didn't have to sit balanced on a beam. There was a little nook in the end of the car that someone small like me could crawl into and hide and I curled up in there out of sight with just my head poking out. My goal was to stay awake long enough to bid a final farewell to my switching location if this was the line that passed under the bridge, but I drifted off to sleep in minutes.

Around midday, my train slowed down and I watched from my hiding spot as the tracks split and multiplied into a sea of rails. An engine chuffed past with a long line of freight cars as we slowly pulled into the packed train yard and ground to a halt. I still had a clear shot to the woods, so I hopped off and, after a quick scan for cops and moving trains, I ran.

Down below was a river. I figured that if the water smelled reasonably clean and it wasn't too cold, I'd strip to my underwear and bathe in it.

"Soap. That's something else I need for my—oh, crap!"

My train had started slowly, almost silently rolling again. I dashed over, hopped up and grabbed my backpack, then ran back to the river.

I followed a well-worn path through a thin strip of woods between the railroad yards and the river. Scattered along this path were side trails leading to homeless encampments, which I gave as wide a berth as possible. Some seemed abandoned, but some were populated by people who suspiciously watched me pass by. I monitored them from the corner of my eye without looking directly at them and making eye contact. I didn't know if they were actual hobos who hopped trains, or if they just lived there. The whole area reeked of unclean bodies, wet blankets and rusty, rotting food cans.

"Hey, come here, boy," came a voice from off to my left.

I hesitated for a second.

"No, it's OK. We just want to talk to you. We ain't gonna hurt you."

I went nearer, but stayed well enough away to run. I didn't want to piss them off by ignoring them, but I also didn't want to get too close. There were two men that I saw at first. Both had beards and were in, I would say, their sixties. One, who I immediately dubbed "Willy Nelson" in my mind, was thin and wore a red bandana to hold back his long grey hair. The other one was heavyset and had shorter hair.

I could have run circles around both of them. But in this body, if one of them did manage to grab me, I wasn't strong enough to fight back.

"Got any money, boy?" asked the heavy one threateningly.

"Don't be an asshole, Frank," said the thin one.

"I didn't say I was gonna *rob* the kid, Bernie, I just asked if he had any money!"

"He don't have no money, look at him. Hey kid, you got any money?"

"Ten cents," I answered.

This seemed to rile Frank: "Ten cents? What the hell you gonna buy with ten cents? What're you doing out here anyways? How old are you?"

"Fourteen," I lied, tacking some years onto how old I'd supposed I was.

"Shit! If you're fourteen, then I'm a hundred!" snapped Frank. He turned to a younger, thin, dark-haired guy who was a little ways off by himself, just sitting and watching me sort of ominously and intently from the open end of his tent. "Hey," (some name I didn't catch—Clary? Clyde?), "how old you think this kid is?"

"'Bout ten, I would guess," Clary/Clyde answered quietly, his eyes never leaving me.

I hadn't noticed that guy until now. '*He* might be fast enough to catch me,' I thought uneasily.

"What're you doing out here?" Frank asked again.

"I just hopped off of a train."

Frank got even more worked up: "A fourteen-year-old boy don't have *no* right to be out here," he stated, and spat.

Bernie said, "Aw, settle down, wouldya Frank? He ain't fourteen—*look* at him!"

"I never said he *was* fourteen, Bern."

I inwardly rolled my eyes and stifled a smile.

Clary/Clyde was still staring at me from his tent. Quietly, almost hypnotically, he said. "You hungry, boy? C'mere, I'll give you something to eat."

The hell he would. I did what little kids are supposed to do when they think they are in danger: I ran. I turned around fearfully to see if I was being chased, but they didn't bother.

Clary/Clyde wanted to do more than just give you food, you know.

'I know. This ain't my first day at the rodeo.'

I wondered if Frank and Bernie would have come to my rescue.

No, they were as scared of what's-his-name as you were. They would have either left, or pretended not to hear.

'Or stood guard. That's why I stay away from people.'

Maybe not, but that didn't help me in my situation. The way I saw it, a bad person who wanted to harm me wouldn't care that I was a little kid out here on my own. But a good person who wanted to help me would feel that it was their moral duty to turn me in.

I needed food and supplies, but I had no way to make money. I knew I looked too young to just stand on a sidewalk and panhandle, but I might have no choice. Once clear of the homeless camps, I slowed my pace and admired how scenic it was along the river. That is, if you ignored the toxic-smelling smog that pervaded the area. There were traces of black, soot-like deposits on the leaves of low-hanging branches. I supposed that people in 1967, when thinking of the future, would grimly imagine skies hopelessly obscured by pollution. In my experience, the air was cleaner in the future.

I hiked quite a ways, right on past the other end of the railroad yard. Down below me, there was a gravel road that meandered along the river. There were little parking areas with picnic tables and metal barbeque thingies on poles. I cut down through the woods and ambled along the gravel road as I scanned the riverbank for a nice place to swim.

As I rounded a curve, I saw a yellow VW Beetle parked in one of the little pull-offs. The smell of the barbeque drew me nearer, and when I could see the person, it was a girl about twenty years old. Her car had Pennsylvania plates and was plastered with all kinds of bumper stickers.

She had the car radio playing what I took to be an oldies rock and roll station and I absently wondered why someone so young would be into sixties music.

This is *the sixties, you idiot.*

'Oh yeah, duh.'

My inner voice shook its head sadly.

'I hate sixties music.'

Well, you'd better get used to it.

I stood off to the side behind some bushes and watched. Just as I was debating how I'd get my hands on some of that food, she got up from the picnic table to go to her car.

She saw me and we met eyes.

"Hey there, whatcha doing?" she asked in a friendly manner.

"Not much, just hanging out," I answered.

She looked at me strangely. Did people use the phrase "hanging out" back now? I had absolutely no idea.

"I'm looking for somewhere private to swim in the river," I explained.

"In long pants?"

"I was just going to go in my underwear."

"Oh. What's in the backpack?"

"Nothing."

"So why are you carrying it?"

Because if he takes it off of his back for five seconds, he loses it.

"Well, I had food in here but I ate it all last night," I said, hoping she'd take the hint.

"Last *night?*" She asked. "Where did you come from?"

"New Jersey."

"Alone?"

I nodded.

She narrowed her eyes and challenged, "How'd you get here?"

"I hopped a freight train."

"So you ran away from home," she concluded with disapproval.

I shrugged.

"Well, did you or didn't you?"

"I don't have any family to run away from."

"What happened to them?"

"They died in a car crash."

Her mouth opened in an "o" and her eyebrows went stern. "That's really mean! Your family didn't die in some car crash. You're making that up. You'd sure better hope they don't die now or you'll feel awful, like you cursed them."

I sighed and chastised myself for making up such a stupid, little-kid lie. "Sorry. But I really don't have a family. I'm all alone."

"How am I supposed to believe anything you say now?"

I stood silent. I wanted to just leave but, oh, what was she cooking over there? Burgers? The smell was making my mouth water.

"Can I have something to eat?" I asked.

"Sure, there's plenty," she said. "My boyfriend's supposed to be here with me, but he's too lazy to get up."

I ate anything that she would put in front of me, and washed it down with a can of Coke that had the old pull-tab that comes right off. I'd forgotten about those.

Every so often I could hear them slamming freight cars together up in the railroad yard, and I looked forward to riding off into the sunset on a train.

It was fairly warm out now and I wanted to take the sweatshirt off, but I was embarrassed by how badly I stunk. I didn't have underarm stink, but just a general unwashed smell. Not as bad as the whiffs I'd caught coming off of the homeless guys, but not good. When I raised my head up from eating, I could smell my oily hair.

I was especially embarrassed in front of such a pretty girl. Her name was Lauren and she had honey-colored hair and greenish eyes. She wore no makeup, and she had the same kind of natural beauty as the river valley we were sitting in.

'If I was her boyfriend,' I silently thought, 'there couldn't have been a "too early" to get up to be with her.'

She had a plain, no-nonsense frankness about her and was obviously intelligent. Although she dressed as though she was poor, I had a feeling that her parents had a lot of money. One of her bumper stickers said "Lehigh University," so I figured she went there.

"Thanks for the food," I said as I got up to leave.

"Wait—where are you going?"

"Over to the river. After dark I'll find some food somewhere and then catch a freight train out of here."

"Just like that? Do you have any money?"

"No. Well, ten cents." I smiled at the irony of that.

She got up quickly and moved towards me. I snatched my backpack and ran out onto the dirt road, ready to run up the hill.

"Wait, easy, don't run!" she said, her hands held out in a harmless gesture. "I wasn't after you. I was getting something for you from my car. I should *not* be doing this," she chided herself as she rummaged around in her car.

I felt a little foolish for running, so I went back to the picnic table. Lauren came back with a blanket for me.

"Thank you," I said and stuffed it into my pack.

"Here," she said softly, holding out a folded bill. "My dad makes me carry this for emergencies, but he has plenty of money. I'll just tell him I lost it."

I hesitated.

"Go on," she said, "take it. You need it more than I do. And if you do have a family, hopefully you'll buy a bus ticket back to them."

I took it and unfolded it: a twenty-dollar bill. "Wow, thanks!" That was a lot of money to give away in 1967.

"Peace," I said as I shouldered my backpack and headed down the road.

I hadn't walked fifty feet when I saw a cop car through the trees at a bend in the road. I probably could have just kept walking and said hello to him as we passed, but I figured if the conversation went any further than 'hi' I might have problems. So I rushed back and sat at the picnic table by Lauren.

"Back so soon?" she asked.

"Cop coming."

"So? You're not doing anything illegal. What do you think, he's going to read your mind?"

"I just didn't know what to say to him if he wanted to talk to me, that's all."

"You could just say that you walked over here from Allentown. He wouldn't know."

"I didn't know of a town name to tell him if he asked, so I figured I'd just sit here with you as he drove by."

"Oh yeah, make me the bad guy."

The cop slowly passed us and gave us a friendly wave.

Lauren slowly assessed me from head to toe. When we met eyes, her expression said, "Honestly, kid, is this the lifestyle you want?"

"If you want help, I could take you somewhere . . ."

I smiled and shook my head. "I'm OK. Really, I am."

I thanked her again and went on my way.

I found a secluded spot to swim, nap, and generally laze about. At dusk, I went up to the tracks and crossed the river on the railroad bridge. A short time later, a train crept out of the yard. The first decent thing I saw to ride that had a hiding spot was a bulkhead flat car (a flat car with walls at each end of it) that was loaded with wooden poles. I didn't sit by the poles. Although they were strapped down, if they shifted I could be crushed. I sat on the end of the car with the end wall to protect me. My view was of the couplers and the wheels of the next freight car. There were little nooks behind the ladders that a small person like me could hide in.

At some time during the night, we stopped at another rail yard. I made my way to the other end and hopped right onto another hopper car on an outbound train. I dozed a little, but I came fully awake as the train slowly came to a stop in what looked to be a bad area of a big city. I felt more vulnerable sitting on the train than I would by getting off it and hiding in the brush, so that's what I did while waiting for it to move again.

It was just starting to get light and I needed food and especially something to drink, seeing as my canteen was empty. I figured if there was ever a "safe" time to walk through a bad area, this would be it because all of the drunks and drug-gies and rowdies would be sleeping. I abandoned my train and carefully made my way to the streets. No one bothered me and the few people who were out and about even said hello. I walked down some narrow, scary, row house-lined streets and past some mammoth, decaying factories. Finally I found a busy boulevard and headed towards what looked to be downtown in what turned out to be Phila-delphia.

8.

I didn't really know how to get back to where I'd hopped off the train, but I wasn't worried. I didn't feel like pressing my luck heading back that way, and anyways I'd already walked a considerable distance and scoped out my next ride. I planned on catching a freight over near the zoo. My target was a line that traversed a long bridge before dropping downgrade to merge with a very busy passenger line. At least one freight train was almost always stopped on the long bridge waiting to proceed in what I assumed to be a southerly direction. I'd have to be very careful, though, because at the junction of the two lines there was a tall, narrow railroad building next to the tracks with lots of big windows so the guy could watch what was happening. If that plan didn't work out, there was another busy rail line tucked in below the buildings along the river on the city side. Mixed in with the crushed stone along the tracks in this area were millions of little, round, what-looked-to-be iron ore pellets.

I made my way to a mostly empty park and found a secluded spot to sleep most of the day away. In late afternoon, as I lounged on the grass and admired the view of the city, a young man limped along on a nearby walkway and stopped to greet me. I smiled and nodded. He seemed quite harmless, but even so I was a coiled spring, ready to run.

"Running away from home?" he asked as he stepped closer.

"No."

He nodded his head toward my pack. "I hope you're not staying here after dark. It can get kind of scary here at night. And with that backpack, you look like easy pickings."

"I'll be gone by nightfall. I'm not running away, I'm just out here on my own."

"Well," he scoffed, "you're way too young to be 'out here on your own,' so . . ."

"You wouldn't believe me if I told you."

"Try me."

"Nah, it doesn't matter anyways. Like I said, by tonight I'll be long gone."

He scrutinized me for a long moment.

"For a kid who's running away from home, you don't seem very upset."

I did a little shrug, letting the "running away from home" description slide.

"Where are you heading?"

"I don't know. South. Then west, I guess," I answered. So far, I'd headed east, west and apparently now I was set on south. Actually, now that I stopped to think about it, I'd gone back east from Allentown to Philadelphia hadn't I? Oops. How I'd done *that*, after heading west out of Allentown, was a mystery to me.

Pretty soon, you'll be going in circles.

'Well, *you* were supposed to bring the compass,' I silently joked.

"Where are you from?" the guy asked.

"New Jersey."

"You walked all of the way here from New Jersey?"

"No, I rode freight trains from New Jersey to Allentown to here."

"*Freight* trains? How do you know where they're going?"

I smiled. "I don't. I look at license plates when the train stops."

"*Man* is that dangerous. How are you going to make money and eat? And keep from getting arrested or beaten up?"

"I hide out a lot, and I'm very careful. So far, I've done OK."

"But, you're so young! Yet," he said pensively, "you're like an adult. How old *are* you?"

"Eighteen."

He shook his head, unamused.

He really was about eighteen to twenty and kind of geeky. He looked Italian. Medium build, a little stocky, dark hair, dark eyes. He walked with a severe limp because one of his legs was really messed up. Funny thing is, when he first started talking to me, he had the demeanor of one who is addressing a child. Now, only a few sentences later, he talked as though he was conversing with an adult. I'm sure he didn't realize this, but I noticed it.

"Where will you sleep tonight?"

"On a train. I sleep well while the train is moving because that's when I feel safe."

"As long as it doesn't jump the tracks," he said.

"Well, yeah, other than that. I sure hope it doesn't."

There was an awkward silence as we both ran out of things to say.

"I, uh … I guess I'll let you be. Nice meeting you, man. Be careful," he said. He turned to leave, but hesitated. "I can't just leave you here. I'm sure you'll say no, and I'm probably crazy for asking, but if you want to come to my place and shower, wash your clothes, stuff like that, you're welcome to. You can leave whenever you want. I'll even drive you to the tracks. I just thought you might appreciate a little help, that's all. No strings attached. It's just—I've only known you for a minute, but I feel funny just leaving you here. Maybe you'll decide to go home."

I didn't answer, just sat there debating. I didn't get any bad vibes off of him and I desperately needed a shower, so I was leaning towards a yes. But then, I didn't feel like having someone guilt-trip me for "running away from home" and me having to make up some story.

"Um, no thanks," I said regretfully.

"I'm a very good listener …"

His kindness and caring made me smile, but I didn't reply.

He hesitantly took about ten more steps before stopping again.

"You're just going to sit there all alone? I mean …" He held up his hands and gestured.

I shrugged.

"Hey, do you want to make some money?" he asked.

I just looked up at him and didn't say anything. Although I didn't think this guy was the type, some people who offer money to runaway boys don't always have, shall we say, the purest of intentions.

He held up his hands in an "I'm just asking, hear me out" kind of gesture. "My partner and I have a painting company, and we have a ton of jobs to do including a suite of offices to paint. But he's in Florida on vacation, and the guy who's supposed to help me drinks and hasn't answered his phone in two days. I have to get this work done and I need the help. I know other people who I could ask, but I figured I'd offer it to you. You're, um … I don't know, man, I just want to know your story. And you could get cleaned up and make some money for your next adventure."

I'd worked maintenance at hotels in the past of my other life, so I was a good painter.

Should I trust this guy? He seemed pretty straight-up.

Just go with the flow, Mike.

"OK," I answered. "Sounds good."

"My name's Gene, by the way."

"I'm Mike."

We walked up to his "G&G Painting" van in the parking lot.

"Who's the other 'G'?" I asked.

"Gary, my partner. Although, I get all of the business, buy the supplies, sched-ule the jobs . . ."

"Pay for the gas and insurance on the van," I added and we both laughed.

"You're pretty grown-up for a kid," Gene noted with a crooked smile.

I just smiled.

As we cruised through a suburb of Philadelphia in his van, it occurred to me that this was the first vehicle in which I'd traveled in 1967—or at least in 1967 in this new life. Although I'd been here for a few days by now, this was the first time that I actually relaxed and took in the sixties scenery in detail. Up until now, I guess the different era was kind of a threat to my security and sanity and I'd subliminally been tuning it out. Now that I could observe it from the safety of a vehicle, every detail seemed special. We stopped at a traffic light and I watched across the corner as citizens came and went from a main street hardware store. For a few brief seconds, I could feel all of the eras that ever were and these people going about their lives in a long-gone era brought me both joy and sadness.

"I remember running away from home when I was a kid," Gene reflected. "But I only went as far as my best friend's house and hid out in our tree fort. I mean, I never would have had the guts to . . . to do what you're doing."

He was quiet for a few minutes, and so was I.

"I guess when I did it . . . I guess I wanted to be found, you know?" he added.

He glanced over at me, but I didn't have an answer for him.

"If things are that bad for you at home . . ."

I hated to lie, but a story was needed. I told Gene I'd grown up in a hippy commune, never really knowing who or where my parents were.

A commune? That's a little hacky, don't you think?

'Well, this is the sixties, so that's why I chose the commune thing.'

Next time, you could say that you got separated from your family on a camping trip when you were a baby and you were raised by wolves.

'Woof! I like that one!'

Gene was mulling it over. Next he'd probably ask questions such as: "Where did you go to school? What happened when you got sick?" and I'd say, "We had a teacher and a doctor living there." On and on it would go until I'd made up so many lies about a living in a commune (something I knew absolutely nothing about) that I wouldn't be able to remember them all. That's what sucks about making up lies.

I figured it was time for a change of subject.

"What happened to your leg?" I asked.

By the look on his face, boy did I ever strike a chord. The question did what I wanted it to do, though. It jolted the conversation into a different direction.

"Polio as a kid," he said disgustedly.

"But I guess it kept you out of 'Nam, right?"

"Yeah, I know it did."

"So, better to have a limp, than to come home with no legs, right?"

He grunted agreement and then added ominously, "My friend whose tree fort I hid in as a kid is over there."

Gene lived in a suburb of Philadelphia in one of those awful sixties garden apartment complexes that I've never liked. White-roofed, red brick buildings with small windows. Silly, faux-white shutters with fake hinges which, if you actually could close them, would only cover about a third of the window area. The grounds were landscaped with widely spaced yew bushes that were carved into various un-natural shapes—some as big gumdrops, some with perfectly flat tops, etc.

Aside from the sixties-style furnishings, Gene's apartment didn't look any-thing like the hippie crash pad that I'd imagined. But then, Gene didn't look anything like a hippie. He could have strolled down the street in 2015 and no one would have batted an eye. This guy seemed to be like I was in my old life: not swayed by latest phases that the country was going through.

He gave me a pair of his huge clothes to bring into the bathroom with me and instructed me to throw all of my stuff out the bathroom door. Although the apartment complex had a lower-level laundry room, he said he was going to his mother's house to wash it and then pick up a pizza on the way back. He invited me to shower and make myself at home. Then, to my amazement, he left me alone in his apartment.

I watched through a crack in the drapes as he pulled away. I figured there was a ninety percent chance he'd come back with the cops, but this was one of the *very* rare times that I decided to just let fate take its course.

This was my first shower in my new body, and just as I'd let myself accept the sixties scenery, I relaxed and accepted my new self. I think the moment I noticed how high the water faucets in the shower were was my turning point.

Afterwards, I examined my face in the mirror. It was only the second mirror that I'd seen since switching into this world and the first time that I had the chance to study my image at leisure. It was still a little unsettling that I didn't look like my old self anymore—or at least a younger version of my old self. And yet, I didn't—actually, I should say I *wasn't able to*—feel as though it was a stranger's face I was looking at.

"I *know* you," I whispered.

A smile turned to a grin and then into head-shaking laughter.

"I just can't believe I really went through with switching lives. I'm actually here, right now, *living* it."

And then: "Look at those little 'stick arms!'" I laughed again.

Then I turned serious. At some point in the last twenty-four hours, I subconsciously vowed that if this kid I'd become had run away and there were parents sitting home worrying, I'd get this body home to them and then deal with whatever happened from there. And who knew? Maybe that was the whole point of switching lives, to get this kid home.

I leaned in, close enough for my breath to fog the mirror. "Now let's go see if anyone's looking for you, young man."

I quickly scanned Gene's newspaper. No mention of a missing kid, but would a missing North Jersey kid make the news in a local Pennsylvania rag? Doubtful.

It was impossible not to get absorbed in the headline stories. What amazed me was—in a broad sense—how similar the sense of impending doom and the issues of 1967 were to those in 2015. There were the crooked politicians being investigated and street protesters being barricaded by police in riot gear. The United States, as always and apparently forever, had our big, evil, "enemy-of-the-month" foreign villain who threatened to destabilize our comfy world.

Indeed, one could almost create a newspaper template for the ages and merely edit a few details and change the names of the main players every few months.

I surmised that if I perused a newspaper from 1941, it would be a similar deal. Ditto for the future: "In other news, fighting with the Veldors from the X-36 solar system continues over ownership of Tetron, which is the sole inhabitable planet in the M-45 solar system. Protesters argue that the only reason Earth covets the disputed planet is because Orion Mining Corporation (which donates generously to the Moon Party) wants to exploit the planet's abundant supply of craptomium-9. Meanwhile, continuing development of the Black Hole Annihilator by the Zweirconians threatens the existence of the entire galaxy . . ."

If I got nothing else out of switching to another era, I at least gained this unique perspective.

I found a phone book in the first place I looked—under the phone, in the drawer of the end table next to the couch.

I picked up a framed picture of Gene and a girl on a beach. Her hands were draped around his lower waist from behind and she was smiling seductively at the camera. I figured it must be his girlfriend.

"Police, police, where is it?" I asked as I flipped through the "P" pages. "Pecker? There's really someone named *Pecker!?* And I thought *I* had problems in school! Hey, I wonder how many Morrisons there are."

Tick-tock Mike. Gene will be back soon.

"Oh, yeah, right."

Then I remembered that the police and fire department numbers were listed on the first page of most phone books. 9-1-1 didn't exist back now, but emergency and non-emergency numbers were listed for several towns.

I dashed back into the kitchen and scanned Gene's mail to see where I was. Back now a call to the next town could be a toll call. There was no sense in running up a bill (and leaving evidence).

I smiled as I inserted my finger in the proper number slots and turned the dial. By 2015, they'd taken all of the fun out of using a phone.

"Upper Darby Police, Sergeant McCann speaking, how may I help you?"

"I'd like to inquire about a runaway kid."

I mentally pictured him gesturing the other cops to gather 'round.

"How so?" he asked.

"Well, I just wanted to know if anyone reported him missing."

"What's your name, ma'am?"

"I'm not a 'ma'am'," I replied dryly. "I'm a boy."

"I see. I'm going to put you on hold."

I was glad they didn't have caller ID back now. But didn't they trace calls on those old cop shows? They had to stall to keep the caller on for a while. Did the technology exist in the sixties? I hoped not.

Gene could return at any time, so I grew more anxious by the minute. I shouldn't have wasted so much time screwing around. Just when I was about to hang up, an Officer Something-or-Other came on and asked me my name. I said I didn't want to give it, so he asked me to explain.

"Well, I met this kid in the park—"

"What park?" he interjected.

"Um . . . a park near my house and he said he ran away from home. Oh, from New Jersey. On August twenty-fourth," I added weakly and rolled my eyes. Then it occurred to me that this kid's body might not even be from New Jersey. For all I knew, he could have ridden trains from California to meet me. Oh well, I had to start somewhere.

The cop asked for a description and then he asked where the kid was now.

"He ran off," I answered. "But I think he's living in the park."

"Son, I need to speak to your parents."

"No. I mean, they're not even home and besides, I'll get in trouble for not telling them first. Can't a person ask a question anonymously?"

"We're making some phone calls."

I could hear him discussing it with someone else in the background. I figured this might take a while. Back now the cops wouldn't have a computer screen in front of them with a searchable runaway kid database. So unless they distributed fliers on runaway kids the way they did for the "Ten Most Wanted" criminals, a police department in southeastern Pennsylvania probably wouldn't know anything about a missing New Jersey kid.

I heard the muted thud of a car door closing out front.

"I'll call you back," I said hurriedly and hung up.

It wasn't Gene; it was someone else arriving at a different apartment. I wished I knew how much time I had.

"Come on, come on," I muttered as I redialed. The phone that had seemed so quaint only minutes ago now was a hindrance. There was no quick way to make a call. The mechanical dial wasted precious seconds just resetting each time.

"Upper Darby Police, Sergeant McCann speaking, how may I—"

"It's me, that kid again and I want to—"

"Hold on."

"Son of a bitch," I said under my breath as I glanced towards the front windows.

"Son," Officer Whatever said when he came on the line, "I need to know where you are."

"OK, *I'm* the one who ran away, all right? If my parents reported me missing, I'll turn myself in. I *just* need to know where they—"

"We just spoke to them. Now, they're not angry, but they're very worried about you and they want to take you home."

"You're just *saying* that! OK, so what town do my parents live in, huh?"

"I can't give out that information over the phone."

"You're *lying*!" I slammed the phone down in its cradle. Then I grabbed the phone book and hurled it across the room. It narrowly missed one of Gene's expensive-looking stereo speakers before it struck the wall.

Mike, you really need to calm down. You're acting like a child.

"I *am* a child, you dumb-ass!"

I plunked down cross-legged on the floor and buried my face in my hands. I was ashamed of the hair-triggered temper tantrums I'd been having lately and perturbed by the fact that, despite my previous experiences as an adult, I'd handled the call like a juvenile. Had I done it in a sensible, grown-up manner, I probably could have gotten some useful information.

You should have let them think you were a "ma'am."

I puffed a humorless little laugh and nodded agreement.

He was still asking you where you were, so at least they didn't trace the call.

I did a long, calming down sigh. 'Yeah, at least there's that.'

"What a bunch of idiots," I grumbled as I checked the phone to make sure I didn't break anything during my tantrum.

The phone book didn't dent the wall, although you could plainly see where it'd hit if you knew where to look at it from an angle. I retrieved it from behind the stereo speaker and put it back where I'd found it. As I tried to close the drawer, the bent pages caught, so I turned the book face down to hopefully flatten them out.

Gene returned about twenty minutes later with clean laundry and hot pizza. I thanked him profusely, but then I fell into a sullen silence as we ate.

"You OK?" he asked.

"Yeah, I'm just tired."

'Of being me,' I added silently. 'And worried that I might have abducted a child, and wondering if I'm a missing person in 2015.'

"Well, we'll both get a chance to sleep a few hours before we go paint," he said.

Gene retired to his bedroom and I crashed on his living room couch. It seemed like I'd only been asleep for five minutes when he woke me to go to the offices and paint.

At about four in the morning, Gene and I took a break from painting and finished up our pizza in an office. Gene helped himself to a cigar from a wooden box and then reclined in the guy's big leather chair, with his feet up on the desk like some high-powered executive.

"You're a better painter than Gary," Gene said as he pretended to puff on the unlit cigar.

"I'm gonna tell him you said that."

He laughed. "Go ahead. How'd you learn to paint so well?"

"Well, we did everything ourselves at the commune."

"So, what really did happen there? Could you go back if you wanted to?"

"Nah, everything went to crap."

"What happened?"

"I don't know . . . I guess even hippies grow up, eventually."

He looked at me for a long moment.

"What?" I asked.

"Nothing," he said, but kept looking at me.

"What?" I asked again.

"It's just that sometimes, you're like an adult in a kid's body."

I smiled.

"There—right there, that wizened old man smile," he quickly added, pointing at me.

I laughed and then turned pensive.

"I've been through a lot, Gene."

"Maybe someday you'll tell me?"

I closed my eyes and shook my head no.

I helped Gene with other painting jobs for the rest of the week before we worked all night to finish up the office suite on the holiday weekend. We left there at dawn on Labor Day and went back to his place.

"Did you mangle my phone book?" he asked without preamble after he closed the door.

'Oh, my *God*,' I thought, wide-eyed. 'That's what sucks about being a kid: grown-ups find out about every stupid little thing you do.'

"Um, yeah," I answered, "I called the cops to see if anyone bothered to report me missing. All they did was give me the runaround. I kinda threw your phone book."

"I 'kinda' noticed."

"Sorry."

"What did it hit?"

"The wall behind your left speaker."

"You're lucky it didn't hit the speaker or you'd be painting for free."

I nodded in shame.

"Well," Gene said, "I wish you would have told me you were going to do that, because I could have saved you the trouble. My brother-in-law is a state trooper. I asked him to check on it the day I met you."

Quickly dismissing the fact that he'd secretly checked up on me (I would have done the same thing if I was him), I made an "and?" gesture using my hands as well as my eyebrows.

"I guess you were telling me the truth."

'Well, I'll be damned.' I silently said to myself. Although I still felt bad about lying to Gene, a huge weight was lifted from my shoulders.

"Hey, didn't your brother-in-law tell you to turn me in?" I asked.

"I told him I met you in the park, but you ran off. I'm not stupid, Mike." Upon seeing my reaction, he added, "I'm glad you find that so amusing."

"No, I'm not laughing at you. It's just that I said the same—"

"Mike, we need to talk," Gene interrupted. "Gary's gonna be back to work on Wednesday, so he and I will be painting again. You're welcome to stay with me, but we're going to have to . . . talk to someone official about . . . you, because I don't want to get in trouble."

"Gene, I didn't mean to put you—"

"You're not *putting* me through anything. You can stay as long as you want, but you need to, ah . . . I think you need to get your priorities straightened out."

A long silence hung between us.

"I'm going to sleep for a few hours," he said at last. "You can either sleep or watch TV."

With a summer day dawning beyond the closed curtains, I felt trapped. Unless I was going to let Gene try to adopt me or something, the sooner I left, the better. I felt awful about it, but adventure and the open road beckoned.

As Gene was heading into the bathroom, I said, "Um, Gene?"

He paused in the doorway.

"I, ah . . . I guess maybe I ought to just split," I said.

Gene's back stiffened. "You could wait until tonight and I'll drop you off. You said you only ride trains at night, and this way you'll get a fresh start with a full belly."

That would have been a better idea, but now that I'd started to make the break, I wanted to finish it.

"N-no, that's OK. Maybe I'll just walk or take a bus."

He swung around to face me. "So, you're *really* going to do this." It was the only time I'd ever heard him raise his voice. "Until what? Until you wind up dead in a ditch somewhere?"

He glowered and I looked down and shrugged.

Gene imitated my shrug in an overacted, sarcastic manner. "That's your answer to everything, isn't it?"

Stupidly, I shrugged again before I could catch myself.

He shook his head in disgust, went in and slammed the door.

I loitered outside the bathroom. Eventually, Gene came out and said, "Excuse me," as he shoved past. I followed him as far as the kitchen doorway.

"After all I've done for you," he said as he busied himself at the counter. "You and Gary would probably get along great. He took off in the middle of a big job to go to Key West and get drunk with my ex-girlfriend. Left me to finish it on a holiday weekend with some kid who—you know what your deal is? You're *all about Mike.* You were *hoping* no one reported you missing, weren't you?" He turned, read my face and nodded his head in confirmation. "Yeah, that's what I figured. You need someone to knock some sense into you, that's what you need."

I closed my eyes as his words cut into me.

"Mike, listen to me."

Gene must have seen by my guilty expression that I still intended on leaving, because he curtly snapped, "Never mind." Then he gestured towards the front door with a tilt of his head and said quietly, "Go on, beat it."

I still lingered by the kitchen doorway, but now Gene was in "self-protect" mode. In a businesslike manner, he paid me for helping him paint, gave me change and instructions for the bus and yawned loudly, which I took as my cue to get going.

As I shouldered my backpack, he scribbled his phone number on a pad, tore off the sheet and handed it to me.

"Call if you need me."

But he wasn't looking at me as he said it. A gulf had opened up between us and his expression was similar to that of the old farmer in New Jersey. It said: "I'm offering help because that's the kind of person I am, but at the same time I wish this strange creature would just leave."

"I hope you find whatever it is you're looking for out there," he said quietly as I stepped out into the morning.

'That makes two of us,' I thought as I left.

Gene had mentioned that the busses were on a holiday schedule today and wouldn't run very often. After quite a while, between my impatience, my paranoia (which wasn't unwarranted—after all, both Gene and I had described me to the cops) and the discomfort of standing across the street from the entrance to Gene's apartment complex where he could see me, I decided to walk to another stop. But midway between the two stops, the bus stirred up dust and left a trail of foul-smelling diesel smoke in its wake as it growled past me. I hadn't even had time to try to flag it down. I figured I deserved to walk anyways. After a few miles, I came to my senses and waited at a stop.

I got off as soon as we crossed a river into an area of Philadelphia that I already recognized. I walked a block back to the river, which a sign at the bridge identified as the Schuylkill. I looped down through trash-littered woods and made my way to the river.

Gene's last statement was a corny, over-used cliché, but it still hit home. What *was* I looking for out here? For that matter, what was I looking for when I went to the bridge in 2015?

And man, did I ever feel like crap over the whole situation with Gene.

'Well, it's not like I was gonna marry the guy or something . . .'

No, you only made friends with him and abandoned him to worry about you. A classic Mike Morrison "hook and dump."

I sighed. 'Maybe it would be best if I don't get too involved with people for a while.'

And that's a classic Mike Morrison cop-out.

That really touched a nerve because lately I'd been thinking that I'd carried the same emotional baggage from my old life into this new one.

'But I couldn't just . . . *stay*,' I reasoned. First of all, I'd lied to Gene about where I came from. He deserved better than that. Second, I didn't know if I even existed as a real person. Sooner or later someone would want to know who I was and why I wasn't in school.

"Oh crap, that's right! When's school starting? All the other kids will be there. Except for weekends, now I won't even be able to be out in public during the *day* without attracting attention."

"Did I *really* just say, 'all the other kids'?" I rubbed my hand across my forehead. "I don't even know who I am anymore."

An overwhelming wave of isolation and depression washed over me. Even the thought of striking out across the country felt like a silly, childish idea. And trying to do it in this kid's body? The odds were solidly stacked against me getting very far.

'Maybe this whole thing wasn't such a great idea.'

I noticed a creepy, homeless-looking guy studying me as he headed in my direction. I was afraid of him so I slunk off into the scraggy woods and clambered up the hill to the streets where there were people around. Too late I saw two cops standing near. I could feel their suspicious eyes boring into me, and even more so into my backpack.

'I'm going to hear one of them yell, "Halt!" in five, four, three, two . . .'

But no alarm sounded. I stole a backward glance and the cops were animatedly conversing with some blond lady with big breasts.

Relax, Mike. The whole world doesn't revolve around you.

'I never said it *did*, you self-righteous nitwit.'

But maybe letting Gene help you isn't such a bad idea. You're a kid now, Mike. So go back to school and live a normal kid's life.

'And what happens if I don't actually exist as a real person?'

Only one way to find out . . .

'This is ridiculous. I'm not going back to school. I hate kids. I couldn't wait to get out of school just to get away from them.'

Oh, you don't hate kids. And despite your lifelong effort to avoid them, kids actually like you. You're just judging them all by the ones who used to pick on you.

'Whatever. I'm just playing a part here anyway.'

Mike, you willfully switched lives. You are *this person now.*

'Well, come nightfall, "this person" is moving on.'

Right—because that's what Mike Morrison does when faced with conflict or emotion, isn't it? Mike "moves on."

'How did everything that started out so simple turn so complicated?'

Have you ever seen yourself naked? I don't mean physically. I mean facing your true, exposed self all the way down to the depths of your soul. With your ego and all of the little positive things that you tell yourself to cover the truth stripped away.

Well, that's what I was experiencing as I reached the Delaware River at Penn's Landing, only to discover that it hadn't yet been turned into the nice tourist attraction that I remembered from the future. Although, I must admit, it was a hell of a lot more interesting now.

I explored the dilapidated, but fascinating pier areas along the Delaware River. Everything was sagging and rotting into oblivion, but still somewhat in use. The switch to containerized shipping, which would shut all of these old piers down for good, was only now starting to occur. So although this area was past its peak and quite doomed, I felt lucky to see the last flicker of an American shipping era.

In the late afternoon, under increasingly cloudy skies, I headed back across town towards the zoo. A part of me wished that Gene would come by in his van to save me from myself.

You do *have his phone number . . .*

I did. But I stubbornly kept walking to the tracks to catch a freight train to who knows where.

<h1 style="text-align:center">10</h1>

Just as I'd planned on the day I arrived in Philadelphia, I caught a ride on a train as it slowly came down off of the long bridge near the zoo. I hopped on a covered hopper car, although this wasn't the kind with the little compartments that you could hide in on the ends of the car. There were some empty boxcars with the doors open, so I planned to move to one of those at the first place the train stopped. I still hadn't slept, but the ride was so exciting that I didn't want to. This train was flying! And if that wasn't enough, passenger trains would shoot past in the other direction at ridiculous speed. First I would see the lights coming on an adjacent track (I think there were four tracks) and then the train would go past with an astonishingly loud *whup* followed by rapid *whoosh, whoosh, whoosh, whoosh* and then a fading *hisssss* as the train vanished into the night. Passing other freights was also cool. They weren't going as fast, but seeing the changing patterns of the cars flying past, sometimes about three feet away from my moving train, was an experience I'll never forget.

I did doze off a little, because I woke up as the train was slowing down. I watched from my hiding spot as the tracks grew on either side until there appeared to be a sea of rails. The railroad line I was riding had overhead power lines for the electric locomotives, and now they also fanned out, seeming to hang over every track. The wires looked like a giant spider's web, silhouetted against the city light-brightened overcast sky.

I hopped off and hid in the brush alongside the tracks when the train stopped. The railroad yard was next to a bay or something and far off across the water there seemed to be flames floating in the air. It took me a few minutes to deduce that they were those flames you see over refineries, burning off waste gas. I worked my way up to the other end of the railroad yard, where a freight train was slowly departing. Fortunately it stopped for a few minutes so I had time to find an empty boxcar with doors open on both sides. Shortly thereafter, we left the yard.

We were soon flying along and I went into a corner and fell fast asleep.

I awoke when the train slowed down, hours later. We were slowly moving on an elevated track through a city. I had no idea which one until I saw the Washington Monument from one side of the boxcar and the Capitol out of the other. I never knew that there were railroad tracks going right through Washington, D.C. It seemed strange.

Dawn was breaking as we pulled into a huge railroad yard. I knew I should hop off, but I didn't. I stayed aboard as we slowly threaded our way through the yards. Eventually my train stopped and after a few minutes it made a loud "whoosh" air sound that I'd already learned to associate as a "this train ain't going anywhere soon" sound.

Seeing as it was still lightly raining and I was hidden and comfortable, I went back to sleep. Someone walking in the crushed stone ballast next to my boxcar woke me. I peeked out and saw it was a railroad worker. I heard a hissing air noise coming from the freight cars as he worked his way down the train. And then a strange moaning sound. I thought it was him making the moaning sound and I wondered if he was sick or something. But it turned out to be a sound coming from the freight cars because of whatever it was that he was doing. I sensed that it was time for me to get moving. Now that I'd slept half the morning, I'd have to sneak out of the yards in daylight. At least the rain had stopped.

Unfortunately, I had to cross many tracks with freight cars on them in order to get out to the road. The cars I crossed could and did move at any time as stray freight cars, rolling on their own without engines, loudly coupled into each other. It was very unnerving doing this, and just totally, irresponsibly, unnecessarily dangerous. I swore that I would never do something so stupid again. I was super careful, and it took quite a while to cross all of these tracks. Now I knew why I should get off of a train before coming into a yard. Then I had to get across an open area, a road at the edge of the yard, and a chain-link fence.

I ran to the fence, threw my pack over it and then froze for a few seconds as I debated whether to climb over and risk the barbed-wire top or to try to squeeze under. A railroad cop in one of those old International SUV-looking trucks spotted me and highballed my way. I quickly chose to dive under the fence it where it didn't quite reach the ground. On some chain-link fences, the ends of the wires are bent backwards so there is no sharp point. But on this one, the wires just ended where they were twisted together.

The sharp end of one of the thick wires caught the skin on the back of my hip, hooked deep and yanked me right back into the yard. The second time, I made it under.

"Come here! Get your ass over here!" said a very angry, red-faced cop from the other side of the fence.

I walked over. There was nowhere else to go but out to a busy road where I'd still be in plain sight.

"If I wave you over to me, you'd better come over, not run away," he yelled, furious. "Now, stay the hell out of here, you hear me? You kids know better than to be playing around in here. If I see you in here again, I'm arresting you, you got that?"

"Yes, sir."

"Now, go home before I change my mind and call your parents!"

"Yes, sir."

Hadn't he seen me throw the pack? I was standing right near it now, but it was hidden where it landed on a weedy little hill. I was afraid to pick the backpack up in front of the cop, so I reluctantly left it there and made my way out to the road. I figured he'd go on his way and I'd run right back and get it, but he was still watching me as I headed down the road in the general direction of D.C.

'Dammit, I don't want to leave my backpack there—some bum's gonna find it and steal it.'

The cars all had Virginia license plates. Had I missed Baltimore completely? Was that where I was watching those flames over a bay?

I was feeling exposed out on the busy road and I was nervous that someone would question why I wasn't in school right now, so I ducked into a park and hung out there for quite some time. It was a pretty cool place to hang out, with the trains passing by on the elevated tracks and jets low overhead as they came into the airport.

I couldn't really see my hip where I'd caught it on the fence. I pulled the skin forward as much as I could and examined it by touch. The cut wasn't real long, but it felt real deep. The flesh had been bunched to one end and, after pulling my underwear up to cover it (it was cleaner than my grubby fingers) I pushed it back in place as best I could. I figured it probably needed stitches and I knew that I needed a tetanus shot, but I damn sure wasn't going to go to a hospital. I'd just have to get stuff to clean and dress it myself and hope for the best. At least the swelling had staunched the blood flow.

I wiped my fingers in the grass to get as much of the sticky blood off as I could and walked back to a burger joint I'd passed earlier. I ordered a whole bag of little tiny burgers and two huge Cokes, paid with filthy fingers that now had dried blood under the nails, and hurried back to the park.

I figured I'd risk catching a bus into D.C. I got on a commuter bus that seemed to be heading in that direction. I was the only kid on the bus and I felt the eyes of the riders on me as I asked the impatient driver where the bus was going and how to pay.

Once I was seated and looking out of the window, it occurred to me that I'd need to know the name of this town in order to get back here later and retrieve my backpack.

I turned to a lady next to me and asked, "Excuse me, can you tell me where I got on this bus?"

She looked straight ahead and ignored me.

"I mean the name of the town where I got on?" I prompted, still getting no reply.

"Alexandria," answered a man in a suit in the next row up.

"Thank you very much, I appreciate the help," I said as I glared at the side of the lady's face. I resisted the urge to lean over and ask her what planet Alexandria was on. The driver was watching me in the mirror that faced back towards the passengers. These people were making me feel like some kind of criminal.

Don't forget, Mike, you're a little kid out alone on a school day, filthy from riding freight trains, with long hair and a New Jersey accent, who has made it clear to everyone on this bus that he has no idea where he is.

'I guess it's a good thing I don't have my backpack.'

Some bum is probably wearing it by now.

'Har, har.'

As I toured D.C., I repeated the name *Alexandria* over and over so I wouldn't forget it.

Late in the afternoon, I caught a bus back to Alexandria. In D.C., I didn't feel like I had an accent. But just a little ways away in Virginia, I felt like I was down south, where I did have an accent. I debated how far south I really wanted to go. This wasn't 2015—this was 1967. It probably wasn't like the era where I came from where you go to somewhere like Florida and half the people you meet are from New York, New Jersey, or Ohio. North and south probably had more meaning back now. I figured I should at least get a haircut and try to talk with a southern accent.

I was going to dart across the road and get my backpack, but then I spied a grocery store a little farther on and I figured I'd buy some supplies first. No sense being out in public with a suspicious-looking backpack any more than I had to.

Just as I was approaching the edge of the parking lot, a mother and her kids were heading back the way I had come. The mom towed a laundry cart loaded with paper grocery sacks and that gave me an idea.

The simplicity of product choices in the grocery store amazed me. I don't mean that it wasn't well stocked, because it was. What I mean is, if you wanted a can of, say, chicken soup, there it was: Campbell's Chicken Soup (condensed). No "super chunky, low salt, extra super chunky, low calorie, home style, home style super chunky" and so forth. The toothpaste choices were a few different brands, but they were "fluoride toothpaste." No "whitening, brightening, gel, striped, with mouthwash, scrubbing crystals," etc. Orange juice was just orange juice (frozen concentrated). However much pulp was in it was how much you got. Aspirin was aspirin, Corn Flakes were Corn Flakes, milk was milk, and a Hershey's bar was a Hershey's bar. Could people really survive in 1967 without having to make ten thousand choices on every damn product they bought? Call me old-fashioned, but *I* sure as hell could. People were calmly walking around selecting products. No one had their nose buried in an iPhone. Whiny little kids were still whiny little kids though. Some things never change. I bought toothpaste, a toothbrush and a bar of soap and asked the young gum-chewing cashier for a couple of extra bags. She gave me three.

When I went to retrieve my backpack, I noticed that the fence wasn't even the railroad's—it apparently belonged to the company that fronted the street and had I run one hundred feet in either direction, I could have missed the fence altogether and not gotten injured. I rolled my eyes, shook my head and laughed at myself. I stuffed my backpack in one of the paper bags and sauntered towards the town center with what looked like a sack of groceries. I was so proud of my little disguise.

There was a train station just past town, so I went up on the platform to await nightfall.

But people were gathering as they waited for a passenger train, so I walked back closer to the yards along the road, crept partway up to the railroad embankment, and waited in solitude for complete darkness.

A little later on, I lay low as a southbound train departed. A few ashes shot up into the night sky with the diesel smoke as the engineer gave it the throttle. For some reason, I had a sort of vision of me lying there hiding and gazing at the scene.

This is one of those snapshot moments that you'll remember for the rest of your life.

Of course, I remember many moments from my trip. But somehow that particular moment in time—young, hiding in the weeds, ready to jump on a train to Anywhere, USA— just seemed to encapsulate the whole adventure. I can't explain it any better than that.

I didn't get a ride on that particular train because the entire train was "reefers" (refrigerated boxcars) and all had their doors closed. No ride on the reefer train, but I didn't wait long before I did get a ride. A train with some open boxcars on it came slowly out of the yard and squealed to a stop. I chose a boxcar with the doors open on both sides. I quickly found some chunks of wood, tossed them into the car, and climbed in. I jammed my chunks of wood in the door tracks so the doors wouldn't slam shut (I was experienced now) and waited. It wasn't long before my train departed.

As we got up to speed, the breeze stirred up fertilizer-smelling dust in the boxcar. I breathed through my shirt while hoping that the dust didn't contain some type of poison. We flew along for hours without slowing down. It was very dark in most areas, and sometimes roads paralleled the tracks, separated by a thin strip of woods. I watched with fascination as the headlight glow in front of cars passing on the road would slowly grow brighter, and then finally the car would zip past. We were going faster than cars that were going in the same direction as we were. Trains traveling in the opposite direction frequently passed us on the other track.

My boxcar had a disconcerting habit of rapidly wobbling back and forth a few inches, as though the wheels were sliding side to side against the rails. On curves the ride was smooth, but every time we got on a straight track it happened again. There was no chance of getting off of this car at the speed we were going, so all I could do was to hope it wouldn't derail. Amazingly, I managed to get a few hours of sleep. But even through my blanket and jeans the side-to-side motion left a friction burn on the side of my hip.

At one point in the wee hours of the morning, the train did slow down a bit. The change in noise level woke me and I watched as we rolled right down the middle of the street of some town. From a train, usually you only see the backs of houses and buildings. Other than my wobbly boxcar, I was really enjoying myself.

14

When I awoke in the morning, we were in a city and slowly approaching a yard. I hopped off while there was still enough cover to do so. I walked around the industrial areas for quite a while, fascinated by this sixties southern-feeling city, with its mills that were still in operation. Up above, freight trains rumbled along on a bridge that appeared to wind along the river for miles.

'OK, I don't know or care where those trains are going but I've just gotta ride a train over that bridge when I leave!'

Now that I'd scoped out where I would catch my next ride, I risked a trip into town and discovered that I was in Richmond, Virginia. I was a little tired of train riding, so I decided to go somewhere to chill for a while. I located the bus station, but it took me several minutes to get up the nerve to enter because I figured I'd immediately be pegged as a runaway. The name "Virginia Beach" beckoned me from the departures board and I decided to get a ticket—if they would sell me one, that is.

I don't think the ticket agent would have cared if I flat out *told* him I was running away. He was so busy bitching to his co-worker about something that he barely gave me his attention. Even so, I bought a two-way ticket so as not to look too suspicious.

In retrospect, I needn't have been so apprehensive. Parents in the sixties gave their kids a lot more freedom than they do in 2015. Most people would say that's because the world was safer then—not so many child molesters around and all that—but the statistics don't back up that claim. In the sixties as well as in 2015, a child was most likely to be molested by a known adult. The depressing thing about the sixties was that it was more likely to be hushed up.

Just to be on the safe side, as I waited for my bus, I sat near adults so it would look like I was with them. But I was too restless to just sit inside and wait, so I drifted out front. I wasn't really thinking about what I looked like as I stood out there. Actually, I'd momentarily forgotten how young I was.

All I can say is that if you are a road dirty, long-haired, scruffy-looking kid wearing a backpack in a strange city and you don't want to attract the cops, then don't stand in front of the Greyhound bus station. The first cops that cruised slowly by, seemingly looking for just such a character, stopped. Two cops were getting out of the car as I slinked back inside. As they turned the corner by the pay phones, I was standing in plain sight, loudly conversing with a dial tone.

"No, Ma, Uncle Ernie didn't work me too hard on the farm. Huh?"

(Dial tone)

"Richmond."

(Dial tone)

"Because I have to transfer to a different bus here."

Young man! How could Uncle Ernie send you back looking like such a mess? I'll have his balls on a platter!

Stifling a smile, I thought, 'Come on, stop screwing around, this is serious!'

Just trying to help fill in good old Mom's part.

'Come on, now you distracted me. Where was I?'

Something about Uncle Ernie's balls on a platter, if I remember correctly.

That one did it, and I had to face away from the cops as I laughed.

"Um, hold on," I said, and cradled the phone between my shoulder and my ear as I pretended to check the schedule in my hand until I could talk without laughing. "I should be there at three-twenty."

The dial tone stopped, so I wrapped it up real quick in case the receiver started making one of those loud "phone is off the hook" noises.

"OK, thanks, Ma," I said, nice and loud. "I love you too. Bye."

I hung up and genuinely smiled and said "Hi" to the cops as I passed them on my way back to the waiting area.

'Oh man,' I thought, laughing again, thinking about this whole adventure. 'I don't know how I got through the daily grind in my old life. I don't think I've ever had so much fun!'

I was pleased to see in a newspaper that someone had left on the bus that today was Friday. That meant that I could walk around Virginia Beach all weekend without attracting unwanted attention for being out on a school day. If I'd planned this trip a little better—or I should say if I'd been offered a choice of dates—I would have started this adventure in the beginning of summer vacation.

About an hour before arriving in Virginia Beach, I sat and relaxed in my dry, comfortable seat and watched as water droplets streaked across my window. The bus trip took much longer than I thought it would. We never got on a road that even resembled an interstate highway and we seemed to have stopped at every town and general store in Virginia. Apparently, some guy had even just flagged down the bus in the middle of nowhere.

As I reluctantly left the dry bus station for the wet streets, my plans of buying a pair of shorts and hanging out on the beach vanished. To make matters worse, it was dusk and even if I could've afforded to spend money on a hotel room, no one would have rented to a little kid alone. I walked over to Atlantic Avenue, the main drag, and then wandered over to the beach. Here the weather seemed even worse, although that may have been because a cool ocean breeze was adding to the misery.

'Is it just my imagination, or has it really rained every single day that I've been living out here?'

I trudged south along the beach until I was under a bridge that crossed an inlet. Although I was out of the rain, I was soaked and the breeze felt even chillier. Luckily, even though I'd wanted to put it on the second I left the bus station, I'd left my sweatshirt in the backpack to keep it relatively dry. I took off my wet T-shirt and draped it over a bird shit-covered rock, put the sweatshirt on with the hood up, and sat down on a boulder.

'Here I am again, shivering under a bridge to be out of the rain. Maybe coming here was a bad idea.' It wasn't that it was such a bad idea, just that my options were so limited by this weather and by my age.

So: Warm, safe, dry, grown-up Mike at home in 2015 or little kid Mike here?

I drew my knees up tight to my chest and gazed through my wet hair at my surroundings. "Here," I stubbornly answered and then added with a whisper, "God help me."

Having too much time to think can sometimes be a bad thing, especially in the wee hours of the morning. As I tried to get comfortable on the sharp rocks, the concerns I'd been trying to suppress over what became of my "warm, safe, dry" 2015 life pushed their way to the surface.

It would be somewhat disingenuous to say that I cared *passionately* about my old life, because I'd always felt slightly disconnected from it. Could *this* be my real life and I dreamt that one up?

Microwave ovens. The space shuttle. Cars with airbags. Home computers. Global Positioning Satellites. Vinyl records giving way to eight tracks giving way to cassettes, giving way to CDs, giving way to iPods. Digital cameras, future U.S. presidents, 9/11. The World Trade Center, for that matter.

'Hmmm, but seeing as those things don't exist back now, I could have made them up. I haven't actually gone to a library and researched whether they're in development. And in 1967, one can't just Google this stuff.'

Google! That's another good one, thank you.

I rolled my eyes. 'Jeez, as soon as I said it, I saw you lobbing that one back at me like a fastball.'

You just want to pretend your 2015 life was a dream so you can brush off your guilt over abandoning your family and friends.

'Gee, thanks for bringing that up. Like I wasn't depressed enough already. Listen, *I* didn't know what was going to happen at the bridge, OK? Besides, I *was* a little overwhelmed at the time.'

Oh, really? The damage you could do never crossed your mind, huh? Are you sure about that?

I covered my eyes with my hand and shook my head as I recollected that, just before I switched lives, I dismissed my concerns over the people I might leave behind with, "Fuck them."

How touching. Did you think your loved ones—or should I say "people who are unfortunate enough to try to love you"—would say the same thing about you when they realized you were missing?

I shrugged.

Can't shrug this one off, kiddo. But just as Gene said back in Philly, you would hope they didn't care so you could get off scot-free.

I rolled my eyes. 'Because I'm all about Mike.'

Yes. You're a self-centered little ten-year-old and you've always been a self-centered little ten-year-old.

Just when I'd thought my opinion of myself couldn't get any lower, my inner voice had managed to take it down another notch.

I reasoned that, in a way, my childish attributes weren't completely my fault; I just never matured beyond that stage. I've never known what it was like to be in love with someone. I don't even know what it's like to *make* love, or kiss passionately or any of that stuff. But in my own way, I could love my family and friends, a dog or a cat, stuff like that.

You forgot to mention your mountain bike. Just so you know, that's the way a ten-year-old loves. That's who you are and why switching was so easy for you and that aspect of your personality will probably never change. But you could be a ten-year-old and still show more concern for others.

I looked down and nodded.

But what else could I have done? Leave a note telling them that I may or may not be going away for an indeterminate amount of time—possibly forever—to somewhere that I can't tell them about? Oh, and that there's no way I'll be able to contact them? It was an "all or nothing" moment.

'Anyway, right after the switch, I saw the adult me go back. So if he/I went back, I actually didn't disappear on them. He's . . . living as me?'

That couldn't be right. The same damn paradox that bothered me when I watched "myself" walk away from the bridge that day was bothering me now. How could I be in two places at once? How could I be carrying on with my life in 2015 New Jersey while I was sitting under a bridge in Virginia in 1967? How could this me not know what that me was doing when we were both the same person? I found myself wishing for a pad and a pen to write down the timelines.

Mike, it's not that complicated. You switched into another person's body and came back to 1967. Little kid original you is doing whatever you did in the past at this moment. Forget about him. You are adult you, but in a different body and time. Only during the transition at the bridge could you see your adult self. After you were fully switched, he disappeared because—follow me closely here, Mike—you're only one you.

'So, what's he doing?'

My inner voice sighed. *You tell me.*

'How the hell would I know? He probably quit my job and—ohhhh, I get it!' I smiled and nodded. 'He's not doing anything because I'm him and I'm here!'

And the light bulb comes on! You can't be off in the future doing things if you're here. Obviously, if you decided to switch back to 2015, you'd go back to the moment you switched away. Did you really think that you would just switch back to some random, arbitrary moment?

I pondered that for a while, amused by the fact that there might be practical, reality-grounded rules governing something that was theoretically impossible to begin with.

Once again, the weight of guilt was lifted from my shoulders. But although, just by fate, I hadn't disappeared on people—I mean, my *loved ones*—in 2015, there was no denying the fact that I would still do it if it was necessary. I wish I could say that I'd learned a lesson, but . . .

You're just lucky the world has provisions to protect you from your own childish decisions.

Now that *that* was settled, I killed time by playing visual games with the nearest flashing buoy that marked the entrance to this inlet. I tried closing my eyes and opening them for a second at the exact flash sequence so that it appeared to be always on. My record was eighteen flashes in a row before I'd screw up and open my eyes just before or after a flash.

You know, they really did pick the right person to turn back into a kid.

I smiled and further entertained myself by thinking up funny scenarios of switching back and forth:

To an observer in 2015—say someone walking into CVS who stopped to watch me, wondering what I was up to—I would walk across the highway, disappear into the woods for a second and then walk right back and get in my truck and drive away. The novelty of it gave me a happy, tingling feeling.

I could get a job at the CVS across the highway from my switching spot and go on a two-year sabbatical on my lunch break, with time to spare to actually eat lunch before going back to work!

I could try switching while talking to someone on my cell phone, just to see if the call would be terminated or if it would still be active when I came back. "I'm sorry," I'd say, "I was gone for five years for a second there. What were you saying?"

I could even have someone with me.

"We've gotta make a little pit stop here at CVS," I'd say.

"Why, what do you need from CVS?"

"Nothing, I just have to run across the highway for a few years. I'll be *right* back!"

I bundled up against the damp breeze as best as I could and settled in for a long, chilly, sleepless night. This wasn't my first time in this type of situation, and unfortunately it wouldn't be my last. It never sucks any less, but you do sort of get used to it, I suppose.

Sunrise was beautiful, but the skies threatened more rain. In the rosy early morning glow, I walked down to the water's edge on the mostly deserted beach and touched the Atlantic Ocean. Then I backed up a little ways and sat in the wet sand. I'd touched the water in case I made it to the Pacific Ocean. If I made it that far, I'd touch the water again. I figured it would mean more to me on the west coast if I ever got there.

By the nineties (the last time I'd been in Virginia Beach), modern, nondescript high-rise hotels lined up like concrete dominos starkly defined the boundaries between nature and city. Utilizing every bit of their available land for moneymaking purposes, these buildings blocked the afternoon sunlight on the beach, forcing sunbathers to crowd the narrow sunlit areas between them. They all featured private, look-alike balconies where the guests could observe—but not have to interact with—the main attraction.

Although 1967 Virginia Beach was not as neat and well kept, it was wilder in a charming, natural way. These old hotels didn't assault the landscape, but actually seemed to enhance it. Their architecture was of a comforting design that one would expect to see near the ocean. The structures only used up a portion of their lots and the rest was left for common areas such as lawns, shuffleboard courts, swing sets, huge covered porches, places where part of the experience would be to actually interact with other guests.

I was getting a firsthand comparison not only of how America has changed since the sixties, but also how rapidly the rate of change from small and quaint to oversized and ugly seemed to be accelerating.

The weather was hot, sultry, and sort of unsettled but at least it didn't rain. Seeing as it was nearing the end of the summer season and much of the clothing in the stores was half off, I bought a dark green T-shirt. The store had bright, embroidered Virginia Beach patches that came with the shirt. You chose the one you wanted and they'd iron it on. I asked if I could just buy the shirt without the patch and the perplexed, long-haired, bearded Jesus-of-Nazareth-looking clerk agreed. I had a feeling that he'd been sneaking to the back and taking hits off of a joint between customers.

I walked the beach shirtless and barefoot, with my shoes tied to my backpack by the laces. A mile or so north of the touristy area, I lay on the warm sand and slept in the sun.

Around late afternoon, I went back into town to get something to eat and catch a bus back to Richmond.

12

The Richmond locals eyed me suspiciously as I walked down a run-down residential street that dead-ended above the railroad tracks. I scurried down through the brush to the tracks as a train was coming off of the bridge and another was coming behind me on the other track. Both trains were slow enough to jump, but both were coal trains with nowhere to hide. I made a little hiding spot for myself in the brush and relaxed.

I loosely followed the river and the long railroad bridge that I wanted to ride over in Richmond. I got strange looks from a few people, but spoke to no one. Looking over my shoulder all of the time was wearing on my nerves and it occurred to me that I was spending an inordinate amount of time lately just keeping out of sight.

It was just so damn difficult to be so young on the road. Hitchhiking was out of the question, Greyhound busses were costly and bus stations were risky. Getting any type of job—even as a dishwasher or a farmhand—would be next to impossible. Sure, I had money in my pocket right now, but never knowing when or if I could replenish it was unnerving. Going to soup kitchens, churches, or even the Salvation Army was out of the question.

So go back to the bridge in New Jersey and try to switch back.

And that's where the mental conflict came into play. I wanted to do that and didn't want to do it, both at the same time. Switching back would certainly be the path of least resistance. One thing I missed out here was just going inside and relaxing. I missed reading, surfing the web, listening to music, going to the diner with my friends, stuff like that. Looking at it from here, my old adult life didn't look too bad. I didn't have many responsibilities and I made more money than I actually needed, although I would need that money in retirement.

I hadn't had a midlife crisis, although I suppose one could argue that this adventure was the *ultimate* midlife crisis. Forget running out and buying a young person's sports car or getting a twenty-something girlfriend. No, not me—I went for the gusto, baby! But even that didn't explain why I went through with this, that day at the bridge.

It was your destiny.

But I didn't believe in destinies. And that brings up another inner conflict that I had, which was keeping a clear assessment of reality. What I'd done seemed to be impossible. 'You can't just switch lives with another person—that's absurd,' I'd reason. 'If you could, then everybody would be doing it and you'd never know who was who.' Yet I'd done it and here I was. So I had to accept the theoretically impossible situation that I was in as real, but yet I still needed to feel grounded in the here and now.

So could I fly or turn invisible or do other impossible things? Once the bounds of reality were broken, were there any rules at all? Oh yeah, there are rules all right. Don't wish you could fly, because you just might turn into a bird. Don't wish you could be invisible, because you just might turn into a ghost. And don't step into one of your dreams unless you're prepared to deal with the consequences.

I snuck into the railroad yards and pulled myself into an empty boxcar on a train that already had engines on it. My hope was that it would soon be departing for points west. It did move, but we only pulled up to the end of the yards and stopped. When I'd climbed in, I was between two other trains and in shadow. Now we sat in the bright afternoon sunshine and my boxcar quickly heated up. To make matters worse, I was right in front of the yard offices. I couldn't hop out or even stand in the doorway without being seen.

I took my shirt off and still I was pouring sweat. At this rate, I had about an hour's worth of water left.

Somewhere in my travels, I picked up poison ivy. In my old, adult body, I could wade through it in shorts without worry because I didn't react to it. I found out the hard way that this body was allergic to it and now it was at the point where I'd scratched it so frequently and carelessly that it was bleeding a little in spots and burning from the sweat. And yet, it still itched.

I did get to ride over the long bridge as we finally departed Richmond. The tracks followed the river valley for quite a ways, but eventually we left the river behind and bounced and swayed our way through the mountains. At times the train was down to a crawl and at other times it was going faster on this track than it seemed prudent to go. We passed many trains that were going in the other direction, and we stopped a few times.

Just after sunset, during one of the stops, I got off in search of water. Under high wispy cirrus clouds that glowed fiery orange in the last rays of the sun, I drank from a puddle along the tracks. This was a bad habit that I really had to get out of. But at that moment I was out of water and too thirsty to care. I really missed being able to walk into any gas station, convenience store, etc., and buy plastic Poland Spring water bottles.

We came down from the mountains and once again followed a river valley. A city appeared across the river, and the train stopped at a rail yard. I stayed on as the engines uncoupled and went into the yard. They eventually came back out with about twenty more freight cars, which they added to my train before we departed.

The next yard we came to looked like a really big one, so I hopped off. I was below some mountain town that was built on the side of a hill. It didn't look like a big city where I could walk around unnoticed. It was daylight now, although it wasn't as bright outside as it'd been a few hours earlier. The mountaintops were shrouded in mist, a drizzle was turning into a steady rain, and I really didn't know what to do.

I ducked into a thin strip of woods between the tracks and a major road. I snuck close enough to the road to read license plates, and I saw that I was in West Virginia.

After filling my canteen in a stream and standing in the rainy woods for five minutes, I decided that hanging out here would serve no purpose but to get me wet. I didn't want to walk into the railroad yard, so I went out to the road. My inner voice strongly advised against it, but I did it anyways. As I ducked my head against the misty breeze created by the passing cars, I walked the shoulder up a hill to a junction with another major road.

"I don't think I've ever seen so many train locomotives in one place before," I said as I took in the scene below. There must have been fifty of the things and many of them were idling. Their combined low thrumming sound seemed to fill the whole valley. A cop passed me on the road and immediately his brake lights flared and he practically skidded to a stop in the loose shoulder gravel.

Without a second's hesitation, I took off. I could hear the car's tires scraping on the wet pavement as he turned around to chase. I knew that by running, I couldn't possibly have done anything to look more suspicious. But what else could I do? Ask for a ride to Aunt Bessie's house? I didn't even know the name of the town I was in. There was no way I was going to let myself get locked up in some little West Virginia town, that's for sure.

Like a rabbit with a fox on his heels, I cut through yards, hopped fences and zigzagged my way through an empty-looking industrial area. Once back down where I'd started, I stopped to catch my breath.

'Man, it seems like every day I'm running from the cops.'

Well, I told *you not to walk along that road.*

"I *told* you not to walk along that road," I mimicked in an obnoxious voice as I darted into the railroad yards. Without losing stride, I hopped on a coal train that was moving west through the yards.

I knew that once the train pulled out into the open, I'd be clearly visible. So with the cover of freight cars on either side of me, I scaled the ladder on the side of the car and looked inside to see if it was empty. Quickly, before I lost my cover, I climbed over the top of the car, staying as low as I could, and slid down the sloping end wall and into the car. I had to stop myself from sliding right into the little compartment at the bottom where the coal empties out, but the doors on it were closed anyways. I relaxed down there, completely out of sight, unless you were in a helicopter.

"And who'd be out flying a helicopter in weather like this?" I laughed, all pumped up and proud of my escape.

You'd better hope you can climb out of here.

'I can do anything with this body.'

My feet skidded for traction as I carefully made my way up the wet, sloping floor of the car and peeked over the top. Fortunately, the slope had a narrow divider in the center about halfway down, so that when they emptied the coal out, half of it would go to one side of the car and the other half would go to the other.

Once the train was leaving the yards and slowly picking up speed, I climbed over the top of the coal car, down the ladder on the outside corner, and gingerly hopped off. I would have stayed on for the ride, but I was afraid that an empty coal train might be heading to some small mining town in the middle of nowhere.

I still had the same problem that I'd had a few miles back: I was stuck hiding in the woods in the rain. At least I was at the other end of the railroad yards now.

My pants, filthy when I inherited them, were now ridiculously dirty after I'd cleaned out the inside of a wet coal car with them. At some point, I was either going to have to wash these in the river or get new ones. What I really needed was two pairs of pants: one for walking around towns and one for riding trains.

As I watched from my cover, I noted that the cop I'd run from—or at least *a* cop—was slowly cruising the edge of the railroad yard. I always got a rush out of watching from a hiding spot as the police searched for me. I wasn't too concerned, because I didn't expect them to call out the bloodhounds over some runaway kid.

Maybe not, but now you can't even go into town after school's out and get something to eat.

Well, I guess my inner voice had me on that one. Oops.

I laughed and shook my head as I repeated the words, "After school's out."

"Only I could be in this situation and just . . . just run with it as though it's perfectly normal."

As one train crept into the yard, another one was departing on the track closest to me. I watched for a car that would provide a good hiding spot and protection from the rain. Some empty boxcars with the doors open were coming my way, but I had no way to get into them. A boxcar with the doors open on both sides came along, and I quickly formulated an insane plan. I easily outran the outgoing train, and ran up about ten cars ahead of the boxcar that had both sides open and hopped on a tank car. The tank car had a platform on the end that extended the width of the car, so I crossed and carefully climbed down and stepped off.

Standing between two trains going in opposite directions was a strange sensation. Fortunately, both were moving at a snail's pace. I hopped up on a ladder on a car on the inbound and when my empty boxcar on the outbound came along, I leapt across the short three-foot gap and into the boxcar.

You are an insurance man's worst nightmare.

I didn't know or care where this train was going. All I cared was that I was out of the rain and leaving this town. As we picked up speed, I tried to think of a way that I could walk around the next town without drawing attention.

'Maybe I can get a fake beard or something.'

A "fake beard" Mike?

I broke out laughing.

A skinny little midget with a high-pitched voice and a fake beard.

And have you ever, in your entire life, seen a fake beard in a store? 'Excuse me, can you tell me where the fake beards are?' 'Why yes, they're in aisle seven, right next to the macaroni and the magic wands'.

"Shut up," I laughed.

As usual, I awoke during the night when the train slowed down. I wanted to just lie there, but I figured I'd better take a look around in case I was in a bad area. We were pulling into a railroad yard and it was pouring rain.

"Is it just my imagination, or has it really rained every single day that I've been living out here?" I wondered again.

I had no intention of getting out of this car, so I felt around in my pack to see what I had left for food. Not too bad—two little boxes of raisins and some peanuts. The jar the peanuts came in (peanuts in plastic bags weren't available back now) would have taken up too much space in my backpack, so I'd dumped them onto my spare T-shirt and twisted the T-shirt into a kind of knapsack around them. But they'd all dumped out into my filthy backpack, so I dined on raisins and gritty peanuts mixed with what I hoped was just sand and bits of leaves. "I need to get a flashlight or some candles." At least my canteen was still three-quarters full.

The sound of the rain hitting the metal boxcar roof was soothing. My only immediate problem was that I didn't know what time it was. It could be eight o'clock at night or three o'clock in the morning. I had absolutely no idea, and therefore absolutely no idea how long I could hang out here before daylight.

The rain let up, so I ventured out to snoop around. It wasn't really a huge railroad yard, like some of the ones that I'd been to. My train made the now familiar "preparing to depart" hissing air noises. I headed back to my boxcar, seeing as it was the only one with both doors open. I found a huge sheet of cardboard in a boxcar on the adjacent track. I carried it to my car for something to lie on and, much to my delight, away we went.

13

I was in Kentucky, walking the tracks in perfect weather, doing my best to keep out of sight. A little ways down a residential street that dead-ended at the tracks, a man who was working on his car wearily watched me approach him. He was black, I was a white boy, and this was a summer of race riots.

"Excuse me, sir," I asked in my northern accent, "Could you tell me if there are any stores or Laundromats around here?"

His hard look immediately softened. I hadn't treated him with respect in any false way. I came from a different time, where I had as much respect for him as I had for myself or anyone else.

"Where'd you come from, boy?"

"New Jersey." I may as well have said "Mars."

"*New Jersey?* And you just out alone walking the railroad tracks in Louisville, Kentucky? That don't make no sense." Then he took in my general condition and my backpack. "You a boy on the run, ain't that right?"

I shrugged.

"What you been gettin' into? You look like you fell in a tar pit."

"I've been riding freight trains."

He glanced over at the tracks. "Didn't nobody ever tell you that you supposed to ride *on* the train, not *under* it?" He laughed.

I smiled. "Well, I was running from the cops and I hid in a coal car and I kind of got stuck in there for a while."

"A little white boy running from the cops and gettin' stuck in coal cars!" He laughed some more, shaking his head. "Wait 'till the boys at the shop here about this!"

Then he turned serious.

"Your momma sitting home crying?"

"No sir. I have no family"

"So why you on the run then?"

"Well, I'm not really 'on the run'—I'm just, um, traveling."

"Uh-huh. Boy as young as you, just traveling. So if a cop come down this street right now, what you gonna do—ask for directions?"

I smiled and said, "I'll just pretend that I'm your son."

He laughed. "Oh, you trouble, yes-sir-ee I seen that right away." Then he got serious again. "I don't need no trouble. I got boys of my own and if I *ever* seen them jumping on one of them trains . . ."

"OK, I'll move on. Could you tell me if there are any stores around here?"

"None that a white boy can walk to." He stood and considered me for a few moments. I was going to ask him at least which direction I should be walking in order not to get killed and to find a store. I couldn't hop on another train without resupplying.

"My old lady gonna kill me for this," he stated and started walking towards the house. "Come on."

I followed. He had me wait on the porch while he went in. I heard a heated discussion inside, and then someone stormed to the door and yanked it open. A heavyset black lady looked at me with cold eyes. I gave her my most pathetic and innocent look, but she wasn't placated.

"Go home, boy," she ordered.

"Yes ma'am," I said. I stepped down off of the porch, paused on the grass, looked back at her and said, "I don't have a home." Without waiting for an answer I walked out to the street and back towards the tracks.

"You gonna get you throat cut walking them tracks," she called after me.

I just shrugged and kept walking. "At least now I know not to bother walking around here," I muttered to myself.

I went back the way I came on the tracks and managed to avoid getting my throat cut.

I saw a thrift shop that I'd missed when walking in the other direction. I desperately needed affordable clothing, so I figured I could get away with shopping there if I did a quick in-and-out. I hid my backpack and made a beeline for the thrift shop.

The tinkling of the bell on the door and my appearance silenced the group of people hanging out at the cash register. I stood out like a sore thumb in every possible way: a little white kid in the wrong neighborhood alone, on a school day.

'Oh, man, what size am I?' I wondered irritably as I headed for the clothing racks. I'd been meaning to look at the size on the jeans I was wearing since I'd switched, but I always forgot. 'I never had kids and it's been so long since I *was* this age.'

Those look about right, my inner voice teased as my eyes settled on a tiny pair of pants that a toddler would wear.

I shook my head and smiled. 'Smart-ass, you're not helping.'

My temptation was to just grab a pair that was obviously too big, roll up the cuffs and buy a belt. But I was afraid that mis-sized clothing would make me stand out even more as a runaway kid.

Michael, I hate to be the one to break the news to you, but you couldn't stand out any more as a runaway kid if you hung a sign around your neck.

I snatched a few pairs of pants that looked about right off of the rack and headed for a curtained-off area that served as the changing room.

'So much for a quick in-and-out.'

Aw, look on the bright side: how many people in this town could make the statement "It's been so long since I was this age"?

'The novelty is wearing off.'

Is it really?

I glanced at my image in the mirror and couldn't help but smile.

'No, not in the least.'

I bought two pairs of jeans (one to cut off for shorts). The lady's face at the cash register finally softened and she smiled. I think she felt sorry for me.

"Too bad they didn't sell socks and underwear," I said as I headed back up towards the tracks.

Socks and underwear in a used clothing store? Ewwww!

'It would be less disgusting than what I'm wearing.'

Which was no underwear at all: in desperation, I'd used it as toilet paper some time ago. This morning, I had to settle for using wet leaves.

At least they weren't poison ivy leaves.

I hightailed it out of that general area, heading back the way I came. I really didn't expect black people down south in the sixties to call the cops over some stray white kid, but you never knew. At least the city in the area where I jumped off of the train was sort of neutral—more industrial, but with areas where I could hide out. I hadn't gotten off at a rail yard, so I had no idea where one might be.

"I hope the thrift shop washes the used clothes," I mumbled as I hid in some brush next to the tracks and changed my pants and shirt. I turned my train-riding pants inside out (so everything else in the pack wouldn't get filthy) before packing them. I hid the backpack and headed off in search of something to eat. I found a little dive where the local factory and warehouse workers probably ate. I went straight to the men's room and washed up, then sat at the counter like any normal person. I knew eating out in diners wasn't the best way to stretch my money, but I needed a burger or something with some protein value. This body had been thin when I'd inherited it, and by not eating enough I'd become a really skinny kid.

I was certainly the only kid in the diner.

"Help you, honey?" asked the waitress.

"Coffee and a menu, please."

"You're a little young for coffee, ain't you?"

I shrugged. I'd ordered coffee so automatically that I'd momentarily forgotten that I wasn't a grown-up.

"My maw lets me drink it," I answered, in a ridiculously overdone southern accent that made me inwardly roll my eyes.

She served me the coffee, and then surreptitiously watched me add milk and sip it.

Two cops walked in and greeted the waitress. It was obvious that they came in every day. They gave me a long sideways glance as I studied the menu, but they left me alone. I was lucky because if *I* was a cop, I would want to know what this little kid was doing sitting in a diner on a school day. A long-haired blond guy a few seats away around a bend in the counter noticed me watching the cops out of the corner of my eye as I ordered a burger.

"Shouldn't you be in school?" the waitress asked, way too loudly, looking towards her cop friends.

I knew she was going to do that. But for once, I already had a good story made up.

"Aw, they say I have pinkeye," I answered just as loudly, both for the cops' sake, and to see the startled expression on her face.

"You do?" she asked as she backed up a step.

"Not no more, but you can't tell them that. Guess which eye it was in?"

"They both look OK."

"Uh-huh, but they won't listen to my maw. She knows I'm here. She works right at—" (I can't remember the name, but it was a factory down the street where

I saw ladies outside on their break sitting at picnic tables, smoking. The only reason that my feeble memory could recall the factory name at the diner was because it was on the calendar that I was just looking at. One of the factory workers must have given a calendar to the diner. Above the calendar pages was a picture of some type of machinery. What an exciting photo shoot *that* must have been.)

"I'm gonna ride home with her," I added.

"What does your ma do there?" she asked.

Oh, for crying out loud.

"I don't know," I answered impatiently, forgetting to use my accent. "They make some kind of machinery or something."

"What time is her shift over?"

I stuffed my mouth full of fries, shrugged and said, "Umhm mahuma." A chunk of French fry fell out of my mouth and I plucked it off the counter and stuffed it back in.

She shook her head as though I was a lost cause and she walked away. The long-haired blond guy lit up a cigarette and as we met eyes he smiled at me as though we shared some secret. I smiled as well and dug into my burger. Fortunately, the cops didn't bother with me and they took their bagged food and left.

As I headed across the small parking lot, I heard a whistle from the side of the diner. Longhair was standing by his beat-up sixties muscle car, smoking another cigarette. He looked like trouble, but I went over to him anyway. Seeing him outside, I realized that he wasn't as young as I thought he was.

"On the run, huh?" he asked.

"Just trying to lie low and stay out of trouble, man."

"Um-hmm," he said, looking down at me with perplexed interest. I guess my last line really wasn't typical talk for a kid my age.

"Where you headed?"

"West."

He smiled and nodded as if to say "of course."

"Where you start from?"

"New Jersey."

He smiled and nodded. "I knew that accent was fake. You made it a long ways. It must be tough, keeping from getting busted out here, being so young and all. I mean, I've seen kids on the road before, but . . ."

'Yeah, yeah, I know. They weren't nearly as young as I am.'

"Only time I get to relax is when I'm on a moving freight train," I said.

"Freight train? If you were going west from New Jersey, how the hell did you wind up down here?" he asked.

I described my scientific method of itinerary planning, which consisted of "jumping on anything that moves, and then checking license plates when it stops."

He shook his head and laughed along with me.

"What's your name?"

"Mike. What's yours?"

"Danny," he answered, offering his hand. "Do you think you'll make it to the west coast?"

"If the cops don't catch me first." I told him about West Virginia and my coal car fiasco.

He took a last drag off of his cigarette, dropped it and crushed it. Mostly to himself, he said, "Running from cops, hiding in coal cars." He didn't find it as amusing as the last guy I'd talked to had. "So tell me something, Mike. Was it worth it?"

"Was what worth what?" I asked, although I thought I knew where he was going with the question.

"Was life on the streets worth leaving home for?" he clarified.

Wow, all of the soul-searching that I'd done lately, all of the debates in my head about switching lives, keeping always on the move, hiding from the cops, not having anywhere to get off of the streets. . . the whole thing could be summed up in that one simple question.

"Have you even *tried* calling home?" he asked in response to my silence.

Sure, I'd called home just to make sure that I was still there. But how could I be here and there at the same time? Who the hell was I, right here and now in this conscious state? And when we switched lives, why didn't I just become the adult him?

Then I remembered that Danny was still waiting for a reply. I had a bad habit of letting people wait for me to answer while I had conversations with myself. As if I don't have enough time alone to talk to myself!

"I don't have a home or a family to call."

He considered that for a few moments, probably questioning the validity of it.

"I'll tell you what, Mike. I'm a trucker and I'm heading to St. Louis in a little while if you want to come for the ride, get a break from risking your life riding trains and maybe have someone to talk to. I normally don't take riders along, other than my own boys. But I want to hear more of your stories."

Wow, St. Louis—the "gateway to the west." I wondered if the arch was there yet. But did I trust this guy? Yeah, I guess I did. But then, where was his truck? Was I supposed to get into his car and really believe that we were going to some truck yard?

"Um, I don't know. I have my backpack stashed over by the tracks. I'd have to go get it," I said, both telling the truth and giving myself an excuse to get away from him if I wanted to.

"Well, go get it. I'll be over there by my rig," he said, pointing to a warehouse across the street.

"But what about your car?" I asked.

"Huh? This ain't my car—my car is in Missouri."

Oh.

As Danny headed for the warehouse, I walked down the street to fetch my backpack.

Was it worth it?

I knew the second that Danny asked that question that my inner voice would latch onto those words and plague me with them.

'Yeah, it was worth it.'

But what about the damage you're doing to this kid's life? Skipping school, living on the streets . . .

'Oh, come on, that's just not fair!'

"The damage I'm doing to this kid's life," I sarcastically repeated as I retrieved my backpack. "Like I don't have enough things to worry about, now I gotta worry about the life of some kid I—"

I had one of those epiphanies when everything seems crystal clear. I loudly inhaled, with a goofy, surprised smile on my face.

"Yes, of course! *I'm* the kid under the bridge! I dreamt me up!"

I looked up at the sky and yelled, "Ha-ho, you'd better *believe* it was worth it!"

As I jogged down the street, I threw my backpack in the air and yelled, "Whoo-hoo!"

Could you possibly make any more of a scene?

'I don't know—got any firecrackers?'

14

There was plenty of activity at the warehouse, but I didn't see my new long-haired friend. After awkwardly standing around for a few minutes, I approached a guy that was standing in an empty truck bay.

"Do you know where Danny went—the truck driver with the long blond hair?"

"Yeah, he'll be out in a few minutes. Are you one of his sons?"

"Yeah," I stupidly lied.

"I figured that by the long hair. I'm Bob, I'm sure Danny's mentioned me," he said, offering his hand. "Which son are you?"

He's the idiot who's not a son, who really should think before he talks.

"I'm Mike," I said. And then, figuring that the odds were too long to gamble on that Danny had a son named Mike, I added, "I'm not really one of his sons. I ran away from home in St. Louis, and he's taking me home."

"Oh," he said. "That's funny, because I think Danny really does have a son named Mike."

I sighed, and rolled my eyes.

"How did he find you?" Bob asked.

"My mom called him."

"How?"

Damn, I kept forgetting that there were no cell phones back now. Did the truckers have CBs yet? 'How the hell should I know,' I answered myself irritably.

"I don't know," I answered Bob. "She told me to meet him at the diner."

"The 'diner,' huh?"

Crap. They didn't call them diners outside of the New York/New Jersey area, did they? Come to that, they didn't speak with New Jersey accents either.

Bob seemed amused, but not in a mean way, at my little kid stupidity as I trapped myself in lies.

"I guess the grass isn't always greener on the other side of the fence, huh?" he asked, smiling kindly.

"No, it really isn't," I answered honestly.

Just then, Danny came out. I wanted to get to him before Bob did, but no luck there.

"Hey Dan, I hear you're doing your good deed for the day, taking Mike home to his ma."

I closed my eyes and put my hand up to rub my forehead.

Dan shot me a look, but he didn't miss a beat. "Yeah, she owes me one for dragging her little runt home for her,"

Dan and Bob stood on the dock and talked for a while. I busied myself re-packing my backpack.

"All right, Bob," Dan said, wrapping up the conversation while closing the trailer doors, "Let me get this kid home."

"Are you going to L.A. this week?" Bob asked, and boy did *my* ears perk up.

"No, I'm home for a few days, then Nashville, then Dallas," Danny answered, "I'll see you next trip. Oh," Danny said, looking down at me and handing me a dollar, "run over and get us coffees, would you? I take mine same as yours—milk, no sugar. Bob, you want one?"

Bob declined the offer. I threw my backpack in the cab and then I lingered out of sight for a few seconds.

"It's good of you to take him home," Bob said to Danny. "But I can tell you right now that he'll run again. That boy's too wild to stay in one place for long. And you can't believe a word he says."

I couldn't catch most of what they discussed next, but I did hear Danny comment: "The kid seems like he's already lived . . ." before I snuck away out of earshot to get our coffee.

. . . A whole lifetime, my inner voice filled in.

'And that's just in the last two weeks!'

Danny was fascinated with my stories, and he told me that I should write a book someday. I wished I could have told him the ultimate story about switching lives. Next thing I knew, I awoke as we rolled along in late afternoon sunshine. I'd obviously slept many hours and I apologized for dropping off in the middle of our conversation.

"That's all right, you obviously needed the sleep," Dan replied as he negotiated the turn into a truck stop/general store. "C'mon, let's get some grub."

"Where are we?"

"We're almost to St. Louis."

We got seated at a table, ordered coffee and food, then took turns going to the bathroom. On my way, I noticed that they sold some clothing, including socks and underwear. Maybe they wouldn't have it in kids' sizes, but it was better than nothing. I rushed over and told Danny that I was going to buy some.

"Hold off a few minutes," he said. "Our food will be here soon. Just relax. You can get your stuff on the way out."

He was right, of course. I was only hyper because I'd gotten so used to not being able to get to a store to buy anything.

Danny told me about his wife and kids and church life. He was a kind, smart, upstanding family man, and I felt ashamed that when I first met him I'd pre-judged him as just some scumbag.

"We got a little problem here," Danny said.

"Yeah, I know," I said, reading his mind, "You feel bad just dumping me off on my own in some strange city."

He sipped his coffee.

"You didn't put me out here, Dan. I put myself here. I don't have a home, a family, foster parents, nothing. Do you know what my last address was?"

He shook his head.

I stopped talking as the waitress brought our food and gave us more coffee.

"My last address was 'under a bridge, somewhere in New Jersey,'" I continued after she'd left. Then I told him the commune story, which I'd had time to refine and make more believable. "I'm better off on my own than in an orphanage or something," I concluded.

"I don't think they call them 'orphanages' anymore."

"Well, whatever they call them."

"Bob seems to think that I shouldn't believe a word you say . . ."

I studied at my plate as I drew patterns in the grease with my fingertip.

"See, it doesn't matter where you came from," Dan said. "It doesn't make sense that a kid as young as you are should be out here on his own. No matter how smart you think you are, you need schooling, for one thing."

That sort of hung there between the two of us for a few minutes.

"Do, ah . . ." He tugged on his ear as he thought his offer through. "Do you want to come stay with us until we . . . get this sorted out?"

"No, thank you. I'm not as young as I look, Dan. I'll be OK. God takes care of me. Things are the way they're supposed to be for me right now."

He lit up a cigarette. "There's a big story behind your story, isn't there?" he asked as he squinted through the smoke.

I smiled. "There's a *huge* story behind my story. Someday you can read about it in my book."

He smiled as well, took a drag off of his cigarette and blew the smoke up towards the ceiling. "Is that commune story even true?"

I silently arranged the items on the table in front of me in an orderly manner for a few moments. "No, I made it up. But it is true that no one's looking for me, missing me, worrying about me, nothing. I touched off at the Atlantic Ocean in Virginia Beach and I'm—"

"You rode a freight train right to Virginia Beach?"

"No, to Richmond. I took a bus to Virginia Beach. Although, there were tracks that went to about two blocks from the ocean. They're probably torn up by now," I mused, mostly to myself.

But Dan caught it and frowned. "How long ago were you there?"

Oh, crap. When I said they were probably torn up by now, the "by now" referred to 2015.

"Well, I was only there in August, but it looked like they were getting ready to tear them up," I said dismissively and quickly continued, "Anyway, I'm going to travel to the Pacific Ocean and touch off again. Then, once this is hopefully out of my system, I'm going to walk up to the first cop I see and say 'I'm homeless, and I have no family' and then just . . . ride the wave, man. See what happens next."

He smiled as he shook his head. "You're a kid, but you're not a kid," he mused. We were totally connected, as though we'd known each other all of our lives. The bustle of the truck stop around us seemed muted beyond our private bubble.

"Where did you get the guts to do what you're doing?" Dan asked.

"You know what the funny thing is?"

He shook his head.

"I *don't* have the guts for it," I said with an ironic smile. "I'm a complete wimp." I held up my hands and shrugged. Then I pointed at his cigarette. "We all take risks. You want to live to see your grandkids?"

He gave me a "what the hell kind of question is that?" look.

"Oh, they don't hurt you," he said as he snuffed it out. "You sound like my wife," he grumbled as he perused the check.

"They kill you in many slow, horrible, gruesome ways."

He sighed. "Yeah, yeah, yeah. Well, *doctor*, where am I dropping you off?"

I glanced through the window at an outdoor world of danger and uncertainty that I'd temporarily forgotten existed. It was getting dark and I didn't want to go back out there. I just wanted to stay here in this truck stop in safety.

"I don't know," I finally answered. "Not right in town—especially at night." I explained that I was used to feeling my way into a city from the edges, usually in the early morning when the streets were safe.

"You have a system."

I nodded.

He shook his head. "Bob was right," he said quietly.

I didn't reply because I was eavesdropping when his friend Bob was making comments about my wildness. And who knows what Bob said after I went for coffee?

I looked at Dan questioningly, but he just dismissed it with a wave of his hand.

"Let's go," he said as he tossed down a tip. I dug into my pocket for my share of the bill, but he said, "No, no, no. Put your money away."

As he paid at the cash register, I selected some supplies.

"What've you got here?" he asked as he scanned my socks and underwear. "Are they gonna fit you?"

"I was hoping an adult small would be OK," I said.

"Nah, leave them here. We'll stop at a five-and-ten."

In 2015 lingo, he would have said, "We'll stop at Walmart."

I silently debated making the break now and letting him drive off without me.

As if reading my mind, he said, "Come on, let's go. You don't want to stay here. This town's worse than St. Louis."

I got to see the arch as we entered St. Louis over the MacArthur Bridge. Danny told me that in a few months the highway would go over the new bridge down the river from here. Underneath us were freight trains, so I guess I had some idea of where my next ride would start.

We drove to an industrial area to drop the trailer. The area was similar to the one we'd left earlier in Louisville, although more urban. It wasn't all that far from the arch, and there were even railroad tracks, although the tracks didn't look like they got much use. There were areas to hide out and sleep, though.

"Um . . . I don't suppose that there's a cheap hotel around here that you could help me get a room in, is there? I mean, I'll pay and all, it's just that they wouldn't rent a room to me." I could really use the break from sleeping outside in the danger, the weather and the bugs and I desperately needed a shower. I'd wanted to get a haircut so I wouldn't stand out so much, but my hair was always too dirty to even bring to a barber.

Dan gazed up at the night sky and sighed. "Sorry, kid, if you're not coming home with me, you're just going to have to walk away on your own. This ain't such a bad area. If I were you, I'd lie low until daylight."

"Yeah, no problem, I do this all of the time. Thanks for the ride, Dan, and thanks for dinner. It was really nice meeting you." I kept my voice upbeat and casual because I knew how it was hurting him to leave me here. As he was busy cranking the hitch on his trailer to unhook it, I edged away and vanished into the woods by the tracks. I didn't turn around to look, but I know darned well that he stopped cranking the trailer and turned to watch me walk off into the night.

I could add Danny to the list of people I've met who will now worry about me. I was willing to bet that when he got home, he'd poke his head into his sleeping sons' bedrooms and thank God that they were home safe and not out at night, homeless and alone in some strange city.

In the rain.

I sighed. 'Of course.'

I spied as Dan pulled his truck out through the drizzle, closed the gate that we'd opened on the way in, and drove off. Then I crawled under the gate and got some cardboard out of the dumpster.

"Man, look at this stuff," I mumbled. "They didn't recycle *anything* back now."

I made a little nest for myself in the thin strip of woods between the tracks and the truck yard fence and to keep busy and keep other thoughts at bay, I buried my old socks and stowed the new stuff which, I took a second to notice, was still made in USA back now.

I'd also bought the smallest bottle of shampoo that I could find. It'd obviously made Dan uneasy to watch me buy supplies for living on the road. I think that it was not only the *fact* that I was buying them, but also the *manner* in which I was buying them: as though I was just some kid going off to summer camp. He had that classic look on his face that was now familiar to me: "This kid really doesn't act like he looks."

Ah, don't take it so hard, Danny old boy. Mike doesn't know who he is either!

'Amen to that! I wonder if I'll ever fully grow into this role.'

No more than you'd ever grown into your old, adult role. But look on the bright side—better to be a mature kid than an immature adult, right?

I couldn't argue with that logic.

I lay back on the cardboard for about fifteen seconds, but the drizzle was turning to rain.

"Is it just my imagination, or has it really rained every single day that I've been living out here?"

Are you going to ask that question in every *city?*

"Apparently!"

I felt too vulnerable to relax. There weren't enough woods, and I was too close to the tracks if someone happened to come along. The fence that protected my back from an attack also trapped me in the event of one from the front. Not that I couldn't climb the fence, but in those precious seconds, someone could grab me. I wondered if I snored in this kid body. I know that my adult body snored like, well, like a freight train. Seeing as I'd slept all day in Dan's truck, I really wasn't sleepy anyway. I gave up and ventured forth to explore.

The rain was more than just an annoyance, because all afternoon my throat had been getting scratchier, and now I felt kind of achy and dreamy.

When I explored cities, particularly at night, I kept as much as possible out of actual neighborhoods. Downtown areas were fairly benign, and the industrial areas I favored were mostly deserted. I intuitively knew that I was more likely to run into drug and gang areas in neighborhoods, and people were more likely to mess with me when they were on their own turf.

I found a huge railroad yard. I wasn't ready to leave St. Louis yet, but at least now when I did plan on leaving I'd know where to go. I sat and watched them shuffle freight cars around for a while. I'd wanted to cut the legs off to make shorts out of one of the pairs of jeans I'd bought, but I had no scissors. I got the bright idea to lay the pants on the rail to let the train wheels cut them for me.

"So much for *that* idea," I muttered. Although the wheels had smashed the pants, they hadn't cut them. All I had now was a pair of jeans with a big, wet, greasy smashed line across the legs.

"Go figure. Put a penny on the rail and it gets smashed thin, but cloth doesn't get cut."

I wandered into the downtown area. I didn't think it was real late, but I seemed to be the only person on the streets. I don't know how it is today, but 1967 St. Louis—at least in the area where I was—seemed to be the kind of city where they "swept up the sidewalks at six p.m." and everyone went home to somewhere else. Although I wasn't feeling well, it was cool walking around a big deserted city. Aside from the occasional car, the only sounds were the rain and the sounds of air conditioning units on buildings. I felt like a visitor from another planet.

I spotted an old, run-down-looking hotel on a corner and I figured it was worth a shot. The lobby smelled of cigarette smoke, aged wood, mildew and way too much Lysol. The place had obviously once been a fine establishment. The woodwork, carpet, wallpaper and the huge staircase leading up to the rooms all seemed to lament the old hotel's former grandeur. In the corner of the decrepit lobby was a really cool old wooden phone booth. I wondered if the building was still there in 2015. If not, had they at least saved the wooden phone booth? As I made my way through, I got strange looks from the old-timers who were hanging out in the lobby.

The sandy-haired, middle aged guy behind the glassed-in front desk had also watched my progress across the lobby, but when I stood before him he focused his attention on his little black and white TV as though he hadn't noticed me. I shifted from foot to foot for half a minute and opened my mouth to speak when, without diverting his eyes from what he was watching, he shook his head with his lips pressed tightly together and said, "Not a chance, little guy. We don't rent to runaway kids."

"I'm not a runaway," I protested, but his expression didn't change. I had to admit that even to myself, I sounded exactly like a little runaway kid denying that he was a little runaway kid.

"I guess I'll have to sleep on the street in the rain then."

He finally looked at me. "Or, you could just go home where you belong," he replied without sympathy as he tilted his head in an "out you go" gesture. He briefly met eyes with one of the old-timers in the lobby before he went back to ignoring me. I hesitated for a few seconds.

He reached for the phone and asked, "Do you want me to call someone to help you find your way out?"

"No, that's OK, I'm leaving."

I headed back down to the industrial area, where I found a covered loading dock with a boxcar parked at it. In spots, the overhang leaked where it met the brick wall and water was trickling down the wall and pooling on the loading dock. I raided the nearby dumpster for cardboard and found some dry stuff under the wet top layers. I spread it out on the dock where the pigeon shit wasn't so bad and the human piss smell was the weakest. Then I settled with my back to the wall and closed my eyes.

'You know what's kinda strange? In that hotel, I noticed that I don't feel like a little kid anymore. No, I mean, I *feel* like a kid, but . . .'

But you don't notice because you just feel like yourself.

I nodded and yawned.

Whenever I slept outside, my ears automatically went into a hyper-perked mode, subconsciously listening for any threats. If a sound did wake me, it was as if it was amplified a hundred times. At one point in the wee hours of the morning, it was either a very tiny sound close to me or just a presence that woke me. A big bushy alley cat was up on the dock, silently watching me. I made the slightest little move and it was gone in a flash.

"You should have stayed and curled up with me," I said. "We're brothers, you and I."

Then I drifted back off to sleep.

15

I awoke at first light under a mostly clear sky. My throat felt as though it was on fire and my eyes stung. I shouldered my backpack, picked up my cardboard and, with legs that felt as though I'd run a marathon all night, I hopped down from the dock. As I was tossing the cardboard back in the dumpster, a garbage truck (minus the usual backup beeper that they had in the future, I noticed) was backing up to it. A big, lumberjack-looking man, complete with blue jeans and flannel shirt, got out and hooked chains onto the dumpster to lift it up and dump it into the truck. He turned his attention to me and motioned me closer with a gloved hand. He had medium-length dark hair, a full beard and striking blue eyes.

"You sleep out here last night?" he asked.

I nodded.

"Not in there, I hope." He indicated the dumpster.

"No, up on the dock, out of the rain."

He glanced up at the loading dock and shook his head sadly. "I got a couple of bananas in the truck. You want them?"

I nodded and smiled.

He retrieved them and tossed them to me.

"Thank you."

He nodded, seemed to consider saying more to me for a few seconds, but said, "Watch yourself, if one of these chains breaks, you'll be crushed."

I took that as my cue to leave, so I hid and ate my bananas. I planned on going to see the arch, but it would really be more pleasant if I could do it on a weekend day and relax without being the only kid out on the streets.

'Oh well, maybe there'll be a school field trip or something at the arch. Not that I'd really fit in with a bunch of school kids.'

You could if you'd clean up your act a little. You look like you've slept on a loading dock.

'At least I didn't sleep in the dumpster.'

I yawned. I really could have used a few more hours of sleep.

You should have hung a "Do not disturb" sign around your neck and slept in.

I smiled as I pictured men unloading the boxcar with me lying there on my cardboard and yelling, "Hey, you want to keep the noise down over there?"

It warmed up and the few remaining clouds dissipated.

As freight trains rumbled overhead on the nearby MacArthur Bridge and on an elevated line about a block away, I washed my hair in the river. It wasn't easy getting just my hair wet without the threat of falling all of the way in. I did the best I could to keep the polluted-smelling water out of my ears, eyes and nose. I mostly dried my hair with my T-shirt, and then put the T-shirt back on so it would dry.

When I ran my hands over my hair, I noticed the difference between the rough, dirty way it usually felt and how silky smooth it felt now. The same was true of my teeth. I didn't really brush them very often, so after I did, they felt smooth when I ran my tongue over them. Speaking of which, I brushed them without water because my canteen was empty.

You're not going to rinse in the river?

'That water? It looks like someone washed their hair in it.'

I hung out in an abandoned-looking industrial area by the mighty Mississippi River for quite a while. I was sandwiched between what looked like a place where they loaded sand or gravel on barges and a power or a pumping station or whatever it was. The area nearer to the arch had boats and people around, so I felt more comfortable here. There were a few other homeless-looking people around my general area, but I put out my best "don't bother me" vibes, and no one did.

I finally got restless enough to risk a trip to see the arch. I half buried my backpack in an old gravel pile and covered it with sticks and dead leaves. Walking right up to the arch on a perfect sunny day was well worth the risk of walking around in public on a school day, if you ask me. It didn't look like it was officially open yet, but it was good enough for me. Although there were no other kids there, there were enough people for me to blend with.

Occasionally I would see a cop, but I would stand close to adults so it would look as though I was with them. When I did this, some people looked at me as though wondering, "Why is this kid getting so close?" One guy unconsciously checked his wallet, which made me think of the play *Oliver* where they trained little kids to pick pockets. And then that silly "pick-a-pocket-or-two" song, remembered from a school play in some distant past, was stuck in my head for the next four hours.

I went downtown, where there were more people out than I would have imagined there would have been. St. Louis was still a true city back then, with downtown stores and throngs of people on the sidewalks. My throat was beginning to feel like it was on fire and the warm weather actually seemed to make it worse. I found a Woolworths and bought the smallest pair of scissors I could find, sore throat drops, aspirin and vitamins. After gulping down a burger, I decided that I'd pressed my luck enough and I headed back to my hiding spot by the river to await after-school hours.

Besides cutting off my pants and cutting my hair, I'd wanted the scissors for another idea I had. On my way back to the river, I ducked into an alley, hid behind garbage pails and cut slits into the inside of the waist seam of my jeans so I could hide money there.

I was back down by the river and heading for my backpack when two guys that I'd thought I could just walk past without a problem jumped me. One was white, with long blond scraggly hair and a sparse beard. The other was a huge, heavyset black guy.

"Where you going, boy?"

"Just out walking," I tried to say, while being choked.

"Well, you're walking in the wrong place, man. What's in the bag? Got any money? Search his pockets."

White guy held me upright, with my feet dangling. My arms were pinned at my sides with one of the white guy's arms while he was half choking me with his other arm. I didn't dare try to kick. The other guy searched my pockets. All I had was a comb in my back pocket and money in my front right pocket. He pulled out my roll of bills and threw my comb away.

"Little boy's got some money." He made me cringe as he smacked my face with the bills. "Where'd you get this?"

"What's in that bag he was carrying?"

"Vitamins and shit." The black guy looked at me. "What you carrying this shit for?"

Only a gurgle came out as my reply.

"What do you want to do with him?" white guy asked.

"I don't know; let me think about it for a while." He drew the words out slowly, as though relishing them. If it was meant to scare me, it worked.

When I finally let myself go limp in his arms, white guy threw me to the ground and I gasped for breath. Being choked had done wonders for my sore throat. My impulse was to run, but I got up and stood right by them, which probably surprised them.

"I'm getting really sick, and I don't have a home and I need that stuff and now I have no money," I croaked.

"Oh, boo-hoo," said the white guy as he pulled his arm back as if to hit me.

I cringed, but I forced myself to stay within striking range as though it was three of us standing together. I was hoping that my body language would be a game-changer. I could always run, but there might be a chance of at least getting my bag of stuff back. I had to make every penny last. As he rummaged around in my bag that the black guy was holding, white guy idly kicked my comb away as I bent to pick it up.

The black guy held up the scissors. "What you gonna do, cut your own hair? Man, that's *pathetic*."

"Maybe we should cut it for him," white guy said, turning towards me.

After going after my comb I was far enough away to run, but I held my ground.

"Think he'll run to the cops?" asked white guy.

Black guy looked at me and answered, "He ain't gonna run to the cops. He running *from* the cops."

As I stood there wheezing, black guy exchanged a "he's just a sick, defenseless little homeless kid" look with his white friend, and reached towards me with the bag.

"Here, boy, seeing as you either too brave or too stupid to run away. I don't know which. We don't want your shit anyways. Get your sick, sorry ass out of here and don't come back."

Hoping that I hadn't misread their intentions, I stepped forwards and took it. White guy was now holding my money, and black guy gave him a look. White guy sighed and looked at me.

"You think you're a *tough* little fucker, don't you? Here man, take your fucking money. But I gotta borrow five bucks, *all right?*" he said, giving me back only four dollars. He held my five-dollar bill within my reach, challenging me to lunge for it.

"Sure man," I said, still trying to talk. "All you had to do was ask."

I cringed again as he raised his hand threateningly.

"Don't get smart with me you little asshole, or I'll kick the shit out of you. Now get the fuck out of here before I change my mind."

'Should I go for it?' I asked my inner voice.

Oh, absolutely!

I snatched my five-dollar bill from his hand before he had time to react and ran full tilt to my backpack. I frantically scanned left and right as I tried to remember where I'd buried it.

Are you crazy? Leave it and come back for it.

'Screw that, I'm not coming back here.'

Leaves and gravel flew as I sacrificed a couple of precious seconds to dig the backpack out. I took off at top speed while trying to wiggle my arms through the straps without dropping my bag of stuff. White guy was closing in on me. Black guy was giving chase as well, but was mostly laughing at white guy. I ran along the riverfront all of the way to the gravel barge loading place and dove through a hole in the fence as though I knew it was there and did this every day. I figured that even though the gravel people would be angry at me for charging through their property, they would come to my rescue if they saw two guys pursuing me—especially if I screamed for help.

Right out in the open part of the place, the scissors tore through the paper bag and everything went flying as I ran.

'Well, what the hell,' I thought, looking back to verify that my pursuers had stopped at the fence, 'I can't make things much worse by picking them up.'

So, under the baffled stare of a guy on a bucket loader who'd stopped his machine to watch my antics, I ran back, picked everything up and stowed it in my backpack.

I charged full speed for the street, with my hair flying out behind me and little puffs of dust coming from my sneakers, but I suddenly realized that I was blocked by a huge wall that I hadn't seen over the gravel piles. "Shit!" I ran along parallel to the wall in the last direction that I really wanted to have to go, and ignored the yells from a security guard as I dashed out the main entrance. I jogged away down the street, slowing to a walk as soon as possible so as not to look suspicious.

That's funny, I don't remember seeing a "gravel pit" listed in the St. Louis tour guide.

'I got the deluxe package,' I answered, laughing in exhilaration at my escape and the accompanying adrenaline rush.

I didn't really think the gravel guys would call the cops just because some kid ran through their place, so I wasn't too worried about that. I kept a lookout over my shoulder in case the bad guys had gone to the street another way and were looking for me, but I didn't really expect them to bother, and they didn't. I wished that I could just climb up to the overhead railroad tracks and hop a freight train out of here. I kept all other thoughts at bay until I was hiding in a vacant lot, trying to calm down. Once the adrenaline rush diminished, I crashed back down to reality, and didn't feel like such a badass any more.

"Holy shit, man," I said in a shaking voice that only really happens when you're a little kid, fighting tears, "Holy *shit* that was sc-scary."

In the moments that the guy was holding my small, skinny body off of the ground, a thousand scary thoughts were going through my head. I'd briefly belonged to them, and they could have done any cruel thing that popped into their heads. Beat me, cut me, burned me, choked me, tied me up and thrown me in the river to drown, anything.

OK, but they didn't, so stop it. Calm down.

I was so worked up that I got the hiccups.

"Th-things like that really *do*—hic—happen to people, y-you know. I didn't know *what* they were going to do."

Shhhh. Yes, they happen, but not to you. Just calm down.

As I tried to pull it together, I muttered, "Hic—Guess I'm not such a 'tough little fucker' after all."

I dug into my backpack for a bottle of Coke that I'd bought last night from a machine at a closed gas station. I figured I could really use it now. I let out a half-laugh, half-cry when I realized that it wasn't in a plastic bottle like I was used to in 2015 and I didn't have a bottle opener. Back now they had a bottle opener right on the Coke machine. I managed to pry the cap off with my scissors. The bottle had gotten shaken up in my backpack and Coke came fizzing up out of the top, covering my hands. As I quickly sipped some Coke foam so as not to lose too much soda, I hiccupped, spraying foam and soda everywhere. I found this humorous, and I sprayed more soda all over my face as I suppressed a laugh. I reflexively licked my upper lip, tasting sweat, Coke and snot. Then I said "bleah!" and spit it out, drooling some down my chin.

You're a real class act, kiddo. Don't let anyone tell you otherwise.

That last comment made me laugh even harder.

As I tried to sip Coke between hiccups, I reached down and reassuringly felt the barely detectable little bulges in the waist of my pants. Hidden in the waist seams of my pants, where I'd put them after making the little cuts with the scissors in the alley, were two tightly folded rolls of twenty-dollar bills. I'd left the alley with only enough cash in my pants pocket to satisfy a would-be robber. Now I put the nine dollars in there as well.

Don't get too cocky. Your vibes might have told you to hide money, but you still walked right into a trap.

"And just when I'd started—hic—trusting people."

'Damn, I meant to buy salve at Woolworths for the cut that the fence in Virginia made in my hip. That's probably why my throat hurts. I'm probably getting lockjaw.'

Shhhh. No more disaster scenarios, OK? Calm down.

The siren song of a freight train horn in the distance helped to calm me down, as the Coke soothed my throat.

I didn't have to look far to find trains to ride, just for a way to actually get on one that was heading west. There were multiple lines and yards to choose from.

In preparation for leaving, I went into a small grocery store to resupply my food and drink. Before going up to the register, I stood in one of the aisles and tried to get money out of the waist seam of my pants without actually unzipping them. A pair of tweezers would have helped because I kept pushing it in deeper every time I tried to grab it and people kept looking at me, wondering what on earth I was doing. I finally I got my nine dollars out. I made a mental note to dig money out of my pants seam before walking into a store from now on.

I felt uneasy and exposed as, in late afternoon, I headed back towards the rail yard where I was last night. Here it was after-school hours and I was still paranoid.

I vowed that I'd either be on a train heading out of town or at least hidden out somewhere within an hour. But the area where I planned to hop a train was too open to attempt it in daylight. A cop car came cruising down the street, so on impulse I detoured through the gate of a car repair shop. The yard was like a junkyard, complete with barking dogs. I continued straight into one of the bays, just to be out of sight. A radio in the back somewhere was blasting sixties rock and roll and guys were working on cars.

"Can I help you?" asked the guy closest to me. He was obviously irritated by the way I'd barged in.

"I'm looking for my uncle Roy," I said, hiding behind the narrow divider between the bays. "I think this is the place where he works?"

"No one here by that name," he said.

'Oh, thank God,' I thought. I don't know what the hell I would've done if he'd yelled "Hey Roy, someone here to see you." That would have been funny.

He watched me watch the cop drive by and waited for me to say something.

"Oh," I said, trying to look baffled. "Is there another repair shop on this street?"

"Couple blocks down," he said, giving me a doubtful look and indicating the direction with the wrench in his hand.

"Thanks," I said, heading off in the opposite direction than he'd indicated.

A few mechanics gathered by the door, watching me. I could picture the conversation:

"What did that kid want?"

"He said he was looking for his uncle, but I think he was just hiding from the cops."

'All right,' I chided myself irritably, 'I've really got to get off of the streets.'

Sometimes I grew tired of the constant threat of being caught and I'd get an impulse to just give up, let a cop nail me and see what happened after that. But the last thing I needed was to be thrown into a juvenile detention center with a bunch of St. Louis city kids, so to give myself a break I ducked into a little strip of woods next to some type of electrical supply company. I really don't know what I expected to accomplish by letting the hour get later. Walking here at night would be even more suspicious looking, and possibly dangerous. The railroad yards were not far from me, but were inaccessible from here due to the fact that they were down below the roads and you would have to get down a high wall to get to them. So I still had some walking to do in order to get myself into a position where I could catch a train out of here.

There was a water spigot behind the bushes next to the front door of the building I was near. I'd been watching and wondering whether everyone inside had gone home so I could use it. That is, if the spigot worked. Unless they were on a house, ninety percent of the water spigots that I tried, even the ones on churches, were either turned off from inside or needed a special handle to operate them. This one had a handle and a hose on it and it worked, so I let it run until the water no longer smelled like hose, drank as much as I could, then rinsed and filled my canteen.

I stuffed my backpack in my grocery bag and walked out to the road to continue moving towards the rail yards. The grocery bag tore and I was giving up on it and stuffing it in my backpack when a car pulled up alongside of me.

"Still looking for your 'uncle'?" asked the driver. It was the guy from the repair shop leaning over to talk to me out of the passenger-side window. Another guy was in the passenger seat, also dressed in mechanic's clothing.

"Sorry I barged in like that. I wasn't looking for my uncle, I was hiding from the cops."

"Yeah, we already knew that," he said in a condescending manner. "Running away from home?"

"No, I don't have a home to run away from. I just live out here and I didn't want to get hassled."

"How could someone as young as you be living on the streets?" asked the passenger doubtfully.

"Oh, it's a long story, but it's no big deal. I like living out here."

The two of them exchanged glances and discussed something. "Hey," said the driver, "Where are you heading? You need a ride?"

"I'm heading to the other end of the railroad yard to catch a freight train west."

I wish I'd had a camera, because they both had the exact same, comic-book perfect, "holy shit" expressions on their faces.

"Seriously, man? You really do that shit?"

"All the way from New Jersey."

Again, need that camera!

"You need food? Come and get something to eat with us, man. You know what, my brother and I have an apartment. You can come to our apartment and clean up if you want. The Kansas City Line is only about a block away and the trains stop there all of the time, so you can catch a ride there."

The passenger must have been his brother, because he looked at the driver with a "what the hell are you doing?" look on his face. He was obviously not pleased with the idea of helping out a kid who was on the road.

"I don't think your brother is real happy with that idea," I said.

"No man, it's cool," said the passenger, opening the door and pushing the seat down so I could climb in back. "It's just that my brother thinks he has to help every lost dog or cat that comes along and now I guess that includes kids . . ."

Common sense would dictate that I shouldn't be getting into a car with two men who were strangers. After all, they could be trying to abduct me for who knows what reason. I knew as I got in that if things went bad, I was pretty much trapped back there. But they showed trust in me by letting me sit in back of them with my backpack. I could have had a knife or something in it for all they knew.

The driver's name was Alejandro ("Just call me Alex,") and the passenger's name was Jorje ("Just call me George"). We drove to their apartment, which was in an old house that had been divided up into apartments. It wasn't too far from where Danny had dropped me last night. George cleaned up and left to go to his girlfriend's house. Alex showered and told me that the bathroom was all mine. He said his girlfriend was coming over in about a half hour and we would go eat.

"Aw," said Alex's girlfriend, Rose. "Alejandro didn't tell me what a little cutie you were."

She was strikingly beautiful and she made me blush.

"He needs a haircut though," said Alex.

"You want me to cut it for you? I can do a real nice job for you. Make you even more *chulo* (cute)," she teased, enjoying watching me blush.

"You should let her—she's good. She cuts mine," said Alex.

I grimaced as if to say that his hair looked ridiculous, and Rose and I snickered. He laughed and threw a pillow at us. Rose went over to him and he feigned anger before she melted him with a kiss.

We gorged ourselves on Mexican food at a restaurant owned by Rose's family (they wouldn't let me pay for anything) and returned to the apartment where I *finally* got a haircut. George turned on the TV and clicked through the channels with the dial. On one channel, I heard the name "Saigon" and I automatically knew it was bad news about the ongoing war. He settled on a cop show. I recognized the music from long ago, but I couldn't remember what show it was. Then they sat down on the couch together watching TV and kissing while pretty much forgetting I was there.

As so often happened, I felt a twinge of sadness and loneliness as I left their apartment and walked off into the night.

16

Riding through the night on a westbound freight, I felt pretty good as I watched the towns and farms slide by. With my hair cut, my head felt ten pounds lighter and my hair didn't reach my eyes when it blew around. Rose had wanted to cut it shorter, but I asked, actually pleaded with her to leave it longish. Afterwards, I admired it in the mirror. I thought that shorter hair would make me look older, but it didn't—it made me appear even younger.

Enjoy it while you can, kiddo.

'I feel like I'll always be this age.'

All kids think that.

'Yeah, but unlike the other life, where your body constantly changes and you never really catch up with who you currently are, I think I can stay this way.'

That would make you a real life Peter Pan. Do you mind if I call you Peter?

'Do not ever call me that, or if I write a book about this someday, I'll refer to you as Tinker Bell. I swear to God I will.'

Then your readers will just think that you got in touch with your inner child and your inner female.

"Boy," I laughed, "if I'd had just ten minutes with Sigmund Freud, I could have had him running for the hills!"

God really did seem to be taking care of me out here. As long as I could leave it at that and not wonder why He would take care of me and let others suffer, I was fine. Any time I saw a picture in a newspaper of, say, hysterical kids blindly running from a flaming village in Vietnam, the likelihood of God taking the time to protect a vagabond American kid who'd switched lives to get here seemed far-fetched.

Someone seemed to be watching over me, though. My sore throat was feeling better. And it was comforting that, for the most part, people just impulsively helped me out. In this last case, all I'd had to do was to barge into someone's repair shop and then leave without asking for help to get help. On top of that, if I hadn't dawdled in that strip of woods next to that electrical supply place, the guys that helped me and I would have missed each other. The timing was amazing.

Even the two losers who'd robbed me felt guilty and gave almost everything back. The funny thing is that if they'd just asked, I would have *given* them $5.

No you wouldn't have, "Saint" Peter (Pan), you would have said that you were broke.

'I hate you sometimes, Tinker Bell.' It was true; I would have said that I was broke. But part of the reason I would have said that is because on the streets, you never show that you have money in your pocket, especially if you are a defenseless little kid.

I was riding in an empty gondola car, which is like a big, long, open-topped box on wheels. I couldn't see over the six-foot high sides unless I climbed up. There were ripples on the ends of the car and I used them to boost myself up and watch the world go by. When my legs got tired, I lay against the back wall of the car and gazed up at the stars as the occasional railroad signals slid past. It was the perfect temperature out here, even with the breeze from the moving train.

Freight trains are a strange thing when you are hopping them. If you consciously think about it, you are aware that there are at least two people up in the engine and at least one person in the caboose. Yet, it almost seems as though the train just exists on its own—moving when it moves and stopping when it stops. It becomes just this "thing"—this mechanical beast and when it's not paying attention you can hitch a ride on its back.

Even the railroad tracks themselves seem to just *be*. You have the hills, the river, the railroad tracks, the trees . . . it's as though the railroad tracks are just another natural feature. Maybe that's why it's so tough for railroads to keep trespassers off of the tracks. Of course, I was the worst trespasser of all. What I was doing bordered on stealing. I mean, it's not like I was *taking* something, but if you threw a sack of flour that was my weight on in a boxcar in New York and took it out in Los Angeles without paying, it would be stealing, right?

Mike, the train is going where it's going anyways—whether you're on it or not.
'So is a 747.'

But on a 747, you would be taking up a seat that was for a paying passenger. Jeez, you never cease to find ways to beat up on yourself.

I awoke when the train stopped and walked to the other end of the gondola and pissed through a hole in the floor down onto the tracks. It was very early morning and the sun hadn't come up yet. I hadn't really slept too well in this car because there was so much debris that I was afraid to really lie down in it. I'd gotten on the train in the dark, so now that it was getting light I got a look at what I'd been avoiding.

There were a few small, thick chunks of rusty steel and many thin, extremely sharp pieces of scrap that were kind of chrome-looking. They appeared to be what was left after circles had been punched out of very thin sheet metal. If you drew a bunch of circles that were touching each other on a sheet of paper, the thin scrap was the shape of the area between the circles.

Besides the debris, objects had been dropped into this car with such force and frequency that the metal floor of the car sagged in between the underlying struts. The floor was in such bad shape that I was surprised that there weren't more holes in it. In addition to the scrap pieces, oily "mud"—consisting of millions of tiny, razor-sharp metal filings—had settled in the sagged depressions. I really would have appreciated some cardboard. I'd never get this stuff out of my blanket.

A few times when I used my hands to get up, I wound up with tiny shards in my palms and fingers. Lacking tweezers, I picked them out with my teeth and did my best to spit them all out. I imagined if I accidentally swallowed them, they might slit my intestines. At *least* I'd remembered early on to change into my filthy, coal-stained "train hopping" pants, standing on my untied shoes as I did it so my socks wouldn't touch the floor.

I don't know why the train was stopped. I would have loved to go get some breakfast, but the area was way too suburban and residential for me to get off and risk getting stranded here. The sun was coming up, so I'd also lost the cover of darkness. I felt trapped.

I sat down cross-legged and pouted.

Hey, cranky pants.

'What.'

You're not going to have another meltdown on me, are you?

I shook my head and rolled my eyes. I picked up a piece of scrap metal and, after discovering that it was magnetic, I amused myself by getting the piece of scrap metal all "furry" with tiny metal filings that stood on end as they were attracted to it. I gradually lifted the little piece of metal higher and higher while sweeping it slowly above the filings to see how high I could get it before gravity overcame the magnetic power of the metal.

You know, they really shouldn't leave sharp toys like that on freight cars that small children ride in.

Laughing at my inner voice, I tossed away the scrap metal.

'OK, I entertained us for five minutes, now it's your turn to entertain us for the next eleven hours and fifty-five minutes until nightfall.'

I hummed a Pink Floyd song as I sat there. It occurred to me that, if I was the kind of person to do so, I could probably make a fortune in 1967 as a songwriter by stealing songs from the future.

That would really put a damper on the positive karma that you've come to depend on in this adventure.

'Oh yeah, it would totally kill it. I wouldn't do it anyways, just out of honesty. But imagine if some of the famous inventors, like Thomas Edison, had actually done what I did and that's how they got the ideas for the things that they invented.'

Yeah, but someone still had to invent them originally.

An eastbound passed on the other track, followed by a westbound passenger train.

"I bet they're serving breakfast in the dining car," I bitched. I poked my head above the side of the gondola to survey the situation outside.

"Man, this train is going nowhere. You know you've been sitting for a long time when dew is starting to form on you."

I heard footsteps in the crushed stone, coming from the direction of the caboose. After the person had passed me, I poked my head up to see what was going on. It was one of the railroad guys, inspecting the train for something. There was another guy facing me as he headed this way from the engines and I jerked my head back in as soon as I saw him, hoping he hadn't spotted me. About ten minutes later, I took another peek around. The two guys were standing there talking where they met—about fifteen car lengths away from me. Another westbound passed us on the other track. Eventually, I heard the guy walking back to the caboose.

Someone in one of the houses must have been cooking bacon because I could smell it. I got some water and a package of those bright orange crackers with the peanut butter in them from my backpack.

"Gee," I said as I tore the package open with my teeth, "these don't look *too* artificially-colored."

Well, if you don't eat them all, you could always grind them up and sprinkle them on the floor of the car to dissolve the metal filings.

We sat there for at least another hour as other trains passed us. To kill time, I created a complicated and artsy mosaic out of scrap metal on the floor of the gondola. If there's one thing that I'd gotten good at lately, it was hiding out and waiting.

What's that supposed to be—a hot air balloon?

'A cat.'

It looks more like a spaceship.

It *did* actually look more like a spaceship than a cat, so I embellished on the spaceship theme. Finally, the train started moving, but only crept along for an hour or so.

I climbed up on the side of the car to have a look around. Boy, was it pretty here in the early-morning sunshine. I glanced down at my artwork on the floor and smiled as I pictured how baffled the next people who loaded stuff into this car would be by it.

They probably would say, "Wow, someone has way too much time on their hands!"

"Yes, time is something I have in abundance," I said happily, as I watched the countryside slowly pass by. At times we were a stone's throw from a wide river and at times there were huge farms between us and it. I guessed that it was the Mississippi River and then it occurred to me that, if I was heading west, I shouldn't be following the Mississippi River at all.

"Oh well. I guess I'll be checking license plates when the train stops."

A short time later, we ground to a halt. I heard the quick "whoosh" of the air brakes as they uncoupled something. My guess was that they were going to switch whichever car had a problem onto a sidetrack.

Perhaps some general railroad information would be helpful to you. Before I actually learned the terminology for this stuff, I'd learned to associate different noises with different actions both by watching and by riding the trains. When the locomotive couples up to a train and the air hoses are connected, it pumps the train's brake system up with air, releasing the brakes. This is the now-familiar air hissing noise that I've described as a "preparing to depart" noise. This noise can also be heard when the engines are still attached, but with the brakes applied. As the brakes are released, the hissing "preparing to depart" noise is heard.

The quick "whooshing" noise is pretty much the opposite. It is the sound of all of the air instantly leaving the brake system. It can mean one of several things: with the train stopped as it was right now, it meant that a car had been uncoupled somewhere. This is what I just heard.

If the train is moving, really the last sound that you want to hear (besides, say, the sound of the freight car that you are riding leaving the rails and bouncing off into the fields somewhere), is the same quick "whooshing" of air that I just described, because it means that the brakes are in an emergency application and something bad is happening. It could be that an air hose has blown, or because a coupler broke. Worse, it could be that a trespasser walking the tracks or a car at a railroad crossing is not getting out of the way and the engineer has intentionally put the brakes into an emergency mode. The very worst-case scenario is that it could mean that the train on which you are riding has derailed.

My best guess as to why we stopped and then proceeded so slowly is because someone inspecting the passing train at a junction saw something amiss. This was reported to the crew, and they had to investigate and inspect the train—which I saw them doing. Apparently finding that there was indeed a problem, they crept along until they could put the problem freight car on a sidetrack. Everything that passed while we were stopped was going fast, which indicated to me that this train, and not the tracks themselves, had a problem.

Using this delay to my advantage, I climbed out, went to the bathroom, cleaned up my hands in the river and searched to no avail for a better car to ride. There were a few hopper cars that I would have ridden at night, but I would be too exposed in daylight riding them and I couldn't take the chance of being seen at a road crossing or a junction.

There were plenty of boxcars and some were probably empty, but some railroads actually followed the "close and lock doors before moving car" rule, which was stenciled on the sides of some boxcars. The last thing in the world I would do is start opening boxcars to see if they were empty (not that I was strong enough to). Just riding these trains was illegal enough. Getting caught opening freight cars is a sure-fire way to wind up in trouble. And in contrast to the cat-and-mouse game that I'd been playing with the cops so far ("What's the charge, officer? Being too young to walk about on the planet unattended?"), if I was seen opening boxcars, the cops really *would* bother to search for me after I ran away.

The train started making the hissing "preparing to depart" noise, which told me that the engines were back on, so I hurried back to the car I'd been riding.

"Oh, isn't that nice," I said as I climbed in and admired my artwork. "That is, by far, the nicest scrap metal snowflake that I have ever seen!"

I think it's supposed to be an island with a palm tree on it.

"Ah yes, of course it is. Now I can clearly see the whiskers!"

As my train once again slowed, I kept my eyes open for signs that we were approaching a railroad yard. I didn't want to ride this car into such a place in daylight and risk either being trapped in here in hot sunshine because the car was too exposed for me to exit, or have to cross many active tracks like I'd done in Virginia. It did appear that we were about to enter a yard, so I put my backpack on and decided to leave while there was still sufficient cover to do so. I bid farewell to my artwork as I climbed down the outside of the car and hopped off. I had absolutely no idea where I was. It basically looked like Suburbia, USA. Definitely flatter than New Jersey, though. I hid in the brush along the tracks and tried to figure out what day it was.

'Let me see, Louisville was Wednesday and Dan gave me a ride in his truck, St. Louis Arch was Thursday, um . . . did what's-her-name give me a haircut the same day that I checked out the arch? How many nights did I sleep out in St. Louis?' It seemed like so much had happened in such a short amount of time.

I deduced that today was Friday. I'd been hoping that it was a weekend so I could restock my supplies in town in the middle of the day without attracting attention.

'Oh well, it's been a slow day. Nothing like being chased by the cops to get the old blood flowing . . .'

And you're providing a valuable community service by keeping them in practice. But seriously, Mike, it's a bad idea.

I nodded. It was a bad idea even if I did it without my backpack. I didn't want to stash the backpack and venture out because I wouldn't want to head back this way for it later.

I kept as close to cover as possible as I made my way along the fringe of the railroad yard. I hoped I'd see somewhere to resupply close by and just dash across the street so my public walking would be at a minimum. I was quickly running out of cover along the tracks, though. Up ahead on my left was a railroad utility truck parked next to a row of freight cars. An older, heavyset guy was bent over looking under a boxcar. I walked up closer and he noticed me.

"Wow, you can't be here, little guy. What are you doing here?"

"I just hopped off of a train from St Louis."

The guy just looked at me, trying to decide if I was being a smart-ass or if I was serious.

"Who are you talking to?" asked a voice from under the boxcar.

"The world's youngest hobo," answered the guy that I was talking to.

"Let me see him," said the voice from under from under the boxcar.

"Hello," I said as I ducked under.

He was lying on his back in the center of the track beneath the wheels with a gas cutting torch and tools. He didn't look much older than eighteen. I wondered why he hadn't been drafted for Vietnam. Maybe his eyesight was too bad—he wore very thick-lensed glasses.

"Wow, you really *are* the world's youngest hobo!" he exclaimed. "Where did you come from?"

"I just hopped off of a train from St. Louis."

"You really did?" asked the older guy, "Well, you'd better skedaddle, because if the bull catches you, you'll be in big trouble."

"The bull?"

"The railroad cop in charge of this yard. He burns hobo's gear, beats them up and throws them out."

"But if he caught a kid as young as you riding trains," added the younger guy, "he'd lock you up and throw away the key, man."

This was terrifying to me, and I looked back the way I'd walked. Suddenly, there didn't appear to be any cover to hide in at all. I also kept my eyes darting in both directions, now fearing "The Bull."

"Can I fill my canteen?" I asked as I eyed up the big water cooler mounted on their truck.

The older guy sighed. "Kid, you really have to get out of here if you can. Go on, fill your canteen. But we could get in trouble with you here. You really have to leave."

I tanked up on water and then filled my canteen.

"Ron, hand me the punch, will you?" asked the guy under the car.

"Thanks guys, sorry I bothered you," I said, figuring that I'd better just head the shortest route out of here and take my chances on the streets.

"No, hold on, don't be walking around here," said Ron as he scanned the area. "Climb under and stand on the other side of the boxcar and talk to us. I don't want the bull to see you."

"I don't want to get you guys in any trouble," I said.

"Don't worry about it man," said the guy under the car. "It's our pleasure hiding you from that asshole. Stay here for a while and we'll get you out of here when we go to lunch."

I watched quietly as they worked on the boxcar for a while. "Um," I asked hesitantly, "Is this train going anywhere any time soon?"

"You'd need to go to the departure yard and you'd never make it there without getting arrested."

"And we'll get you off of railroad property, but we won't drop you off at a train so you can hop it," added Ron. "So, what's your story? Are you running away from home, or what?"

"I'm a homeless orphan and I just live out here."

"And you wouldn't have it any other way, would you?" asked the younger guy, looking at me closely and smiling.

"No," I answered, in a kind of crooked smiling frown, wondering how he seemed to instantly pick up on what I was about. "What's your name?"

"Ed, and if you get caught out here, you never met us, got it?"

I nodded.

"How long have you been living on the streets, anyways?"

"Oh," I said and shrugged. "A while."

"Where are you from?" Ed asked. Then he asked Ron for something as he handed him back a few tools. Ed was lying on his back and the smaller of the two parts that Ron handed him fell out of his hand and landed beside the rail. "I dropped it—where did it go?" he asked as he twisted his hand to feel around for it.

"Here," I said, after crawling under and putting it in his hand. "What are you fixing?"

"A brake rod. The pin fell out and the rod got all twisted up, so we had to heat it and bend it back in place."

Then to his partner he said, "Hey Ronny, crank the handbrake just a little bit."

Ron went to the end of the car and turned the brake wheel slowly until Ed could get the holes lined up.

"Good!" Ed yelled, as he put the connecting pin in place. Then he put in the wiry-looking piece that I'd handed him. He felt around for the pliers, and I handed him those as well.

"See, if Ron wasn't too old to climb under here, I'd be handing *him* tools," Ed said to me and winked.

"I'm not so old that I can't hear your wiseass comments," Ron busted back. They obviously enjoyed working together.

They hid me in the back of their truck and got me out of there.

"All right, little guy, you're on your own," said Ron as I looked around doubtfully. I was in the exact situation that I'd wanted to avoid in the first place: a little kid wearing a backpack, out on the streets of a strange town in the middle of a school day.

"You were walking the yard so the cops wouldn't see you on the streets, weren't you?" asked Ed.

I nodded. "Thanks for the water and for saving me from the bull."

"Hey," said Ron, "You never did answer. Where are you from, anyways?"

"New Jersey."

"*New Jersey!?*" they exclaimed in stereo. Ron just shook his head. Ed said, "For a few minutes back there, I was wishing I was you—just free as a bird. But seeing you standing here now, I guess you're not really so free, are you?"

I smiled and did a "what can I tell you?" shrug.

As many people seemed to do when they met me, Ron and Ed paused for a few moments as though they wanted to say more and didn't want to leave me all alone. Then they sort of reluctantly drove off. Ed seemed like the kind of person that I could tell my true story to and have a fair shot at someone believing it. He seemed very intuitive. He even understood that I wasn't quite as free as one might think that I was.

I hustled over to a cemetery next to a church across the street to hide out.

Pure freedom requires that you give everything up for it.

"Well, I've got *that* department covered," I muttered.

'Actually, it's almost as if pure freedom requires that you become a slave or a prisoner to it. How's that for an oxymoron?'

Not as crazy as you might think. We can become slaves to whatever our true passions are.

I was sort of hoping that the preacher in the church would see me out here and offer me no-strings-attached help, but it really didn't look like the church was occupied at the moment.

"Damn, I forgot to ask those guys where I am."

Hey, watch the swearing. You are *in a churchyard . . .*

"Oh, yeah," I giggled, covering my mouth. "Oops."

I had no choice but to pass time, so I went to a brushy area in the back of the graveyard where they dumped all of the dead flowers and made a little nest for myself. I'd slept only a few hours last night, so I kicked off my sneakers and fell asleep.

The sound of a barking dog and kids playing in a yard abutting the graveyard woke me, some hours later. I was sweaty and uncomfortable. It had gotten much hotter and more humid since I'd gone to sleep. As I got up and brushed the leaves off of my filthy train-riding pants, hearing the pulse of the town around me depressed me in the same way it had at the bridge in New Jersey.

"All around me are normal people living calm, predictable, productive lives, and here's Mike, sleeping in a cemetery," I said. I felt like a bum, just a plain old bum. "If I didn't have the excuse that I was a little kid, I'd be contemplating suicide right about now."

At least they wouldn't have to go far to bury the body!

"You're such an asshole," I laughed.

Language, watch your language. Churchyard, remember?

Shaking my head and smiling, I changed from my train-riding pants into shorts, combed my hair, buried the backpack in the leaves, and went out to the street. Walking around in daylight like a normal person felt good, but I didn't dawdle. As I walked through some neighborhoods, sweating in the humidity, I noticed how many kids were playing outside compared to the era that I traveled from. Actually, it seemed to me that *all* of the kids were outside. Many houses seemed wide open—all of the windows and doors open with just a screen door closed.

Something else (besides all of the clotheslines) seemed strange in all neighborhoods I'd walked through since switching into this era, but I could never put my finger on it. Then I realized what it was: the lack of so many cars. I associated cars in the driveway with people being home, but back now there were still probably many one-car households and dad had the car and was still at work.

I got my supplies and headed back to the graveyard for my backpack.

"Pfff, of course," I said sarcastically, seeing someone was there putting flowers on a grave right near where I had to duck in and get my backpack. I walked around a bit and went back. This time, someone else was there at a different grave, but I just ducked into the brush for my backpack anyway.

I carried the backpack in a grocery bag as I walked a street parallel to the tracks until I passed the end of the yards, then I veered down a dead-end industrial side street to check out a slow-moving westbound train. There were "auto racks" (multi-tiered cars with automobiles on them) going past. The vehicles looked so vulnerable, just sitting on the railroad cars. In the era I traveled from, auto racks were fully enclosed to protect the cars from trackside stone-throwing kids. A hobo had told me never to ride either auto racks, or "piggyback cars" (flat cars with truck trailers on them)—at least not in daylight—because the railroad police kept a closer eye on them.

It wasn't looking as though I was going to find a good car to ride. I was extra hesitant anyways, because my vibes told me that I shouldn't hop on right now regardless. On pure instinct, I'd stayed in the partial cover of the trackside brush. It's a good thing that I did, because as the caboose rolled past, the guy was standing on the end platform, leaning out a little and watching ahead, down the side of the train.

"Always trust your vibes" was a mantra that I lived by. It might sound superstitious, but ninety percent of the time my vibes were right on the mark.

I wasn't well hidden, so if the guy had been looking straight out at the side of the tracks he would have seen me. At least all he would have seen would have been a boy standing near the tracks, holding a grocery bag. As it was, we'd passed by so closely that I was surprised he didn't sense me and look at me. I stayed stock-still and lowered my eyes so he wouldn't "feel" me looking at him.

You know how it is when you are out in public somewhere and you look at someone, however briefly, and they somehow sense it and look at you and you meet eyes? Well, for that very reason, if I'm hiding and watching someone, I try not to look directly at them. It sounds silly, I know. The funny thing is that it only happens spontaneously. I've tried *making* it happen by looking at someone and thinking, "I'm *looking* at you . . ." but it rarely works that way.

I stayed in the general area, killing time until dark. I could have stashed the backpack and walked around, but this wasn't such a big town. While exploring earlier, I felt as though everyone was watching me and knew I was a total outsider.

18

At nightfall I hopped onto yet another gondola on a slow-moving, westbound departing train. Seeing that this car was empty, I decided to stay put. Empty gondola cars had apparently become my freight car of choice. I'm sure that would change the first time that it started pouring rain while I was riding in one.

Well, this ride was a switch for me. This time, I'd hopped a freight that was heading *into* a city. We crossed a river and wound between the river, a huge railroad yard and a city, but we didn't stop, which pleased me greatly. I neither knew where I was going, nor where I was leaving. I'd managed to be close to probably hundreds of license plates without thinking to take note of the state I was in.

The train gradually picked up speed and I stood with my feet resting on the ripples on the end of the car, my arms on top and my chin on my hands. A distant building had a huge neon sign on it that said "Montgomery Wards." For a brief moment, I thought that I'd just seen half of the sign burn out because most of the letters went dark. Then I realized that the sign alternated between saying "Montgomery Wards" and "go Wards."

We passed a long, low warehouse that was right next to the tracks and had open, wooden slat sides. Inside were bundle upon bundle of what must have been tobacco, because the whole area smelled like pipe tobacco.

As usual, once my knees started shaking from holding me up there so long, I lay down against the wall of the car on my blanket (which was now itchy from the metal filings) and went to sleep.

I awoke sometime in the middle of the night and dreamily stared up at the stars. The wheels beneath me went "clunk, clunk" as they rolled over the joints in the rail (no, they didn't go "clickity-clack.") Sometimes, often on curves, the joints in the rail were welded together, making one long strand of rail. The ride was a lot quieter on those sections.

A couple of times, I thought I saw a faint flash of light on the opposite wall of the gondola. I climbed up to investigate and saw that we were heading into a wall of thunderstorms. At one point, the train stopped and I stood alongside the tracks in the wind-blown grass, mesmerized by the fast approaching, frequent lightning. It wasn't until a bolt arced through the clear overhead sky and struck somewhere off behind me that it occurred to me that standing next to or sitting on a mile-long metal train that was on hundreds of miles of rail in a lightning storm wasn't the smartest thing to do. Plus, I'd been riding in an open-topped car. I cursed myself for wasting so much time watching lightning as I frantically searched for a boxcar with wooden floors. Even the wooden floors sometimes had a thin strip of metal every three or four boards, so I'd still have to be careful.

Rrrrip, BOOM! A bolt struck the field behind me and I cringed so hard, I pulled a muscle in my neck.

My train started making the air hissing "preparing to depart" noise, so I settled for riding the end of a covered hopper. I tried squatting down so only the rubber soles of my sneakers were touching metal, but I kept finding myself holding something metal for balance or having my back against the metal wall so I finally gave up and just sat down. I watched one of the best thunderstorms I've ever seen. Although some lightning bolts were damn close and the wind felt like it would blow the train over, I enjoyed every second of it.

At least I stayed fairly dry and I never did get zapped. Shortly after we started moving, we noisily crossed directly over two sets of tracks that were on a ninety-degree angle to the ones I was riding. (I later learned that the spot where two tracks cross each other like this is called a "diamond").

The storms passed and the sky turned crystal clear other than a few fast-moving, craggy-looking clouds—the edges of which were illuminated by the bright moonlight. The temperature must have dropped twenty degrees in an hour.

I rode trains for days and nights, as though this was the most normal lifestyle in the world. At times, I felt like I could live this way forever and be happy. Other times, I was aware that living on the road like this—uninterrupted by some normal living—was slowly taking the novelty out of it. I was still enjoying myself, but now I didn't have the incentive from that initial thrill of the unknown that I'd had at the beginning of this adventure. Now, the risks necessary to do this sometimes didn't seem worth it.

The farther west I traveled, the better things got for me. For one thing, now

I wasn't always the only person out riding the freight trains. There were other people, which added both a sense of danger that didn't exist for me before, but also a sense of camaraderie. We were all outcasts of some type, running from something, running from ourselves, or running because we had nothing better to do. I preferred to think that I fell into the third category. One of the best aspects of talking with someone who'd been doing this sort of thing for a long time was that they actually knew where they were going and how to get there.

The "bulls," which is slang for the railroad cops in the yards, were the stuff of scary legends. They were rumored to do anything from having you thrown in jail to burning all of your belongings, beating you with clubs, or even waiting until you were in the middle of nowhere out in the desert before throwing you off of the train. The stories terrified me. I guess I would select the burning of my stuff and the beating over being thrown in jail.

Most of the hobos I met had at least one scary story about being robbed and beaten by thugs, but I noted that alcohol was involved in ninety percent of their stories. They'd just come from a bar where they'd had an altercation or they'd gotten drunk and slept in an urban park and gotten assaulted or some similar situation. I wouldn't sleep where they slept to begin with and I especially wouldn't do it with my senses numbed by alcohol. I'd never even had a drink in my old, adult life.

Many of the people I met had at least been in jail and some had done serious prison time. Some told me that they'd gotten thirty days in jail just for hopping freights.

I was warned numerous times that it would be very easy for a kid my age to get raped out here. Some guys seemed to talk too much about this risk, which made me suspect that they might be the very ones to do it. Mention it to me once and I'll just take it as a warning. Keep mentioning it and I'll start wondering why it's on your mind so much . . .

Some guys would seem OK at first, but then go off on angry rants about the mistakes of Vietnam or how society was going to hell with all of the hippies and drugs and war protests, or the "corrupt" government, or the race riots or whatever. I would listen politely (always situated far enough away from them to run) as they worked themselves up to rants that often no longer even resembled cohesive thought. I'd tear myself away from them at the first chance I got. If things started to get scary for me or if there were a bunch of people together that were looking for trouble, I just flat out ran away.

Some of the hobos seemed angry or resentful that I was so young out here doing this. I guess I understood their resentment. After all, other than the hippies that were out here riding the rails (who were basically well-brought-up suburbanite kids who chose this life as a rebellion against their parents), I was still just out here playing around for the hell of it. There was no reason for me to think that I didn't have a bright future of my own choosing. Anything's possible. If anyone in the world knew that, I did.

The hobos and bums depended heavily on charity meals. They would discuss which church was serving meals on which days. They often referred to the "Sally," meaning the Salvation Army. Many of these guys rebuffed sleeping at the free shelters because you had to be in by dusk and out at dawn. And of course, you couldn't bring your bottle in there with you. None of this mattered to me because I was too young to go there in any event.

I rolled into Pueblo, Colorado, and decided to hang around that general area for a while to take a break from traveling and to restock my supplies. The first night, while searching for somewhere to sleep, I came upon what looked to be a seldom-used railroad line that branched off from the main track and headed out into the wilderness.

Something about the night scene was so enchanting that I couldn't resist it. The old, sun-bleached railroad ties shone bright in the moonlight and shortly after starting my walk, the railroad line crossed a rocky stream. I hiked for miles out into the countryside until I grew tired and relaxed. I bedded down in a gravelly area by a stream under cottonwood trees that gently swayed in a chilly night breeze and cast shifting, dappled shadows on the whole scene.

The next day I alternated between swimming in the icy cold water and lazing on hot rocks in the sun. I washed my clothes, my body and my soul while relaxing in such a beautiful place.

It occurred to me that I had become pretty wild. I'd been living outside for so long that I felt like I would never be able to sleep indoors again, or even be in a room with the windows and blinds closed.

As I ambled back towards town, I reflected on some of the perplexing aspects of my switching experience. What made this whole thing possible to begin with? Did some cosmic forces just happen to come together at the right time and open some portal? Could other people do it, or was I the only one? In order to complete the switch, I'd felt as though I had to "let myself die." Not many people would be willing to do that in order to step into the unknown.

'Well, I guess people with nothing to lose—like some of the bums that I've met out here—might.'

How shallow of you to place such a low value on someone else's life. What is your unit of measurement? Yourself—a Peter Pan idiot who's running around the country dodging cops? Do you think that any of the bums you've met wouldn't fight for their lives?

'Yeah, OK, scratch that. How about someone who is considering suicide?'

I know a certain someone who came close a few times when he was living as an adult. Can you think of who that might be? I'll give you a hint: his initials are PP.

'My initials aren't PP, *Tinker Bell*, they're MM!'

I already had it in the back of my head that I'd write a book about this someday, but now I wondered if I should just keep it a secret. What if I publicized my secret and others discovered they could switch and they tried to get rich or change the future?

'Of course, most people would assume it was fiction.'

Trust me on this, Mike: everyone *would think it was fiction.*

Either way, could I handle people reading a story about my deepest, innermost secrets, flaws and adventures and maybe saying it sucks and it's really crappy fiction?

On the outskirts of the rail yards, some hobos told me which lines went where. North would take me past the line I'd walked and on to Denver. I restocked in town and at dark, on a whim, I hopped a northbound. A weekend was coming up, so I figured I could explore without worry of standing out. It was still night when I arrived in the city, so I hid out and tried to sleep. Here in the "Mile-High City," although it was a beautiful sunny morning, summer was clearly over. Soon I would need a coat. I already had a bit of a cold. I stashed my backpack and wandered through an industrial area on my way towards the tall buildings of downtown.

Uneeda biscuit?

"What the hell *is* 'Uneeda Biscuit' anyways?" It seemed like every city I visited, Denver included, had an old broken-down brick factory that had those words painted on it in peeling paint. I smiled. 'If I see a box of those in a store now, I'm going to laugh my ass off and buy it.'

Every city I went to also had at least one tall, abandoned-looking windowless warehouse that said "cold storage" on it. I guess these were a throwback to the days before mechanical refrigeration was common.

I took a break from exploring and sat on the sidewalk and leaned back against a factory wall. It was so nice and warm in the sun that I dozed off and on for a few minutes. A group of well-dressed oriental men came out of the factory. They looked out of place on this decrepit industrial street. One of them noticed me and said something to the others. They watched and waited as he came over and silently handed me a five-dollar bill.

"No, that's OK," I said, even though I really could use the money. "I have some money."

But he wouldn't take no for an answer, so I took the bill and thanked him. They all got into a huge, shiny black car and drove off.

Later on in the late afternoon, I retrieved my backpack and returned to the area where I'd planned on catching a ride back south. It was just too damn cold here and if I was going to continue west, it would be warmer if I went south first.

I talked to a couple of hobos, one of which got disproportionately angry over some little thing that I'd said. But I was used to unpredictable behavior from street people. As we conversed, a train slowly proceeded south. I didn't go for it because it had four engines but only about twenty cars, meaning that the guys in the engine and/or caboose could have seen me jump on—especially in broad daylight. The bum who'd gotten mad at me got even angrier that I passed on hopping the freight.

"It's too short," I said. "It's probably just a local." (Meaning a freight train that leaves the yard, but only serves the local industries before returning to the same yard).

"It's not a damn local," he yelled at me. "With four engines on it? That train's going all of the way to Pueblo making pickups and it'll be more than a hundred cars long by the time it gets there. You just missed a good ride."

"Well, I didn't see *you* jumping on it," I mumbled after I'd moved on.

I hopped on a southbound that came by about a half hour later. It was really cold by the time I left Denver but as I rode south and down to lower elevations it got noticeably warmer. We stopped in the middle of the night in some town with a small railroad yard, but I took my chances and stayed on, hoping that we would move on and we did. Later on, I hopped off in Pueblo in the same area where I'd hopped on the day before.

I found a hiding spot up on a raised bit of level ground under a power line pole and I slept. I awoke at first light and noticed that I'd missed sleeping on an ant mound by inches. I didn't know if they were fire ants, but either way I was glad that I hadn't had to scramble up in the middle of the night, tearing off clothing after being covered by stinging ants. I'd felt uneasy sleeping out here in the west anyways, because now the landscape was more desert and I didn't know what kind of creepy-crawlies I had to watch out for.

My choice of sleeping spots was poor for another reason as well. As I wiped the crud from the corners of my eyes and stretched, I realized that I was in plain view of houses on the ridge just above the tracks. Last night in the dark, I hadn't noticed them. Oops.

I stashed my backpack and went into town to get some breakfast. Walking around alone works in some places and doesn't work in others. A hike in the woods alone to some fantastic viewpoint that few people reach: good. Explore a big city alone, where most of the people that make up the crowds are there by themselves: OK. Stroll around a public destination where couples, groups or families go to enjoy—places such as a fair or Pueblo, Colorado: not so good.

Pueblo had many nice, low, southwestern-styled buildings with shops in them. If you were with friends or family, it would be a pleasant town to stroll around in, stop for lunch, maybe get an ice cream cone. But I was alone and I had no destination or purpose and I quickly felt like an outcast.

There was no sense pushing the issue, so I returned to the yards to try to catch something going west. At least if I did it in daylight, I could enjoy the scenery.

I stood in a patch of brush and watched the happenings in the Pueblo railroad yard. Then I went deeper under cover to go to the bathroom. By the time I realized what was happening and hastily wiped my butt, I was under a full-blown attack by tiny, stinging ants. I ran out to the tracks and danced around while frantically tearing my clothes off and trying to shake the stinging ants from my hair. I looked up and saw a teenage kid watching me.

At the moment, I didn't care what he thought. I sat on the crushed-stone edge of the railroad bed in my underwear and turned my T-shirt inside out to check for ants. As I was doing the same thing with my socks, the kid retrieved my backpack, pants and one of my sneakers.

"Thanks. I don't know where the other sneaker went—I kicked them off."

"I see it," he said and plucked it from the branches of a bush.

I thanked him again, checked everything for ants and got dressed.

"You're pretty young to be out here," he said.

'If I had a dollar for every time someone told me that,' I thought, 'I could fly to L.A., touch the ocean and catch a red-eye flight back to New Jersey.'

I dumped the contents of my backpack in order to de-ant them. And there, on the edge of the railroad yard, the young stranger and I got acquainted.

"Your accent sounds like you're from New York City," he commented.

"Close—New Jersey."

He said that his name was Dave, he was eighteen years old and he was, to quote him, "a full-blood Arapaho Indian." He was tall and bone skinny and wore wire-framed glasses. His jet-black hair draped over his shoulders. He said he was just wandering the country like I was, although he stuck to the western half of the country.

He was the first train-hopping person I'd met that didn't seem to be laden with hang-ups or seem to be running from something. We immediately clicked and I was amazed at how two people from such different parts of the country and who grew up in such different cultures could mesh so well.

Dave needed to go into town for supplies, so I concealed my backpack in a bush and tagged along. As we walked, I told him that "Dave" didn't sound like much of an Indian name and asked him if that was his birth name, but he just said "Ah . . ." and brushed off the question. I joked that if he didn't tell me his real name, I was going to call him something silly, like "Running Bull." He laughed but still said that his real name was Dave. Testing him, at one point I quietly said, "Dave," to see if he would respond to that name. He knew what I was doing though, and laughed. Later on, I tried quietly saying "Running Bull." Dave laughed and looked around with mock surprise and said, "Where?"

He suggested that we go to Albuquerque, New Mexico, "Because it's nice and it will be even warmer." That sounded fine by me.

Back at the yards, Dave told me to get my backpack and he'd meet me there. He saw some railroad workers in the yard and he said he was going to go ask them what train was going to Albuquerque.

"Huh?"

"I said I'm gonna ask—"

"Yeah, I heard you, but won't they arrest you?"

He laughed. "No, I do it all of the time. Those guys don't care."

I described how I'd been hiding from every person I saw since New Jersey. Dave said that it was common for hobos to ask the workers—but not the bosses—for directions. But he also said that back east, it was a lot easier to get arrested. He also pointed out that if he was as young as me, he'd let someone older do the asking.

I readily agreed, so I went back to hang out with the ants.

We eventually found our train and a boxcar to ride in. Dave got us some cardboard and away we went.

We both sat in the doorway and watched the countryside slip past for quite some time. Around midday, our train moaned to a halt. From what we could see from our side of the boxcar, even calling this a "town" was a stretch. It was more like a semi-agricultural desert area. Dave was about to get out and open the door on the other side of our boxcar when we spotted a cop or sheriff's car cruising down the dirt road along the train.

"I didn't think local cops patrolled along the railroad tracks," I whispered to

Dave as we watched him approach.

"They do if they are called," he answered quietly. "He could be looking for an escaped prisoner or something and that's why they stopped the train."

We couldn't get out undetected and the door on the opposite side of this boxcar was closed, so we were sitting ducks. All it would take would be for this guy to walk over to check this empty boxcar and it would be game over. Even if we ran, there was nowhere to hide. I longed for the dense woods of New Jersey. I was surprised by how homesick that thought made me. There was another empty boxcar about six cars away from us and we anxiously waited for the cop to get to it to see if he would get out and walk over and look inside of it.

"We'll just stay out of sight. He probably won't bother us if don't we give him a reason to," Dave said quietly and confidently.

I wished that I was as calm about it as he was. I was flat-out terrified. The cop might let Dave go, or at least the court would let him pay a fine. They'd never let me go. I'd rot in jail while *all* of us tried to figure out who I was and where I belonged. It was agony waiting to see what the cop would do . . . and then he drove slowly past the other open boxcar without stopping to look into it. I listened to his tires crunching the gravel as he drove past our boxcar, praying that I wouldn't hear him stop. Whew! Thank God for lazy cops. The cop was only a few cars past us when the train started rolling again. Boy was I ever glad to get out of there!

My usual policy when the train stopped in a town or a city if sufficient cover was available, would be to get off and hide out until it started moving again. Sometimes I did it because I was worried about being caught, but many times I did it because we'd stopped in such a bad area that I felt more vulnerable on the train than hidden trackside in the weeds. This "not having anywhere to hide" thing was a new, insecure feeling for me.

Keeping my train riding activities limited to nighttime was also out of the question out west. Back east, towns and cities were relatively close together, but out west the distances were vast and the environment was less forgiving. During my early days of riding trains back east, when passing through areas that looked to me like the middle of nowhere, I would torture myself by wondering what would happen if I had to get off of the train and get myself out of there some other way. Well, all I can say is that until I came out west, I had no real concept of what "in the middle of nowhere" really meant. Unassisted, you couldn't possibly get yourself out of the desert areas we passed through. You'd walk until you died, plain and simple.

Riding in daylight in remote areas had its advantages as well. You could relax in plain view and watch the countryside slide past for hours. At night, you could climb to the top of a coal car and lie on the coal, staring up at the stars. I had conflicting emotions while traversing the west. One side of me never wanted to leave the long, beautiful views and the unobstructed sky while another side of me felt homesick for the compact nature of New Jersey and the overhead tree canopy.

Dave and I arrived in Albuquerque, New Mexico at nightfall. We camped out on the edge of town and Dave made a campfire. Although I loved them, I seldom made campfires when I slept out alone because I was a creature of stealth. Although the fire itself made me feel safe, sitting near it in the dark made me feel uneasy, as though I was spotlighting my vulnerability. To make matters worse, with your eyes adjusted to the bright light, you can't see anything or anyone lurking in the darkness around you. Possibly very close to you. Possibly about to grab you . . .

I peered into the surrounding gloom.

"I can't believe you've been doing this stuff alone," Dave commented.

"You've been doing it alone," I pointed out.

"Only sometimes, and I'm not . . . you know . . ."

A little kid. "Ah, I'm never really alone anyways," I said in a whimsical reference to an inner voice that Dave knew nothing of.

Just to try to make the concern lines that appeared on Dave's forehead deepen, I darkly and intimately added, "They follow me *everywhere*." It had the desired effect and I burst out laughing. Dave smiled and threw a stick at me.

"Seriously," I said, "I'm used to being alone. I was always alone in my other life. Or, I mean—you know—before I hit the road."

"Why were you always alone?"

I poked at the fire with my stick and shrugged. "I'm just—just different from people, that's all."

"Everybody's different."

"I know."

"Believe it or not, I understand," he said.

I smiled and kept poking at the fire. "So, what's your story?"

"No story. I'm just drifting."

"How did you grow up?"

"In a house."

I waited.

"Lots of fighting, lots of drinking. Everyone acted like a victim of something. I was the youngest and the first one to leave."

In late morning, we headed into the city. But as always, I was nervous about being so young and walking around in public during the day unless it was on a weekend. Just at the point where I was explaining this to Dave and I was going to turn around, we met some other kid on the edge of town near the rail yards who was about Dave's age. The kid had real long hair like Dave's (although it was almost blond) and wore a cowboy hat. I didn't catch his name, probably because I instantly nicknamed him "Tex" in my head.

Dave and Tex started discussing different towns and experiences on the road. Apparently they'd both been to some big concert/party/Woodstock-type event at the same time. I lost track of their conversation as they discussed the music at the concert and then moved on to their favorite rock stars. I think I knew before they did that they would decide to travel together.

I really had no interest in hanging out with the kid because I sensed that he was trouble. He had bags of fake marijuana that he had picked along the tracks somewhere (Nebraska?) and dried out. He said that the Chinese laborers had planted it way back when they were building the railroads, but that now it was no longer potent and the most you could hope for by smoking it was to get a headache. He and Dave came up with a plan to continue into town and sell this to the local druggies and college kids. I wanted nothing to do with it. I couldn't afford the trouble or even the exposure on the streets—not that I was invited anyways.

I told Dave that maybe I would see him back at the railroad yards later, but I really figured that I'd never see him again. That's just the way it is when you live the lifestyle I was living. I liked Dave and would miss him a lot, but from the moment that he met "Tex," it had become him and Tex together and me on the sidelines.

'Oh well, no big deal. I'm used to it,' I tried to placate myself. I headed back towards the yards and the brush cover that made me feel more comfortable.

Hey, lonely boy.

'What.'

Don't worry, I'll never leave you and run off with some long-haired cowboy!

Later in the afternoon, I stashed my pack and ventured into town for food and as many beverages as I could carry for my continued trip west.

When I returned to the railroad yards, I hid out as best I could and ate. I couldn't sit down in the area I was in because there were so many ant mounds. Some were several feet tall and the ants were large. One ant mound would be all red ants and another one would be all black ants. I imagined fierce battles between them as one or the other invaded their territory. Some mounds at first appeared to be abandoned, but when I poked them with a stick, thousands of angry ants would come gurgling out like a gusher from an oil well.

As I was searching for *somewhere* to sit, I heard someone call, "Hey, Mike!"

I looked over at the tracks and saw Dave and "Tex" (actually, my nickname for him was close—his name was Tim) smiling at me as they were checking out an empty boxcar that I'd been watching. I didn't want to walk out in the open, so Dave came over as Tim climbed in.

"How long have you been sitting here?" Dave asked. "Not all day I hope."

"About a half hour. I went into town for supplies a little while ago."

"You waited until school's out." He nodded, as though subconsciously affirming that I was too much of a burden—or at least too young—to travel with. "I thought you didn't like other kids."

"I *don't!*" I said with exasperation. He knew damn well why I waited. I changed the subject by asking, "Hey, how did your fake pot sale go?"

"Good! But now we gotta get out of here," he said, as he nervously scanned for the druggies that they'd scammed. "Me and Tim are going to ride trains or hitchhike down to Corpus Christi for the winter."

"What's Corpus Christi, some kind of festival?" I asked.

He smiled. "No, it's a town in Texas, on the Gulf of Mexico. Nice and warm all winter."

Oh, yeah, duh. For some reason, I'd confused it with Mardi Gras. The old, adult Mike wouldn't have done that . . .

"Where are *you* gonna go?" Dave asked.

Obviously I wasn't invited to go with them.

"I don't know,' I answered. "I guess I'll keep heading west *alone.*"

"You gotta go to the other yards, that way." He pointed helpfully. "Then you can catch a ride west."

"I uh, I guess you don't feel like checking out California, huh?" I asked, a little desperately.

"Uh, no . . . I'm going to go with Tim to Texas. He's kinda more my own age. And . . . no offense man, but you're kind of immature."

I looked down and nodded.

"You know," Dave considered, "I never said this to anyone else out here because I really hate it when someone says it to me, but . . ." He debated whether to say it or not, and then he took the plunge, "You should just go home, man. You really should."

He braced himself for me to go off on him, but I just closed my eyes and let out a little closed-mouth, air blowing out of the nose laugh and nodded.

Dave headed back to his boxcar, where Tim was waiting. By the time Dave would have been in a position to look back, I was gone.

2.0

'Am I really immature?' I asked myself while I headed across town to get to the west side of the other railroad yards.

Let's just say that you've really warmed to the part you're playing.

'No, I'm being serious here. When I started this adventure, people said I was mature for my age.'

I don't remember anyone saying that.

'OK, well maybe they didn't *say* it but they, um, they . . .'

C'mon Mike, don't get yourself all worked up over it, okay?

'*Implied* it—that's the word I was looking for.'

Personality-wise, you're the same as you were in your old, adult life. Sometimes you were the most grown-up person around, and then five minutes later you were like a little kid. You're kind of a scaredy-cat out here, so that's probably what Dave meant.

'Oh, so now I'm a scaredy-cat too!'

You're also as oversensitive about every little negative thing someone says about you as an insecure little schoolgirl would be.

I sighed. 'Do I have any good qualities?'

Mike—enough, OK? Just relax and be yourself.

Just before sunset, I managed to hop a train that I hoped was going west. I was on the end of a covered hopper. This car was what I called a "thumper," meaning that one of the wheels had a flat spot on it, so when the car rolled, it thumped. As it was leaving the yards, the sound was slow. Thump . . . thump . . . thump. Once we sped up, it became more of a bang-bang-bang-bang. When we passed cliffs, the noise was amplified back at me.

I watched a spectacular sunset, although much of the time it was in front of me and I was sitting on the east end of the hopper car. I almost always rode trains facing backwards with my back against the wall because I felt safer that way.

For one thing, when most people watch a train pass, they tend to look in the direction that it's coming from. If I was sitting on the facing end of a freight car coming towards them, there's a good chance they'd spot me.

Another reason is that although the entire freight train can't stop fast enough to throw a rider off, the slack between the couplers, which has been stretched by the pulling action of the engines when the train is moving, sometimes comes rushing back in and can give you quite a jolt. It's only a few inches per coupler, but on a one-hundred-car train, that adds up. It seemed to me that the farther back I rode on a train, the more slack action I felt. There is also some slack action when the train first starts moving and pulls the couplers tight, but that's more expected and is also at a slower speed.

I associated all desert areas with heat, so I was surprised that the farther west we went, the colder it got. By the time we stopped in the morning and I stiffly climbed down, it felt like it was in the twenties. I sat on an east-facing embankment and waited for the morning sunlight. But once the first rays were on me, it seemed to get even colder for a while. I took my sneakers off and held my toes in my hands to try to warm them up. I'd made matters even worse because I'd sat with my legs folded, thereby cutting off the blood circulation.

I didn't bother to go to a road to look at license plates, so I had no idea where I was. I didn't intend on lingering anyway; the line that this train brought me to was two to three times as busy as the line I rode in on. The area was beautiful. The nearby cliffs and bluffs were reddish in color, contrasted by green pine trees. The golden morning sunlight glistened off of the pine needles and brought out every detail in the contour of the land in stark relief.

But I wasn't in the mood for walking around; I was in the mood for traveling. I risked walking along a road for a while and I soon came upon a large, out-of-season campground, empty but for a few Airstream camping trailers parked in the best sites under the pines. Water spigots mounted on concrete aprons were scattered about the site and I snuck up to fill my canteen, but all were shut off.

For a few moments I stood there and gazed longingly around the campground and all it represented: family vacations, togetherness, adventure at a measured, leisurely pace. A break from a routine that's settled enough that "roughing it" is a pleasant diversion.

That's called life, Mike. It takes commitment and sacrifice and dedication.

I nodded.

As long as I was getting away with trespassing, I snuck over to the bathroom/

showers where I cleaned my face and filled my canteen. After I put my backpack on, I checked out my image in the mirror. As always when I saw myself in 1967, I couldn't help but smile. I loved this kid I'd become. It was just as simple as that.

Across the road and down a little ways, a west-facing train was stopped at a signal. About twenty cars from the engines was an empty boxcar with an open door. When no cars were in sight on the adjacent road, I pushed through the brush to the top of the railroad embankment and hoisted myself into the boxcar.

It wasn't until I was in and my eyes adjusted to the relative darkness in the boxcar that I realized that there was someone already riding it. He was white, middle-aged, skinny, and his thick-rimmed glasses made him resemble a scientist from an old fifties technical film. He wore jeans and a flannel shirt. He looked too sensible to be out riding freight trains around.

He spoke first by asking me if anyone had seen me climb on. I assured him that no one did and that I knew what I was doing. He was friendly in a reserved way. He said that his name was Walter and he was originally from Ohio. He couldn't believe that I'd been living on the road since New Jersey.

"You're awfully young to be riding freight trains around, aren't you?"

I shrugged. "Maybe the youngest one ever. Where are you heading?"

"California. You can ride along with me if you want to. I'll look out for you. You have a sleeping bag in there?" he asked, indicating my backpack.

"No, I just have a crappy blanket."

"You can lay your blanket on this cardboard and roll up in it later. It'll get pretty cold tonight when we cross the mountains."

Walter had several large sheets of cardboard. I hadn't really decided whether or not I wanted to travel with him. I couldn't get a reading on him, vibe-wise. I had to decide quickly though. I was sure that as soon as the train got its green signal, we would be departing.

He seems harmless in an intelligent, serial killer kind of a way.

'Yeah,' I considered, uneasily. 'I wonder what he has in his bag of tricks there.'

The hissing of the brakes releasing pushed me even faster to make a decision. Banging noises moved down the train, from the engines on down toward the caboose (the slack action that I described) and we started rolling. I hadn't decided whether or not I wanted to ride with this guy, so I lingered by the door.

He who hesitates gets chopped up by the serial killer.

I dawdled as we picked up speed. We were soon going too fast to jump off, so the decision was made for me.

Aw, I wouldn't worry. If I were him, I wouldn't make my move until tonight when you're asleep.

'Would you please stop that? It's your fault that I stayed on, because you called me a scaredy-cat.'

And it got to you, didn't it? Just like a little schoolgirl.

'Buzz off!'

I watched the western landscape slip past for at least an hour. I wanted to start a conversation with Walter, but couldn't think of how to do it. It was difficult enough to carry on a conversation with someone you already knew in a noisy box-car, let alone get to know someone. I glanced over at him. He was already watching me but he looked away. This was the third or fourth time this had happened.

"So, what brings you out here, riding the rails?" I asked him during one of the times we stopped.

He was sitting against the boxcar wall with his knees up and his hands resting on his knees. "Divorce, wife took damn near everything. I'm traveling around until I figure out what I want to do. You?"

"I don't know. I'm sort of lost in the world. No family, not sure what I want to do, stuff like that."

"You ran away from home, right?"

I sort of shrugged and made a face as though the act of running away or not was a distinction that could be debated. "What did you do for a living before . . ."

"I was an accountant for a bank in Columbus."

"Did you just up and quit and hit the road?" I was hoping my questioning wasn't out of line.

"Yup," he said, looking off while seeming to be considering the ramifications of what he did with his life.

"How long have you been out here doing this stuff?" I asked.

"About five years, give or take."

"So you just got tired of the rat race."

He smiled for the first time. "The 'rat race,'" he said, tasting the words. "I like that phrase. Yes, I got tired of the 'rat race.' Especially considering that I felt like I was going backwards on the treadmill."

I nodded.

"You'll understand when you get older," he added.

I smiled to myself. I'd lived in a rat race in the future that made this one look quaint by comparison. I still felt for the guy, though. If what he told me was true, he'd built a whole life and what didn't come crashing down around him, he'd abandoned in disgust.

"Why are you going to California?" I asked Walter.

"I have some stuff to straighten out in L.A."

I couldn't help but smile as I told him that I'd touched off at the Atlantic Ocean and was planning to touch off at the Pacific. But after that, I told him, I didn't really have plans.

"I have to make some money because I'm almost out. But it's almost impossible for me to make any money out here because I'm so young."

"I'll help you make some money. There are places where you can go to get work for the day. I can go in and register, but you're too young. But when I get work, I can see if I can take you along."

That sounded like a great plan to me.

It got quite cold that night as we rode, just as Walter said it would. I guess we traversed some mountains. Walter and I both rolled up in cardboard cocoons, he in his sleeping bag and me in my blanket. The next morning, I was first up. I sat in the doorway of the boxcar to watch the world go by.

Walter eventually slid out of his sleeping bag, came over by the door and made as if to piss off of the side of the train. I gave him his space by going back to my corner and packing up.

After he was done, he retired to his corner and leaned against the back wall of the boxcar. I was trying not to look in his direction because I would swear that he was masturbating.

"C'mere," Walter said to me.

"No," I replied as I scowled.

"Just come and sit next to me for a few minutes."

I shook my head.

"Just five minutes."

I picked up my backpack and stood in the doorway.

Walter had a mix of anger, embarrassment, and sexual frustration on his face, but by the sound of it, he apparently wasn't too embarrassed to finish.

Needless to say, that put a damper on our relationship. As the train slowed,

Walter said that we were coming into a big yard and that we should get off soon. After we hopped off, Walter said that he was heading towards a hobo camp, but that I wouldn't really be safe going there. That was fine with me and I told him that I was going to head into town. We couldn't travel together any more anyway.

I thought that was the end of it, but after a few seconds, Walter said, "Hey, kid."

I turned and we faced each other across the low scrub.

"Find yourself a home, son. Don't make a lifestyle out of this."

"*You* did," I countered.

He pursed his lips as he searched for the right words. "At your age, you're finding yourself. At my age . . . you're a bum." He arched his eyebrows to drive his point home and turned away.

I couldn't resist checking license plates. I was obviously nowhere near the ocean, but at least I'd made it to California.

<h1 style="text-align:center">21</h1>

As I shuffled towards town in Barstow, California, I could still hear the squeal of freight cars going through the "hump" yard. A hump yard is a section of a railroad yard where the freight cars are shoved up a hill and then uncoupled one by one, to roll on their own down the other side of the hill (or "hump") and are then switched to whatever track they are supposed to go to. There are devices called retarders along the rails that slow the cars down to a prescribed speed before the cars go to their tracks. The squealing that I was hearing was from the wheels of the freight cars being slowed down by the retarders.

I had a rapidly worsening headache and what I really desired was a soft bed in a cool, darkened room. But I needed supplies—particularly aspirin—and seeing as those things weren't about to come floating over to where I'd been sitting under a bush for the last hour, I had no choice but to risk walking around the town.

"Hey man, running away from home?" a kid's voice yelled to me from the porch of a house on one of the side streets I was passing. There was a group of boys hanging out on the porch. I didn't know whether to just keep my head down and keep walking or acknowledge his comment. I sort of half waved and kept going. About three seconds later, I was surrounded by the group. Most of them were bigger than I was.

"Hey man, I'm talking to you," taunted the big, stocky red-headed kid who was apparently the ringleader. He was about thirteen and he looked like the kind of kid who loves to fight.

"What're you doing in our town, man?" asked another kid.

"I'm just looking for something to eat," I said softly.

"What's in the backpack?"

"Nothing much. Just . . . stuff."

"Oh, I'm running away from ho-ome, I'm running away from ho-ome," the redhead sang in an obnoxious voice.

I felt my face flush.

"What are you gonna do for money—suck old men's dicks?" He looked around for support as his buddies took the cue and laughed for him.

I kept my mouth shut, knowing that anything I said would just make things worse. If this stupid kid only *knew* what I just had to put up with on my train ride here.

My heart was pounding in my chest, taking my headache up a notch.

"Do you get into a lot of fights?" he asked.

"I don't get into *any* fights," I answered impatiently.

"Oh yeah? Because Martin here wants to whup you." With this, the ringleader pushed the smallest kid there in front of me. The kid was about eight years old, pale and skinny. His blond hair was almost white and he wore glasses. Now, with his big friends to protect him, he gave me what was supposed to be his toughest look.

If this kid hit me and I lost my temper and hit him back, I'd be done for. They'd never let me win. I'd wind up with ten or so kids kicking my ass or holding me for Martin to punch.

"I think he should fight *you*, Drew," said another kid.

"Oh, yeah? You think you can take me?" Drew shoved me so hard that I slammed into someone behind me. The kid yelled as though it was my fault that I fell into him and stepped on his foot. He shoved me forwards.

"C'mon," taunted Drew. "I'll give you first punch. Don't roll your eyes at me, you little punk!" He shoved me again.

One of the other kids tried to push me back into Drew.

"No!" I said as I twisted around and almost fell.

I frantically looked around for help, but there was none. It vaguely occurred to me that the adults in the passing cars only ten feet away were oblivious to this scene that was playing out in our "kid's world."

"You know what?" I yelled at Drew as I recovered my balance.

"What?"

"How come every time I'm not feeling well, I run into an *asshole* like you?"

"WHAT?!"

And before he had time to react to that, I took off down the street.

You know, one of these days you're going to wise off to someone and get caught.

But I knew that no one had *ever* been able to catch me either in my old, adult body or in this one. The only one who really gave serious chase was Drew. But I knew within a hundred feet that I was losing him. I had the strength of adrenaline and of an incredible rage that rose up in me. Who the hell was he? What gave him the right to beat me up, just for sport?

I've met this kid, in one form or another, many times in my life. If he actually laid a hand on me in the rage I was now in, I would turn him into pulp. It wouldn't be a "put up your dukes" fight between two boys. It would be more like an attack by a wild animal (me) that had been taunted and cornered by a surprised boy (him).

The sole of my right sneaker had been gradually separating from the toes back to about the halfway point and now it was slapping loudly on the pavement as I ran. I stopped running when we neared the railroad yard and so did he. We were about a hundred feet apart.

"Come on, *Drew*," I screamed between breaths as pain seared through my skull. "Follow me into the railroad yard and we'll find out who's *really* tough. Come on sweet cheeks, just *you and me* behind a boxcar. Leave your little pussy friends here to call for an ambulance for you, you piece of *shit*!"

Spittle was flying out of my mouth as I yelled and I was so out of control that I thought I might break my teeth. It takes a certain combination of ingredients to make me really blow my top. It doesn't happen very often. But when it does happen, you want to stand back.

Drew didn't know what to do. He was used to pushing kids like me around. Now here was a real street kid who was obviously crazy and who, at least at this moment, had the power to make him wish he'd never been born. His "friends" had held back to let him face me on his own.

"FUCK OFF!" I screamed before turning my back and walking away.

"You're lucky I'm letting you go," he yelled, a little doubtfully.

"Yeah, *whatever*, asshole," I muttered under my breath. I didn't like the side of me that I was feeling, the years of pent-up rage that could make me do something really, really bad to someone like him.

'Fucking kid. He probably hates himself, so he takes his aggravations out by picking on others. I bet he hangs out in front of a 7/11 somewhere.'

With his skateboard, smoking cigarettes.

'Yeah and when the other kids have to go in, he's still wandering the streets because no one cares about him.'

His mom cares, but she's overwhelmed by life.

'Yup, because she was way too young when she got pregnant—probably with some one-night-stand sleazeball she met in a bar.'

OK, so I wasn't exactly in the most charitable, politically correct frame of mind. My hands shook as I pissed behind a bush.

This all did wonders for my headache. I walked parallel to the railroad yards for a few blocks and headed back into town.

"All I need now is a fucking cop to show up to complete my day," I bitched.

I found a small store and got everything I needed except for the aspirin. The lady at the register wouldn't sell it to me, so I said I'd send my mom in. I stood off to the side of the windows in front of the store, waiting for an adult to show up so I could ask them to buy me some aspirin. There was a pay phone there and I had the crazy urge to call the other me in New Jersey, just for someone to talk to.

A lady in a car with Michigan plates pulled in.

"Excuse me, could you buy aspirin for me if I give you the money? It's for my mom, but they won't sell it to me," I asked her as she was about to enter the store. Her eyes drifted to my backpack as she silently took the dollar from me, gave me sort of a bemused look and went in.

As I shifted from foot to foot while waiting, two kids that I recognized as Drew's friends raced up on bicycles. In perfect sync, they skidded to a stop, swinging their rear tires in a dramatic arc as they did so. One went into the store while the other stayed with the bicycles. On his way into the store, the one said, "Drew is looking for you. You'd better hope he doesn't catch you out here or you're dead meat."

I walked over to the one by the bikes.

"Why are you guys bothering me? Don't I look like I have enough problems?"

"You think you have problems now? Wait 'till we catch you on the street, you little faggot."

So much for that idea. I wanted to say something inflammatory, but the reality was that I would have wound up in a fight with both of them and I couldn't afford to get hurt and need medical care. After all, I couldn't go to a hospital as a kid alone. Besides, I'd already used up all of my rage and energy before. Now I was just feeling spent.

I sighed and ambled back to where I'd been. The other kid came back out with gum, which they both shared. Then they hopped on their bikes and hightailed it back towards, I guess, Drew's house to tell him where I was.

I wished I had the guts to just go and ring Drew's doorbell and when he answered, start walking in as I said "Hey, what's happening, Drew old buddy?" I felt that I should just face Drew and get it over with—and do it now while I was a kid. Win, lose, or draw, I ought to face my fears head-on instead of running away all of the time.

I sighed. "Once a pussy, always a pussy," I mumbled.

"Man, what the hell is taking this lady so long? The store's not *that* big." I bitched loudly, worried that the group of kids would arrive.

Finally, she came out.

"Why are you wearing a backpack?" she asked.

"I was pretending I was an army soldier."

She smiled. "Where do you live?"

"On the other side of town. There's a bunch of kids picking on me and they're after me. Could you give me a ride home?"

"Well, I'm on my way to work," she answered, but then felt bad for me. "Where do you need to go?"

I pointed, indicating the direction of the west end of the railroad yards.

She arched her eyebrows as she asked "Anywhere but here?"

I nodded.

Looking sort of amused, she said, "Hop in."

Once seated, I automatically reached back for the shoulder harness, but I grabbed at thin air because there wasn't one. I felt silly, so I pretended I was stretching.

"This looks good—I can walk from here, thanks," I said after a short ride.

She gave me my aspirin and my money back and waved off my hand as I tried to give her some money. As she sped off, I headed toward some houses, but as soon as she was out of sight I crossed back over the road and headed toward the railroad yards.

'That lady was kind of strange. She was friendly and unfriendly both at the same time. Seems like she has way too many problems of her own.'

She could play the part of Drew's mom.

'Yeah, there you go. She'd be perfect.'

I wondered why she had Michigan license plates. Had she come to California alone to make a new life for herself?

I worked my way across undeveloped miniature mountains and canyons to the tracks. The railroad yards slashed through the mini mountains and I sat atop a cliff and watched them switch trains down below.

'Boy, I hope this aspirin works.'

In my old life, from earliest childhood, headaches every day were just a way of life for me. When I look back at my childhood in my other body and think of a clear, crisp summer day, I also think of a blasting headache. Later in life, I mainly had "cluster headaches," meaning that I wouldn't have one for three weeks or so and then I'd have one for two weeks straight. I've had vacations where I've had a headache the entire vacation. Out of necessity, I became an expert on over-the-counter pain medications, because each one would no longer work for me after a few years. Shortly before my switch to this life, ibuprofen (which wasn't available back now) was the last pain med that worked for me. Aspirin had been the first one to stop working, many years ago. I hoped it would work now in this body.

Between the effect of the headache and the aftereffects of losing my temper earlier, I was unnaturally drowsy. My eyelids felt like they were weighted and I only intended to close them for a second.

22.

I awoke some hours later, just lying in the dirt. Even though my body was shivering, my head felt "light and free" like it always does after getting over a bad headache. I'd been using my arm as a pillow and I'd drooled all over it. The drool had cleaned off my filthy skin in an area and then dried, leaving a chalky patch with dark, dirty edges. I shook my head sadly.

"I'm turning into too much of a barbarian out here."

The last glow of sunset was in the sky—although it seemed to be getting brighter, not dimmer. I couldn't tell which direction the light was coming from. For the first time since I switched to this life, I was disoriented as to what direction was what. Normally, I just relied on my own inner compass, which seldom failed me.

"Let me see . . . the town is north of the yards, so I'm facing south, meaning west is right and east is left, so . . ."

It's getting lighter while you're sitting here debating whether it's getting lighter or not.

I couldn't get it through my head that it was morning and not evening. I scrunched up my forehead, trying to concentrate. Had I even seen the sun set? I looked around for my backpack to get my sweatshirt and realized that it was gone. No wonder I'd been using my arm as a pillow. I usually covered the backpack with either my sweatshirt or a spare T-shirt and used it as a pillow.

"Oh man, this isn't good," I said as I leapt to my feet.

The missing backpack didn't bother me as much as the fear that someone might have come so close to me and taken it while I was fast asleep and vulnerable.

'Did Drew find me and take it? Did he do something else to me that I haven't realized yet?'

Oh, for crying out loud, Mike! Yeah, he put lipstick and mascara on you and painted your toenails. Sheesh! The backpack probably just rolled down the hill.

Hoping that it *did* just roll down off of the hill, I peered over the crest and spotted it.

"Whew," I said as I donned my sweatshirt. "I never would have found it in the dark." Then I remembered that it was morning and not evening.

I drank from my canteen and then I sat there, staring into space. I noticed my unopened bottle of aspirin lying over where I'd slept, so I retrieved it. "Best damn aspirin I ever had," I mumbled. "You don't even have to open it."

You still had aspirin left from the bottle that you bought at Woolworths in St. Louis for your sore throat.

'Why do you delight in reminding me of stuff after it's too late? Like, "Oh, by the way Mike, you left your backpack on that train that's departing"—stuff like that.'

What am I, your personal secretary? When you're all hyped up, you don't take the time to be in touch with your inner voice, that's why. And you want to know another reason? I'm very forgetful.

I finally smiled. 'Of course you are. What do you do while I'm tuning you out?'

I usually plant nasty little seeds of self-denigration and doubt into your brain, but lately I've been trying to hypnotize you into thinking that you're a rooster.

I couldn't help but laugh. I dug the old aspirin bottle out of my backpack so I could combine both bottles into one. Back now, the bottles were glass and I didn't need them banging into each other and breaking. But even with the cotton in the bottle, the old aspirins were pulverized from bouncing around.

Unless you want to spend the whole day out in the blasting sun with nothing to do, you should get out of here before it gets really light.

'Um-hmm. I think I'm sort of coming apart at the seams and it feels kind of good, actually.'

Wonderful. I'm so happy for you. Come apart at the seams after you get on a train, OK?

"Oh," I said quietly, rubbing the sleep out of my eyes and yawning. "I don't feel like riding. I need to get a job. I'm almost broke."

It was only because I slept outside and people gave me food that my money had lasted this long. I fantasized about having a job and a nice little place to go at the end of the day to relax and feel secure. And a hot shower.

'Yeah, a hot shower.'

Of course, every time I pictured a normal life, I pictured me as this little kid living it. The movie in my head showed ten-year-old Mike coming home from work, greeting his adult neighbors in the hallway, etc. It's strange how . . . *natural* that scene seemed to me.

Before my inner voice had the chance to break in and give me the "You can't have it both ways" speech, I shook off my little fantasy. I packed up, stretched and yawned, and put my heavy backpack on. It was always heavy at the start of a trip because I had so much liquid in it.

In an old western movie accent, I said, "This here town ain't *big* enough for me and Drew." I chuckled at myself as I worked my way over to the rail yards.

Out of sheer habit, I kept out of sight as much as possible as I beelined for some trains that had cabooses on them.

'I don't know what to do.'

What do you mean you don't know what to do? You've been doing this almost every day for weeks on end.

'For the first time since leaving New Jersey, I feel like I'm lost. I don't know what to do.'

I'd never felt lost before on this trip, because I sort of felt as though I was "home" wherever I was.

Just to be doing *something*, I snuck across the gravel road that paralleled the tracks and hid myself between the trains. I found an open boxcar and climbed in.

Two tracks over from where I sat, I heard the loud hiss of the brakes releasing. I made my way over to it and frantically searched for a car to ride on that would give me somewhere to hide. I ran out of time as the cars started rolling, and I settled for riding the end of a covered hopper. I had absolutely no idea where this train was going. As long as it wasn't going to Mexico, I didn't care.

'I'll bet *Drew* wouldn't have the balls to just jump on a freight train without even knowing where it's going.'

Are you obsessed with this kid now?

'Doesn't matter; I'll never see him again.'

Until the next town, where you meet him in some other form . . .

'Swell.'

I found an empty boxcar when the train stopped and I sat in the doorway as the desert landscape rolled past. I was so deep in thought that I didn't even notice a crossing coming up. Before I knew it, I was riding past right in front of the waiting cars, so I waved. The girl in the first car in line gave me a big surprised smile and waved back.

'You know, I've been thinking: what if I decide to stay here and grow up in this body? And just for the sake of argument, let's say that sometime between now and 2015 I become the President. President Morrison. Would history books rewrite themselves and reality change around the new events?'

Mike, history and reality aren't about to shift the whole world around for little old you. You're not going to stay and grow up in this body anyway. Right after the switch at the bridge, you had a vision of the adult you going back, remember?

'Holy shit, that never even occurred to me!'

I'd rerun that scene a thousand times since switching, but I'd always concentrated on whether or not someone else was living as the adult me or whether I'd disappeared in 2015. But all this time, I'd missed the significance of *why I saw it* until now. Hell, he/I had even said, "See you around, kiddo." That should have been a clue.

'So, sooner or later I'm gonna switch back. I might be trapped in a cycle.'

You're trapped in a cycle and you know it. You just won't admit it.

'Well, what if I refuse to go back to the bridge? What if I stow away on a cargo ship to China or something?'

Now you're just being ridiculous.

'No, I'm not. If there was ever a person crazy enough to do that, it's me.'

Ain't that the truth. But you won't.

'But I don't *want* to switch back. I want to stay here forever as *this* me.'

I know you do. You got the chance to play Peter Pan and run off to Neverland and you like it. When the time is right, switching back won't seem so bad.

I let out a big, long shaky sigh.

Sorry kiddo.

'So what am I supposed to do now?'

You do the same as everyone else does: live each day to the fullest.

'Yeah, I guess. So much for Neverland . . .'

Ah, don't take it so hard, Mikey old boy. Neverland isn't big *enough for you and Drew anyway!*

23

For some reason, I'd assumed that this train would bring me to Los Angeles and that Los Angeles was a short hop away. But now if I had to guess I would say that I'd been traveling north all day. California was stunningly beautiful, I must say. Back in the sixties, much of the state was still undeveloped. I think this trip set a new record for me as far as just staying on a train and riding. I can't really put a time frame on how long I rode because I slept some of it, but it seemed to me that I'd managed to stay with the same train for over a day. At sunset, we came to a stop in a city. I didn't know if we were going into a big railroad yard or not, so I reluctantly hopped off my ride.

It didn't take me long to confirm that I was still in California. I saw a gas station and thought that it was high time I got a map. My inner voice warned me to ditch the backpack, but I decided against it because I didn't feel like searching for it in the dark later.

"What happened, your car break down?" the attendant joked.

I smiled. "Do you have a map that I could have, or at least one that I could look at?"

He strode into the little building and grabbed one off of a rack.

"Here you go. That'll be five dollars." I looked from the map up at him, but he was smiling. "They're free. Usually people buy gas first, though. Here, cup your hands and I'll sell you some gas to make it legal."

I liked this guy. He had my sense of humor.

"You're in Sacramento, California," he said in answer to my unasked question. "So, running away from home are we?" he asked.

"No."

"No, no, of course you're not. You got lost coming home from summer camp." I smiled.

"Excuse me," he said as a car pulled up, "don't go away."

No "self-service" here, I noticed. He filled their tank, cleaned their windshield and offered to check their oil. I also noticed how cheap the gas was and that the air was free.

We went into the little shop. On the floor near the door sat a bench seat out of a car. There wasn't much else in there except a desk, a few mismatched chairs, a rack with oil and wiper blades and stuff, and the map rack.

"So, as I was saying, you're in Sacramento."

"Yeah, I just . . ."

"Wanted to know where Sacramento was in relation to the rest of the world? Don't open that one—you'll never get it folded again," he said, showing me where we were on a big map of California that was on the wall. "Nearest big city is San Francisco, over here. If you don't mind my asking, how does one arrive in a city without knowing how he got there?"

"Oh, I rode in on a freight train," I said matter-of-factly.

He looked alarmed, but then quickly hid it. Smiling, he said, "They should fire that conductor for not calling out the station names along the way."

"Yeah," I answered, smiling, "the service in my boxcar was lousy."

He shook his head in mock dismay. "I'm Lee, by the way."

"I'm Mike."

"So, Mike . . ." he said and spread his hands in a "what's the story?" way.

I shrugged. "I'm just living on the road, traveling the country."

"Oh, is that all? Seems reasonable enough for a—how old are you—about twelve?"

"That sounds about right."

He smiled. "Is your name really Mike?"

I felt my face flush as I nodded.

"Where are you from?'

"New Jersey."

"First definite answer we've gotten. OK, what town?"

I sat down on the car seat and then took my backpack off after leaning back against it. I raised my hand a little in an "I don't know" gesture.

"I'm sure it'll come back to you," he said as he went out to take care of a customer.

The car seat I was sitting on was on the floor and very low. On impulse, I half stood up and craned my neck to see what he was doing.

'Oh, nuts.'

One of the cars was a sheriff's and I watched carefully as Lee leaned down to discuss something with him. Did I just see Lee glance my way while talking with the sheriff? They both looked my way.

Right next to where I was sitting was a door leading to the garages. There was another door at the back of the shop, but I guessed that it went to the bathroom. I grabbed my pack and tried the doorknob nearest me. It opened, so, staying low, I slipped into the garage. As I closed the door behind me, I realized that it was irrelevant how low I'd stayed; the door was six feet high, so they'd probably seen it opening.

Swearing softly, I quickly glanced around. There were huge, window-filled bay doors with a regular door beside them, but they were right in front.

The only light on was a fluorescent light over a workbench. There were windows in the back and on the sides of the garage, but they were too high for me to get to. On the left-hand wall of the garage, over a large shelving unit, was an accessible window. I ran to it and quickly scampered up the shelves, being careful to stay near where they were attached to the upright supports so the middles wouldn't cave in from my weight. I turned the latch on the window and pulled. The window was hinged on the bottom, so it opened down and to the inside, towards me on a forty-five degree angle.

I took my backpack off and dropped it through the opening. I had no choice but to put my weight directly on the window in order to get through. At least the glass looked like it was reinforced with wire imbedded in the glass in a diamond pattern. I wanted to close the window behind me, but there was nothing to grab to hold myself in place in order to push on the bottom of the frame and move it. If I pulled from the top, I'd close my fingers in it.

For some damn reason, I didn't seem to be outside anyway. By the closeness of the echoes, I seemed to be in a small room that was pitch-dark and smelled like a bathroom. 'Why would someone put a window between a garage and a bathroom?'

I had no way to get down because there was nothing to grab onto and only a tiny ledge on which to kneel. I had to make a move here. Seconds counted and I'd already used up probably most of a minute. I quickly tried to maneuver myself around so I could hang by my fingers before dropping into the darkness. If it was the same distance down in here as it was in the garage, I was in for quite a drop.

Silly thoughts raced through my mind, such as, 'What if there are big, long spikes sticking straight up out of the floor and I impale myself on them?' A more likely scenario would be that I'd land half on and half off of something and break an ankle.

Stupidly, I was holding myself up with my hands on the top of the window and now my weight pulled it shut on my fingers. I panicked and my knees slipped off of the narrow ledge. I was totally trapped, hanging by my arms with my own weight holding the window shut on my fingers. The pain was instantly excruciating in my fingers, arms and shoulders. I quickly brought my knees up against the wall to take some weight off of my arms. But there was no way to get my fingers out. The harder I pulled to get them out, the tighter I pulled the window shut on them.

I heard the door to the garage open and then a moment of silence as the sheriff figured out the only escape route as quickly as I had.

"Where does that window go to?" the sheriff asked.

"It used to go outside, but now it only goes to the new bathroom," Lee answered.

"Was it unlatched before?"

"I don't know."

Could they see my fingers on the top of the window? I wondered.

One of them said something softly, and then said more loudly, "I guess he's gone."

As soon as I heard them leave, by a sheer act of will and ignoring the pain, I pulled myself up and kept the momentum going in order to push the window back open. I started going backwards again, but reached in with one hand and turned it towards me while slapping it into the inside wall above the window. I tried to get enough leverage to keep my knees on the little ledge and down I fell, landing on my backpack in a heap on the floor of the bathroom. As I started taking stock of my body parts to feel if anything was broken, the bathroom door opened and the light came on. "Game over," I mumbled to myself.

"You all right?" asked the sheriff.

"I think so."

"OK, let's go son," he said as he grabbed my arm with one hand and picked up my backpack with the other. "I got him, Lee," he yelled.

The sheriff had a firm grip on me and he wasn't about to let go. Once outside, I tensed for my chance to break away and bolt, but none came.

'No more freedom, no touching off at the Pacific Ocean, no more anything.' I thought glumly.

The sheriff silently brought me back into the office. He tossed my backpack on the desk, dragged the desk chair to the furthest corner from the door and plunked me down in it.

"What's your full name?"

"Michael Jeffrey Morrison."

No, it isn't.

'Shit, that's right!' I silently chided myself. 'Oh, I screwed up already.'

"Di-oh-bee?" The sheriff asked.

I blinked at him.

"Di-oh-bee?" he asked again.

"What's your date of birth?" Lee clarified for me.

"Oh, D. O. B!" I laughed.

The unamused sheriff was still waiting for an answer.

All this time you've been living here doing nothing and you've been too busy to figure out a birth date?

"Lee, you have a customer out there," said the sheriff.

Lee nodded and left.

"Son, we can either do this here or go downtown and do it. Your choice."

Did I sense a glimmer of hope here?

"August 24, 1955." I figured that would make me about twelve.

"Where are you from?"

"New Jersey."

"Ask him what town," said Lee as he walked back to the office door, keeping an eye on the car that he was filling.

"Lee," said the sheriff as he held up his hand to him.

"What town?" the sheriff asked. In a different setting, say in one of the Police Academy comedy movies, that little scene would have been funny. In one of those movies, Lee would suggest asking me what town I was from and the sheriff would say in an official voice, "Lee, I'll ask the questions here. I'm a highly trained police officer." Then he'd look at me and ask, "What town are you from?"

He was still waiting for an answer, but I remained silent.

"How long have you been living out here?"

"Since 1965," I answered, adding a few years onto the time I'd been doing it to make myself seem older and more self-sufficient (as though that would have made any difference to the sheriff).

"What's your parents' phone number?"

"I don't have any family."

"Uh-huh."

Lee had finished fueling the car and was back by the office door. I gave the sheriff my commune story for all it was worth, adding that I never knew my parents. He was looking through my backpack while I was spinning my tale and now he looked up at Lee and asked, "Why do all of these kids assume that cops are idiots and will believe anything?"

Addressing me, he said, "Well, whatever lie you want to tell me, you just can't be living out here and hopping freights, plain and simple. Sorry Lee, I know I promised, but I've got to take this kid in and find out where he belongs."

"Wait, please? Can't I stay here? Lee, I'll work for you. I'll be the best worker you ever had. You don't even have to pay me! Just give me some food. I'm totally honest. You could leave me alone with a million dollars on the desk and I wouldn't steal a penny."

"Totally honest? You haven't said an honest thing since I met you! What town did you grow up in?"

I was getting desperate. 'Should I give him the rest of the other Mike's info?' *No, that'll just make things worse.*

"Please don't take me to jail. I'll do anything—sweep the streets, clean the courthouse steps, the bathrooms—anything."

"Kid, that's not how the system works," the sheriff said tensely.

"Well, we both know *that's* the truth, don't we?" asked Lee.

"Lee, I can't just ignore a runaway kid. Even if he really *doesn't* have parents. My job is on the line here."

"Carl," Lee said quietly and nodded his head sideways in a "let's go over there and talk" kind of way.

"Do not move a muscle," the sheriff ordered me.

The sheriff watched me like a hawk as he and Lee quietly talked. I could hear enough snippets of the conversation to get the gist of it.

"... Did you bring me in here in the first place? Because I ... who he is and ... home. I can't ... You know that. No, but you can ... the kid? I'll take responsibility and then we'll ..."

The sheriff gave his head a little shake and sighed. "All right," he agreed and then turned to me and held up my backpack.

"Do you have anything less filthy in here you can put on?"

I nodded.

The sheriff gave me a doubtful look as he tossed the backpack to me. I dug my clean pants out and went into the old bathroom and changed. The two of them watched as I carefully turned the filthy pants inside out before stowing them.

"He does that as though he's been doing it for years," the sheriff commented to Lee. I made as if to shoulder my backpack and the sheriff pulled it from my hands and said, "Oh, no, no, no you don't. Do you need anything from here for tonight?"

"I guess just my toothbrush and toothpaste," I said timidly.

After I got my stuff, the sheriff took my backpack.

"I gotta go, I'm late for supper. Marcie's probably burned it by now."

They walked outside, talking quietly. I moved to the old car seat by the door because it was more comfortable. They both turned and looked at me. "I won't run away," I said.

"You'd better not. Do you know how to pump gas?" asked Lee.

I nodded. "I've worked at gas stations before."

"How come that doesn't surprise me? Well? Get to it."

We closed up and Lee took me to his sister's boarding house, stopping at Kentucky Fried Chicken along the way so I could run in and get a meal to go. His sister seemed quite stern as she recited the rules to me, but I liked her. She made it clear that she normally doesn't allow children to stay there, but was making an exception.

"Is the sheriff a good friend of yours?" I asked Lee as we walked upstairs to my room.

"He's my best friend. All a cop's friends are cops."

"So, you're a cop?"

"Ex-cop."

Boy, did *I* pick the wrong gas station to walk into.

"I'll be back at 5:30 a.m. to pick you up."

"I don't have an alarm clock."

"I'll knock on your door. And Mike . . ."

"I'll be here."

The communal bathroom down the hall was cleaner than I expected it to be. Back in my room, I moved the bed closer to the window as quietly as I could. I was having a hard time adjusting to the thought of being trapped indoors for an entire night.

'It would probably be a bad idea to go for a walk after I eat, huh?'

Just stay put, Mike. It won't kill you to sleep indoors for one night. What if the sheriff sees you out walking around?

I nodded agreement. Boy, the chicken sure smelled good.

'Didn't that lady say no eating in the rooms?'

No, she said no cooking in the rooms.

'What are you going to cook with when there's no oven or stove in here and microwaves don't even exist yet—a bonfire?'

Where do you go in your head when people are talking to you? She said no hot plates.

'Oh. It's been an eventful day.'

She also said no moving the bed under any circumstances.

'Now I *know* you're messing with me.'

After I'd gulped down every last morsel of chicken like a wild animal and cleaned up with the non-absorbent, useless little paper napkins, I turned off the light and sat in the blueish-green glow of the streetlight outside. In 2015, the streetlights were an orangey color. I reran the day in my head and reflected on how lucky I was to be this boy and be out here on the road. And man, all of the bad things that could happen to you! But I'd stayed safe and sound, aside from a few cuts, bumps, and bruises. It seemed as though every time I wished for something, it happened for me. Any time I was starving, someone fed me. I got more breaks than any person could ever hope for. Today was a perfect example of that.

Emotions welled up in me and there was just no stopping them.

'Why are You so good to me, God? After all of the derogatory things I've said to You, how could You still love me?' I hung my head as hot tears rolled down my cheeks.

Eventually, I pulled it together. I bunched the greasy napkins into one huge wad and blew my nose extravagantly.

Then I sat up until the wee hours thinking.

24

"Why didn't the sheriff take me in last night?" I asked Lee around a yawn in the car on the way to the gas station the next morning.

Lee didn't reply and I decided I'd better not press the issue.

I surreptitiously studied Lee's profile as he drove. He didn't look like a cop—even an ex-cop. He was tallish and thin, with sixties' style light brown hair and sideburns. Carl the sheriff looked the part of a sheriff. He was big and stocky with short dark hair that was greying at the temples.

"A few years ago," Lee suddenly began saying. "Well, now that I think about it, it's more than ten years . . . I was a cop in L.A. and my partner brought a runaway kid in. Nice, good-looking, all-American boy, a little older than you. The kid just came from a lousy home environment, that's all. Couldn't fault him for running away."

Lee stopped and composed his thoughts for a moment before continuing. "Well, his parents didn't want him back, so he got sent to juvy."

"What's 'juvy'?" I asked.

"Juvenile detention. My partner made arrangements to have him protected from the general population, but it never happened. The first night the kid was in juvy, he got his front teeth knocked out and he was raped. Three days after they sent him home, he killed himself. My partner took it to heart and never got over it. All of the things you see on the streets as a cop that you blank out of your mind," Lee said, seeming to be referring to himself, "but this was the one that did it for him."

We rode the rest of the way in silence. I recalled what the sheriff had said to Lee last night: "Sorry Lee, I know I promised, but I've got to take this kid in and find out where he belongs." Obviously, it wasn't Lee's partner, but Lee himself who'd tried to save the kid. Maybe that was why Lee was an "ex-cop" now. So the sheriff had broken protocol as a favor to his friend, Lee. I wondered if I was supposed to slip away from the boarding house last night and make things easy.

The sheriff had already unlocked the office and had a pot of coffee made when we arrived at the gas station. I asked if I could have a cup and the sheriff snapped, "No" in a manner that suggested that my request was as absurd as if I'd asked if I could take a match to the gas pumps. Lee grabbed a cup and wandered off to his morning duties.

The sheriff told me to sit in the chair and he sat on the edge of the desk.

"So," he started after he drained his cup, "do you have anything to tell me this morning?"

I looked down and did a little shrug.

His jaw set and his face flushed with anger. "All right, no more futzing around! Where—"

"No more *what*?"

"Listen, kid. Early morning is not the time to try my patience."

"I have no family and I'm not in any trouble and I . . . originated in New Jersey," I answered meekly.

"You 'originated' in New Jersey." He looked up at the ceiling. "What the hell is *that* supposed to mean? *Originated*?" He held out his hands in a 'come on, you can do better than that' gesture.

"You know what, kid?" he said as got himself more coffee, "I'm beginning to wish I'd never met you. OK, let me tell you your own story: You came from a nice home with two parents who loved you, but that wasn't good enough for you so you hit the road and now they're sitting at home worrying. How's that for starters?" He was getting kind of fired up at this point and when he dumped his milk in too fast, a dollop of coffee leapt up onto his hand. He rapidly wiped his hand on his shirt, swore, and grabbed a rag to clean his shirt. "You obviously had a good upbringing, so you're not running away from some bad situation. You're just gallivanting around the country because you feel like it. Am I close?"

Just as the sheriff was wetting the rag in the old bathroom off of the office, the phone on the desk rang. There was a ringer outside as well, and Lee came in to answer it. When he saw the sheriff lunging for it, he lingered by the doorway.

"Damn, Jack," the sheriff asked the caller as he checked his watch, "what *time* is it there? Wow, sorry. So what did you come up with? Yup, I'm all ears." He sat down at the desk, poised to write in a little pad with the phone crocked between his ear and shoulder. "No one missing by that name—that's what I figured." The sheriff glanced at Lee, then down at the setting stain on his shirt, then at me accusingly. I stifled a smile.

He listened for some time and jotted down a few notes. "No, that would be too far back. He'd be a lot older by now." He looked at me: "How old are you?"

I answered with a blank stare.

"Oh, for God's sake." Then back to his friend on the phone, he said, "Who? That would be a good match except that this kid's hair is dark brown. Oh, don't be ridiculous, a kid is not gonna—Boy, you guys . . . all right, hold on."

The sheriff told Lee to check my hair for blond roots. Lee gave him an incredulous look and the sheriff indicated the phone receiver with his free hand as if to say, "What the hell you want me to tell you? It's what the man said to do so just do it to appease him, OK?"

I sat patiently while Lee checked my hair.

"Nothing but fleas," Lee teased before ruffling my hair and returning to the doorway.

I smiled and smoothed my hair back out.

"He's a natural brunette," the sheriff confirmed dryly. He listened for a second and then laughed. "I don't think he's old enough to have any yet, but if you want to fly out from D.C. and check, I'll pick you up at the airport."

D.C.? I wondered if he was talking to the FBI.

The sheriff laughed again and then got back to business. "And that's in New Jersey? What major town is that near? Why didn't you tell me about him first? Well, don't you have a newer list? Oh."

The sheriff stared at me and screwed his mouth sideways as though debating a long shot. "I, uh . . . I guess it couldn't hurt for you to send me a picture. No, mail it to my house if you would. Uh . . . actually, no, we didn't bring him in. Lee and I." He looked up at Lee. "Jack says hi."

Lee nodded.

"Because we want to return him home in one piece and not in a casket, that's why." He shot a concerned glance in Lee's direction and silently mouthed, "Sorry."

Lee gave him a "Don't worry about it" hand gesture and went out to attend to a car.

"No, he's here at the gas station with us." Even from where I was sitting, I could hear Jack whistle in a "wow" way through the earpiece. "Oh, I don't care. You think I care anymore? I'll take an early pension and go into the gas business with Lee if I have to. Do you have any idea how many cars there are out here?

You should see the highways they're building down by L.A. They look like the Autobahn, for crying out loud. How's Nancy? Is she really? You guys ever gonna tie the knot?" He laughed. "She's good, thanks. Ah, for now, she's doing OK. She'll have to keep getting tested, but, you know. I will. OK, I'll let you go. Hey—I owe you one. No, please just mail it to my house. Nancy has the address, she sends us a Christmas card every year. You too, buddy. Go home and get some sleep."

The sheriff sat and sipped his coffee, lost in his thoughts. He looked at me as though remembering that I was there.

"There's something about you that I just can't put my finger on. Come here," he said as he walked over to the map of California on the wall. "Show me where you came from."

"Um, I can't show you on that map," I said timidly. "I'm from New Jersey."

"Oh, for Pete's sake . . ." Glancing back at the map on the wall as though it had betrayed him, he snatched an "Eastern United States" map from the map rack, spread it out on the desk and stood back with his arms crossed and waited.

As I put my finger on the general area, I noted to myself that the interstate highway I drove out there on in 2015 only existed in bits and pieces on the map back now. "I originated here on August 24, 1967."

"Yesterday you said it was *1965* that you 'originated' there. You're lucky I didn't believe you or I'd have to call my friend back and start the search all over again." He looked at me accusingly and I felt my face flush. "So, you don't have amnesia . . ."

I couldn't help but smile as I shook my head no. "Sometimes, I wish I did."

"Did someone dump you there?"

I shook my head.

The sheriff took a long, slow breath. "Go out and give Lee a hand or something, would you?" he said quietly with his eyes closed.

"Yeah, um, sure . . . but people might wonder why I'm not in school . . ."

"It's *Saturday*," he snapped. Then he muttered to himself, "Kid doesn't even know what day of the week it is."

As I walked out, the sheriff was idly twirling the ashtray on the desk around with the point of the pencil, looking at the map, deep in thought.

I helped Lee at the gas station for the next couple of days, keeping out of sight during the day as best I could. Late Wednesday afternoon, the sheriff came by. He talked quietly to Lee for a few minutes while they looked at something. Then the conversation got quite animated. I wandered over and I could see that the sheriff was holding a photo of a kid—probably the one that his friend had sent him—but I couldn't really get a good look at it. I was dying to bend over and get a closer look to see if it was a picture of me, but I didn't.

Yeah, Mike, it's a picture of you with a tear-stained, handwritten note from your loving mom saying "Please send my little boy home ASAP," but the sheriff chooses to ignore it.

I inwardly rolled my eyes at my sarcastic inner voice as I went off to clean the garage.

It seems as though the sheriff found something out about you.

'Uh-huh.'

And you've always wondered if you exist in the real world.

'Yup.'

Aren't you even going to ask him?

'Nope.'

Okaaaay . . .

I watched through the windows in the bay door as he and Lee argued. Then the sheriff angrily pointed in my direction, pointed at Lee, at himself, waved the whole thing off and drove off in a huff.

Lee came in with a strange look on his face. "Hold down the fort for a few minutes."

I stood, dumbfounded as he too got in his car and scraped his tailpipe as he bounced out onto the road.

"Is he . . . chasing the sheriff?" I asked the silent garage.

Lee returned in less than five minutes and tossed my backpack on the desk in the little office.

"Mike, why don't you take the rest of the day off," he suggested in a strained voice.

I stared up at him in wonder but he glanced away.

"Lee, you don't have to stick your neck out for me."

"Don't *you* stick *your* neck in where it don't belong!" he yelled with disproportionate anger.

I recoiled as if struck. "I'm sorry. I just—"

He strode over to the desk, picked up the phone receiver and poised his finger over the dial. "Ten, nine, eight, seven . . ."

I dug his gas money out of my pocket and laid it on the desk. Then I hesitantly shouldered my backpack and hurried away across the lot.

I didn't waste any time heading for cover by the river, where I sat and tossed rocks into the water. I could still smell gasoline on my fingers from working the pumps. It would have been nice if I'd at least made a little more money working there.

Well, you can add Lee's name to the list of people you've—

'Don't. Please, just don't. I feel bad enough already.'

I still found it difficult to believe that I dreamt me up and this body had no past. Maybe I should have asked the sheriff.

'Oh well, too late now. Anyway, at this age, what's to know about my past? The first time I fell off of my tricycle and skinned my knee?' I made a "*pfft*" noise and waved the whole subject off with a hand gesture.

No, Mike, more like the first time your dad ran alongside your bike and let go because he just took the training wheels off, your first best friend, little unimportant memories like those.

'Wow, that's so deep.' I did a fake sniffle. 'OK, I admit that it really upsets me that I can't remember my first poop without a diaper.' I laughed hysterically at myself.

I actually think you've regressed a few years since August 24. Don't you even want to know if you have a family?

'Listen, if someone was looking for me, I'd be on my way home whether I wanted to go or not. I'm cool with things being just the way they are.'

I don't know what's sadder—the fact that no one cares about you or the fact that you like it that way.

'It's only a problem if you make it a problem, sweetheart.'

What I really needed right now was to just settle down somewhere for a while and live a normal life.

You can't have it both ways, Mike. You can't stay here as a kid on the streets and be totally free but have the security, predictability, and comfort of your old adult life. It doesn't work that way.

'Yeah, yeah, yeah. I think you might have mentioned that about *three hundred times* already.'

Ah, you're just disappointed because Neverland looked so much nicer in the brochure.

I laughed at my inner voice's last comment as I shouldered my backpack and started searching for a train ride out of here. I was at a familiar point that I occasionally reached out here on the road where I completely lost my drive and ambition to do anything at all. It's a recurring pattern that probably happens at some point to everyone who just hits the road on impulse:

Set out on an adventure—the opportunities are limitless!

Adventure loses its luster and reality sets in.

Debate packing it in and going home.

Repeat, simmering over a medium heat, stirring occasionally.

'Next stop: the Pacific Ocean,' I told myself. 'Then maybe I'll just go back to good old N-J. Boy, do I miss that place. If I don't have to switch back right away when I go back there, I'm just going to tour around 1967 New Jersey for a while.'

It would be even cooler if you could go back to the forties or fifties.

'Well, beggars can't be choosers. What would *really* be cool would be to go back to the eighteen—oh look, an ice cream truck!'

I stopped the ringing truck and parted with some of my precious money for a Strawberry Shortcake ice cream.

25.

After dark, I snuck across the river on the railroad bridge. I could hear train horns in the distance, so I followed the tracks to where they joined a line that was actually used. I caught a freight that I hoped was going west. The tracks sort of curved around all over the place, so I wasn't sure. Whatever direction, I had to get out of this town.

In the early morning, we pulled into a yard so I hopped off and quickly made my way to the streets. I walked for miles, discovering along the way that I was in Oakland, California. I got real bad vibes from this town, like the whole place was about to explode or something.

A group of people were waiting at a bus stop. No screwing around this time, having learned my lesson back in Virginia, I asked one of them where the bus went from here, how much it cost and whether you needed exact change or not. Then I stood, looking strange amongst the commuters: a scruffy, obviously runaway boy, heading into the big city of San Francisco.

The commuters all around me on the crowded bus seemed not to notice what an incredible journey this was, but I guess they were used to it. The skyscrapers of downtown glittered and the buildings draped over the hills were bathed in golden sunlight. I was excited and a little scared because this wasn't just one of the mid-sized cities that I'd visited, where you walk from the railroad yard into downtown, resupply, and then leave. This was big time. I must say, though, that the big cities always seemed safer than the mid-sized ones. You'd think it would be the other way around, but not in my experience.

By far, San Francisco was the nicest city that I'd visited. I'd come into downtown in what seemed to be the financial district. The streets were bustling with activity and pedestrians. I was completely ignored by everyone, which was just fine with me. I donned my sweatshirt to ward off the cool, damp weather and I headed back towards the bay.

With the sweatshirt out of it, the backpack was nearly empty. The coal-blackened jeans were long gone—worn out and thrown in a dumpster a few hundred miles back. So I once again carried the backpack in my hand instead of on my back, so as not to attract too much attention.

I sat for a while down by Fisherman's Wharf, where tourists began to gather. I didn't know the lay of the land here. If I walked west through the city, would the other side of it be on the Pacific Ocean? I looked for the gas station map Lee had given me, but I guess in all of the excitement I'd never put it in the backpack. I needed somewhere to go to the bathroom—and soon—so I started walking.

"It seems like you street kids get younger and younger."

Startled, I spun my head around to see who was talking to me. He was short and squat and what little dark hair remained on the sides of his head matched his mustache and beard. He was dressed sort of like a sloppy college professor. He had kind, happy eyes that were so dark brown that they were almost black, with deep laugh lines at the sides of them. But they were also eyes that had seen it all.

"Oh, you scared the hell out of me!"

"Good. Hell is not a good thing for a young man to harbor."

I puzzled over what he'd just said as my stomach gave me a warning grumble. "I've gotta go," I said and began walking.

"Wow, everyone's in such a rush these days," he exclaimed as he kept pace with me. "Where on earth could a runaway boy have to go in a hurry? I'm not a cop, in case that's what you're worried about. I think if you'll listen to me for a few moments you'll—"

"No, I mean I have to *go* go—to the bathroom. Like, right now."

"Oh, oh, follow me," he said and headed across the busy street.

Amazed at myself for doing it, I followed him up the block to a hotel.

"Pass the front desk without looking that way and keep going to the right, across the lobby from the elevators. Here," he said, holding out his hand, "I'll hold your backpack." After two seconds' consideration, I handed it to him and I rushed in.

I came out a few minutes later, feeling relieved and also refreshed. It wasn't very often that I got to wash my hands and face after going to the bathroom. Ninety-nine percent of the time, I went to the bathroom outdoors and buried it.

As he handed me my backpack, he introduced himself as Ryan. He suggested that I come with him over to his youth hostel on Market Street.

"You don't want to spend your first night in the city on the streets, do you?"

"How did you know it would be my first night here?" I asked, while I pointedly stayed put in front of the hotel where there were people around. A bellhop that I'd ignored as I breezed past him in the lobby came out to a cab to fetch a guest's bags and he gave me a "move on, kid" warning look.

"See, you've made them angry," said Ryan.

"You're the one who told me to go in there! *You're* the grown-up."

The bellhop came back out and I pointed at Ryan: "*He's* the grown-up!"

Ryan and I both laughed as we sauntered away.

"So, what's your name?"

"Mike."

"Where are you from, Mike?"

"New Jersey."

"Oh! I guess you've been out on the streets for quite a while then. I thought you were new to this," he said while handing me his business card.

A reverend? And a psychologist? Boy, you could have a field day with him. A one-hour session and he'd become an atheist and have himself committed!

I couldn't help but laugh at that. Then I noticed that Ryan was scrutinizing me. Oops.

"Did I say something funny?"

I grinned self-consciously. "Oh, I was laughing at my inner voice. I do it all of the time." As I told him about our "relationship," he listened with rapt fascination.

"Does it have a name?" he asked.

"No, I'm not *that* bad. It doesn't tell me to do things, I don't 'hear voices', none of that crap."

"So, what did your inner voice say about me?" He wasn't angry, just amused.

I laughed again as I shook my head.

"Come on, Mike, out with it."

I told him and he laughed. I must say, I really liked this guy.

"But don't think that I'm evil or an atheist or something because I'm not. God really takes care of me out here," I added.

"No, no, no, I didn't think that. How about the asylum part?"

"Oh yeah, well *that* part's true."

He chuckled. "I doubt you could tell me anything that I haven't heard a hundred times before."

You'd be surprised.

"Yes, he certainly would be." I answered out loud.

Ryan was right on top of it, though. "No, I wouldn't. Nothing surprises me anymore."

He looked at his watch. "Oh, darn it. Mike, I'd love to stand here and chat with you—*both* of you—but I have an appointment to get to. We don't have time to go to the hostel right now. Tell you what. It's quarter to ten now, so why don't you come to the hostel at twelve for a free lunch," he said, indicating the address on the card he gave me.

"Um . . . are there other boys there?"

"Of course there are other boys there," he said encouragingly, thinking that this would be a selling point. But then he noticed the sour expression on my face. "Teenagers, none as young as you are."

I looked down at my shoes.

"It's a *youth* hostel," he said while holding his hands up in a "what would you expect?" manner. "Is that a problem?"

"Well, I'm kind of a loner. Adults aren't so bad, but I really stay away from other kids."

He smiled kindly. "I'll sit with you and if you feel uncomfortable, we can leave."

I studied the sidewalk. Ryan actually bothered to lean down to catch my eyes. "Just come. I'll make sure that nobody picks on you, OK? In the meantime, try not to talk to anyone out here. Except yourself, of course, you'll fit right in on the streets that way." We both smiled. "People out here will steal everything you own, including your sneakers." He looked down at my sneakers and then quickly back up at me.

"See," I laughed, "*You* have conversations with yourself too! Your inner voice just said: 'But no one would be desperate enough to steal *those* sneakers.'"

His eyebrows shot up and his eyes widened as he laughed and nodded. "Guilty as charged."

There was a moment of silence between us as he had, as I would describe it, a little frowning conversation with his inner voice.

"How old *are* you, anyway?"

I shrugged. "Old enough to take care of myself, I guess. I don't really know."

"You 'don't really know?' I find that hard to believe."

"Well, I use August twenty-fourth as my birthday, but I really don't know what year I was born. How old do I look?"

"Well, looks-wise, I'd say preteen. Personality-wise, I'd say young adult to adult. Put the two together and I have absolutely no idea how old you are."

I smiled understandingly. "Somewhere between ten and a hundred."

"Indeed . . . If you don't mind my asking, how did you wind up out here?"

"Oh, well I really don't have a family or anything and I just sort of decided to hit the road one day and see the country. But don't start feeling sorry for me or anything, because I have it made. I mean, it's a rough life out here, especially being so young and all, but. . ."

He looked at me seriously for a minute, as though scrutinizing a specimen. "Living on the streets hasn't hardened you at all. You're very intelligent and completely aware of. . ." He trailed off and continued after a few seconds. "There's something about you that's . . . that's *different*. But I like it," he quickly added. "I like *you*. We need to talk more." He glanced at his watch and shook his head. "But I can't talk now. See you at noon, OK?"

"Um, I'll try."

I went back down by the waterfront and explored my way south. Cars passed above on an elevated highway that paralleled the waterfront. After asking a security guard at one of the piers the time, I hustled over to Market Street, arriving well before noon. I cautiously confirmed the building number and then positioned myself in an easy-to-escape-from hiding spot across the street and watched. An official-looking car passed me and parked down the street from the hostel. A man and a woman got out and went inside. I didn't know if they were cops or social services people or what, but I figured they were there for me.

"Uh-huh. Always trust your vibes," I said quietly to myself. "That son of a bitch sold me down the river. Or is it up the river?"

No, I think you were right the first time. It's "sell you down the river," or "send you up the river."

'Yeah, up the river to jail.'

A few minutes later, Ryan came out, looked around and glanced at his watch.

'Damn, I really liked that guy. This totally sucks. I still can't believe he sold me—tried to turn me in.'

Mike, you're a little kid. Did you really think that an honest, law-abiding reverend/psychologist who runs a youth hostel for teens and no doubt works closely with the cops and city social workers would just take in a little kid, feed him, and give him a bed to sleep in? He's not operating a runaway hideout.

Now I had to either stay hidden or walk away and risk being spotted by Ryan and the cops inside.

Or you could get on that bus that's coming.

'Or I could get on that bus that's coming,' I agreed. I would be hidden from their view as I got on. I still wanted to watch, though. It really seemed unlikely that two cops would come here looking for a runaway kid. I mean, there were probably hundreds of runaway kids out on these streets.

But not as young as you are.

'Yeah, that's what they tell me.'

Sometimes I was amazed that I'd made it as far as I did, I must say. I'd lived like a shadow though, mostly keeping out of the public eye.

I let the bus pass, but only because I could already see another one coming down the hill. I debated what I should do.

That depends on what your intentions are. It's not like you're some poor, lost little waif. Well, that actually does describe you pretty well, but I didn't want you to go on one of your rants. Seriously, you're not going to accept the type of help he's offering, so don't waste the guy's time. Get on the bus, Mike.

I boarded and fumbled through learning how to pay. Three boys got on the bus at one of the stops. They were about twelve and they looked like well-off, all-American kids. One of them was Asian and he was chewing what smelled like Juicy Fruit gum. I could smell it all of the way in the back where I was sitting. As they laughed and carried on, the gum-chewing kid happened to glance back at me and we met eyes. His smile faltered a bit and he quickly averted his eyes. His friends sensed he'd seen something and looked back at me. I wondered what went through their minds as they saw this younger, dirty, obviously homeless kid holding a backpack in his lap.

The kids stole glances at me as they got off at a stop. A few minutes later, I noticed that the area was starting to look run-down and dangerous. I got off of the bus, crossed the street and caught one going in back the way I came. I didn't need to be riding a bus into a bad area for absolutely no reason. Besides, this way I could see from the bus what was going on at the hostel. But I daydreamed and I only noticed that we'd already passed the hostel when the bus began ascending the big hill.

Later on, I went to a pay phone and called the number on the card Ryan had given me.

Probably not a good idea. . .

'Yeah, I know. But I want to find out who those people were and if he really did turn me in. If he didn't and he promises not to, I'll go hang out with the guy.'

"Hullo?" answered a sullen male teenaged voice.

"Can I talk to Ryan?"

"Yeah. Oh, um, may I ask who's calling?" he suddenly remembered to ask with forced politeness.

Alfred E. Newman

"Alfred E. Newman," I said with a smile.

"OK, uh, yeah, OK hold on. . ."

"This is Ryan."

"Did you sell me up the river?"

"I'm sorry?"

"I was going to come by, but you had the cops waiting for me."

"I don't know what . . . Oh, *Mike?*"

"Yeah."

He sighed. "Michael, I'm sorry. It was not an easy decision, believe me."

Until he said that, I wasn't one hundred percent sure that he really had tried to turn me in. I sighed as well. I was sad and angry at the same time.

Don't start going off on the guy. You have a habit of—

'I'm not gonna go off on the guy. Sheesh.'

". . . and an education, and if there are home problems, they'll help you with that as well," Ryan was saying.

"Who will help me?" I asked Ryan.

By the way, it's "sell me down the river," not "up the river."

'Would you please,' I begged my inner voice. Damn it, now that was the *second* time that I missed hearing who those people were.

"Mike, are you listening?" Ryan was asking. "Where are you? Tell you what, I'll come meet you. I promise to come alone."

He'll probably have some of his teenaged thugs hiding in the shadows.

I covered the mouthpiece and laughed quietly. 'Where do you come up with these things?' I pictured brainwashed, zombie-like teenagers coming out of recessed doorways and out from alleys.

Yeah, and out of the sewers with long strands of seaweed-looking stuff hanging off of them.

". . . the kind of stuff that goes on every day. So let me help you." Ryan was saying.

By taking me off of the streets and throwing me in some youth jail with a bunch of hard-core scumbags? I wanted to ask. But I knew Ryan's intentions were good.

". . . and that's just for starters," Ryan concluded. Oh man, I had no idea what he just said. Boy, was I having trouble keeping track of both of these conversations. Why was I so good at it in a face-to-face conversation, but not on the phone?

"Maybe I'll stop by and see you on my way out of town," I said. "I guess I'm. . ."

"Mike, trust me on this, would you?"

"Trust you?" Anger that he'd tried to turn me in so quickly and in such a sneaky way rose up in me before I could control my mouth. "You know something, Mr. Reverend slash Psychologist? I told you—I'm not a *runaway*; I have no family. And I'm not some charity case; I'm a person. I have a life of my own, you know, and it's a great life. Maybe you should take the time to actually *get to know someone* and find out what they're about before you try to get them thrown in jail. Oh yeah, and thanks for the delicious lunch. For some strange reason, I'm still hungry. Running from the cops has that effect on me."

"Michael, I—"

Mike, don't do it. You'll be sorry if you do.

Ignoring my inner voice, I quietly hung up.

"You had your shot at Mike Morrison and you blew it, Ryan," I said.

I massaged my temples with my hand, covering my eyes. "Shit," I whispered as I calmed down and felt guilty for being such a jerk. "I'm sorry, Ryan. You don't deserve to be hurt by some street kid," I said quietly, even though he couldn't hear me.

I told you that calling him was a bad idea.

'Yeah, I know you did. As usual, you were right.'

The least you could have done was to pay attention to what he was saying.

'I *couldn't*, because you kept—*oh*, you aggravate me sometimes!'

Call him back and apologize.

'Nah, screw it. He *did* try to turn me in, but I guess he thought he was doing the right thing.'

Yeah, by sending you up the creek without a paddle, or whatever that gibberish was that you were trying to say on the phone.

I smiled a little and shook my head. 'I still don't know where you come up with them.'

I wandered the streets for a while, fairly content except for the nagging from my inner voice that I'd better find a place to sleep tonight ahead of time before it actually got dark. I wanted to ride one of the cable cars, find that really crooked street and maybe walk across the Golden Gate Bridge—if it even existed back now.

Up ahead of where I was walking, a 1967 Camaro pulled to the curb and a young man with long hair who looked to be in his teens sauntered over to the passenger window, crouched down and discussed something with the driver.

"Wow, look at that! That car isn't a *restored* '67 Camaro; it's a *brand new one*. How cool is that?"

The guy in the car handed the kid something. I couldn't *see* that it was money from the distance that I watched, but I just *knew* that it was. Maybe the kid was selling drugs? The kid looked directly at me and then stood up and came my way as the car pulled away.

"Hey man," said the kid to me.

I nodded.

"I'm Brad. You new around here?" he asked with a southern accent.

"I'm Mike and I'm just passing through," I said, cautiously.

He seemed puzzled and momentarily speechless by my reply.

"You a runaway?" he asked.

I nodded. "I'm from New Jersey."

He did a "wow" whistle. "Well, that guy in the Camaro wants to talk to you."

Could it be Ryan? No, Ryan probably couldn't afford that car and anyway, he'd just pull up next to me. "Why?" I asked the kid.

"He wants you to take a ride with him. You should go, man."

"A ride? Why would I do that?"

He held up his hand and rubbed his fingers together, making a "lots of money" gesture. "He's loaded, man. You could make a fortune off of him, believe me. Besides, if you go talk to him, I get the other half of this," he said, showing me half of a ten-dollar bill the guy had given him. "And that guy's easy. You don't even have to do anything."

'Ah,' I silently said to my inner voice, 'I think I get it.'

You're not seriously considering this, are you?

'I'm not about to start whoring around, if for no other reason than the risk of being arrested or getting some disease.'

Another good reason is: eeeewww!

'That's another good reason.'

Actually, that should have been your first reason. Still, you're a little bit tempted. . .

Well, the street lure was there and the temptation of easy money . . . possibly lots of easy money. But when it came down to actually letting someone put their . . . up my . . . I definitely wasn't into that—even for money.

Yeah, and that's what they are going to want to do.

"So are you going to do it?" the kid asked me. The Camaro had gone around the block and slowly passed us. Now it was pulled to the curb up the block. "That guy gets real nervous."

"No, sorry man, but I'm just not into that scene," I answered as casually as I could so as not to insult the kid in case he *was* into that scene.

"Aw, that's all right. I don't need his ten dollars. He's a fucking chicken hawk anyways," he said and spat.

Chicken hawk?

He walked down the block to the car to tell the guy. The car drove away and the kid came back to me, beaming because the guy had given him the other half of the ten-dollar bill. "You must be good luck for me," he said while lighting a cigarette. "First time he's ever done that."

"What's a chicken hawk?"

"Someone who likes kids. You're 'chicken' out here. Most guys out here want real men. No offense."

I shrugged. "What did he say when you told him I wasn't interested?"

Brad looked around before answering. "Well, don't tell him that I told you, but he said that you didn't look like you were for sale but you look like you can be bought and in a day or two he'll have you for half of what he was going to give you." He lowered his voice, as though afraid that the guy could hear him from his car a mile away. "So if you do decide to do it, ask for double what he offers you. C'mon," Brad said to me as he started walking.

"Where're we going?" I asked as I followed.

"I gotta go home and take a shit."

I waited out in front of a ratty-looking apartment building while Brad went in to do his business. Once he came out and we'd walked a few blocks, Brad diverted most of his attention to the passing traffic.

"Where are you from?" I asked him.

"I'm from Florida. Hey, I gotta go, man. You'd better get off of this street. The cops will think you're hustling and pick you up for sure. You, they'll make a point of picking up anyway 'cause you're so young. I'll see you later, alligator."

A big, expensive-looking car that had slowly cruised past us pulled to the curb about where the Camaro had stopped.

"Oh, this guy's hooked on me. Hey Mike, come around later and we'll do something."

"Yeah, OK."

He walked up to the car, briefly discussed something with the driver and hopped in. The car pulled away into the afternoon sunshine.

'Wow, just like that. This seems like a weird area for this kind of thing. I thought it would be more like a Times Square-type area. This just looks like any other street. How do people know where to go looking for this?'

Maybe the town council zoned this street for prostitution.

I laughed. 'You are such an idiot.'

A few of the drivers that had been circling the block glanced my way, but none showed any real interest.

'Boy, I hope it's because I look too young and not because I'm ugly.'

All right, that's enough of this. Let's go, Mike. Off of this street—now.

I hurried out of that general area and contentedly wandered around a pretty, hilly residential area. Two guys were walking towards me, talking. "Excuse me," I said. "Could you tell me where that really crooked street is?" They completely ignored me. I know that they heard me because they paused in conversation, but resumed talking and continued walking as though I wasn't there. I had to actually get out of their way to keep from getting pushed aside.

"Rich snobs," I muttered as I shrugged and resumed walking.

A few blocks later, I ran into a guy walking his dog. Although he gave me quick directions that I couldn't follow, at least I learned that it was called Lombard Street.

This place was too urban for me. I mean, as cities go it was very nice. But besides city parks, which I wouldn't even consider going into at night, let alone sleeping in, I hadn't seen a single place to hide out in when it got dark. Sometimes I just wished I was back in New Jersey. I missed all of the woods.

I decided that later on, my best bet was to head back down by the waterfront. I knew there would be countless places to hide out down there and there were railroad tracks under the elevated highway so maybe I could hop a freight. Although, the tracks really didn't look like they got much use. Most of the switches off of the tracks led to abandoned, weedy, rusty sidetracks going to piers or warehouses that themselves looked like they were in their twilight years. Earlier, I'd followed the tracks past the touristy area to where they went into a tunnel, but my vibes told me to stay out of there. Sneaking out onto one of the abandoned piers would be a cool place to spend the night. Then I could spend the day in the city tomorrow and decide what to do next.

My mood lightened as I pictured sitting on the end of an abandoned pier with water lapping on the pilings and distant, twinkling lights reflecting on the bay. I also felt better because I had a plan. Not much of a plan, but a plan nonetheless. For now, I figured I should take advantage of the fact that this was a Sunday and I could freely walk around.

I absently wondered how much the guy in the Camaro would have paid me. I probably could've gotten a shower and a free dinner out of the deal as well.

Mike! Let it go.

'I was just curious, that's all. And what did that kid mean by saying that I didn't even have to do anything?'

I'm warning you, Mike, I will shut down on you and you'll have no one *to hang out with. Then you really* will *find out what it's like to be lonely . . .*

'You'll go to your happy place?' I taunted.

You're really pushing your luck today, kiddo.

27

I found Lombard Street and I leaned into the curves as though I was riding a motorcycle as I ran down it. The sidewalk was so steep that it had steps in it. I felt set apart from the tourists. Yet, as often happened, I felt comfortable—even protective—of my outcast, loner status. Some things in your life start out as something bad but can slowly morph into something that you depend on to keep you in your comfort zone.

The word "loner" often has a negative connotation to it, as in: "Neighbors and co-workers of the suspected killer described him as a loner." Keeping to yourself is a self-defense mechanism that develops early in life because of something about you that's very different from the mainstream. After a while, you really don't want to bother trying to fit in. When you're alone, you can just be yourself. But whatever it is that's different about you doesn't automatically have to be something bad.

'You know what's kind of messed up? In my old life, I never got attached to anything or anyone because I always had it in the back of my mind that one day I would leave it all behind and switch out of there. Now I feel the same way about this life.'

Mike, you see all of these people? They'll all be "switching out of here" someday. They could die in fifty years or in fifty seconds. Yet they still have the guts to love, also knowing that their mate could die at any time. And just like you, they all have secrets that they've told no one. So, don't use the switching lives thing as an excuse. Maybe you should start treating your life as a life and not a temporary fling.

For a brief while, I forgot myself and just enjoyed being a tourist without an agenda. No backpack hidden in the weeds that I needed to fetch before darkness made it impossible to find, no freight train to catch, nothing.

As the late afternoon shadows lengthened, I wandered back towards the area of Ryan's youth hostel. I avoided the hostel, but couldn't resist walking into the raunchy part of town. Here I didn't feel too out of place. Or at least I felt like an outcast who blended in with the other outcasts.

Maybe in a runaway street kid sort of way. But believe me, that isn't a safe costume to be wearing to this party.

The area was like New York's Times Square in the old days: peep shows and sex for sale everywhere, religious nuts ranting on corners and so many street type people and outcasts that no one really took notice of me. I found that I could just meet people and talk to them.

A homeless bum that I talked to for a while told me about how he he'd recently been shot, and he showed me an astonishingly deep scar in his huge beer belly. He warned me to be careful because the same thing could easily happen to me. I asked him how it happened and he explained that he'd been in a bar in the wee hours of the morning and some guy he'd fought with had followed him to the streets. As usual, I was unlikely to be in the scenarios that street people were in when they fell victim to violence.

I sat in a coffee shop with someone named Denise that I first thought to be a female hooker but turned out to be a guy dressed as a girl (hooking). He chain-smoked as he passionately related his dream of getting an operation to become the woman that he was inside. I asked him, didn't the customers become outraged when they found out that he was really a guy, no offense? "I just use my mouth, honey," he replied. I wondered if his real name was Dennis and he changed it to Denise. I felt sorry for him. He was such a lost-soul train wreck.

Later on, Denise got into a shouting match with another transvestite—I think over who had the right to stand where they were standing. Afterwards, he said, "That old drag queen thinks she gonna take my spot? Honey, she was old when Elvis was born. C'mon, let's go for a walk." He shot some expletives at the other transvestite and then boasted, "I read that bitch!" I took that to mean that he'd told the other (guy?) off.

We got some ice cream and then Denise went back to "work" after warning me to get out of this area, stay away from the drug dealers and not to go home with any of "these old chicken hawks." No one really bothered me, though. As usual, I sort of slipped below most people's radar. A few guys gave me long glances and one followed me for a little while, I guess to see if I was for rent, but no one tried to just snatch me off the streets or anything crazy like that.

As it got on towards midnight, I noticed a subtle shift in the types of people around. The curious tourists, adventurous college kids and peep-show patrons seemed to be disappearing as the hard-core street people and criminals came on duty. The frequent police patrols were morphing from warning glances to flat-out "jump out of the car and grab the perpetrator" arrests. It was time for me to make myself scarce.

As I headed down towards the piers, I frequently checked over my shoulder and I was aggravated with myself for pushing the limits of common sense and staying out on the streets until I was scared to be here.

Once down by the waterfront and back in my own element, which is to say "at a location and time where no one else would be there," I felt better. I found exactly the type of old pier that I was looking for. I didn't intend on going into the actual building, but along the outside walkway. It was protected by a dilapidated fence that had been bolstered with corrugated metal. I pushed in on a bent corner so that it was just barely big enough for me to slip through but too small for an adult. I again pictured how cool it would be to sleep out on the end of the pier with the water lapping the pilings and the lights reflected on the bay. I took my backpack off to slide it in ahead of me, when the sudden fury of claws scraping and loud barking on the other side—so close that the metal seemed to vibrate from the sound—sent me reeling back so fast that I fell backwards. The dog couldn't get at me through where I'd pushed the metal because for him, it was bent in the wrong direction and I hadn't really bent it very much, thank God.

Seeing as they didn't have sophisticated stuff such as motion detectors back now, I'd become so complacent that I forgot all about the "low tech" security methods. I shivered at the thought of being halfway through and getting hung up on the metal so I wouldn't be able to back out as the dog attacked. That scenario played over and over in my head as I hid under a truck trailer and waited for my heart rate to return to normal.

Through the dog, I'd almost managed to make the most noise in the area. My competition was some guys who were raising an incredible racket as they loaded stuff into a box truck down the street. Two guys would push a stack of boxes along with a hand-pulled pallet jack and slam the load into the truck. Then one would yank out the jack and race across what sounded like a rough steel plate before bouncing down onto the loading dock with the empty jack. It was almost comical how much noise they were making and it was echoing off of the old warehouses and piers. They were yelling and carrying on in some foreign language.

The dog finally stopped barking and the guys in the truck finally left. The temperature rapidly dropped and a fog started seeping in between the buildings. My feet hurt so much and I was so tired that I debated sleeping right there under the truck. I actually did doze off while sitting cross-legged, but a light woke me and I quickly hid between the tires as a cop car slid by. He was shining his spotlight at doorways and warehouses, but I wondered what good it was doing. Even a kid who was asleep as he approached had time to hide on him and watch him. Wouldn't someone breaking into a warehouse just do the same thing?

The cop's taillights faded into the fog as he continued his lonely patrol. I was hungry again and had no food and no chance of getting any until daylight, and even then it would be Monday so I'd have to be careful walking around. A fine drizzle began falling through the fog and I sighed heavily and crawled back under the truck.

'Oh well, no big deal.'

No, no big deal. You abandoned your old life to switch with a kid from a dream one rainy day. Now you're thousands of miles and forty-eight years away from home and wandering around the abandoned warehouse district of a big city in the foggy, wee hours of the morning.

You're damp, tired, cold, hungry, lonely (not that you'd admit it) and your feet are killing you. Your butt is stinging even worse than your feet because you're usually hiding behind something and in a rush to wipe it with whatever's available when you crap outside. The only sleep you've had in the past twenty-four hours was either a nap on a moving freight train or a nap under a truck trailer. You're so worn down, smelly and filthy that you can no longer even go into a store for sneakers.

I shook my wet hair out of my eyes in defiance. The last thing I needed right now was a lashing from my inner voice.

'Yeah, so what's your point? Gonna ask me if it was worth it? Yes, it was fucking worth it, OK?'

For crying out loud, Mike, take ownership of at least one *of your lives. That's the message that I was trying to get across earlier on Lombard Street.*

I leapt out from under the truck trailer and, as I yelled out loud at myself, my high-pitched voice echoed off of the buildings and the overhead highway and caused the dog on the pier to go into a fresh tirade of barking.

"What—like I haven't been trying? I don't know what else to do, man—I really don't. What the hell was I *supposed* to do? Sit under that rainy bridge in New Jersey crying for the rest of my life, waiting for the other me to come back? Sit there and beg God to turn me back into that poor excuse for a man that I was before the switch? And then what? Seriously, *then* what?"

I wheeled around and screamed, "Oh, would you shut the hell *up!*" at the dog before I sat back down under the truck.

Mike, you weren't the total failure that you thought you were as an adult. And no one said you had to run off, live on the streets and ride freight trains around the country in some self-imposed exile.

'I don't care. Even if I knew I'd wind up right here, right now in the condition that I'm in, I'd *still* do it all over again. How's *that* for taking ownership of your life?'

It's your fantasy, kiddo . . .

'Oh, don't turn it around into a "Mike's crazy-obsessed fantasy" thing now! This is real.'

OK, so you take ownership of the fantasy, but still avoid taking ownership of your life. What are you running away from?

'I'm not running *away* from anything. I've never *felt* so grounded.'

This from the boy who just stood on a deserted street and screamed at himself like a crazy person.

'Fuck you.'

What brought you to the bridge in New Jersey?

'Curiosity. Adventure.'

Uh-huh, but what really *motivated you to search all of those years for the bridge?*

I took a deep breath, closed my eyes and whispered, "Escape."

Bingo. So, what are you running away from?

"I don't know," I said quietly as I dug dirt out from under my fingernails in the gloom, "Myself, I guess."

Kiddo, if switching bodies, going back in time forty-eight years and traveling thousands of miles didn't do it, nothing will. Maybe it's time to start changing what you can change and accepting yourself as you are.

I smiled sadly. 'Yeah, just like that. If only it was that easy.'

Mike, do you like yourself the way you are?

'You mean now as a kid, or back when I was an adul—'

Inside, Mike.

'Of course I do,' I retorted shortly. 'I mean—'

Then I did sort of a frowning, ironic smile and said, "Huh, what do you know about that? Yeah, I guess I actually *do* like myself the way I am."

How had I measured my self-worth? By how different I was from other people? The funny part is, I never coveted anything they had, did, or were. I just bashed myself for being different.

You battled your adult side with your kid side in 2015 and now you're doing the opposite in 1967. Stop fighting yourself. Stop running away. The two sides are what make you you.

I smiled and added, "As the psychologists say, 'Embrace your inner adult.'"

Uh, yeah, something like that.

I vowed that tomorrow night, I'd at least find a way to take a shower and sleep in a bed. Then, once I was clean, I'd go shopping for socks, shoes and underwear and maybe by some miracle find a way to make some money.

Not by getting into strangers' cars, right?

'Of course not, my ass is sore enough already.'

That's really gross, Mike.

'Well, *you* brought it up. . .'

Facing myself was always exhausting and, lacking any initiative to search for a better spot, I decided to sleep under the truck.

28

I awoke at first light, as usual. It never did really rain—just very light drizzle and fog. The drizzle had dripped from the sides of the trailer, pooled on the ground and then run under the trailer in thin rivulets. I wrung out the wet areas of my blanket as best I could and stowed it. Then I took a quick look around, scurried out from under the trailer and got moving.

Considering where I'd slept, I felt pretty good. I was often amazed at how good I felt in the morning after sleeping in some really uncomfortable and dirty places.

'I guess being in a kid's body does have its advantages.'

You lived like a kid in your old, adult body with no ill effects. . .

That was true. I'd treated my old adult body like it was a kid and it had put up with it just fine. I'd bicycled, hiked, run, swam, climbed on stuff, jumped off of stuff and exercised ten times as much as most people my age. Actually, I'd lived like a kid who'd switched to a grown-up's body. But of course I had the rights and options of a grown-up whenever I wanted them—the best of both worlds.

See, even your old life doesn't look so bad in daylight.

'Yeah, things always look bleak in the wee hours of the morning when I'm overtired.'

I crept up to where I was going to squeeze through the fence and onto the pier last night and quietly took a piss—just to aggravate the dog by leaving my "mark." I stifled a laugh as I snuck away.

I hope he finds a way through the fence and bites you in the ass.

I laughed out loud as I walked down the street.

Chided by my inner voice for doing so, I walked back through the gay red-light district, hoping to run into Brad. I went to Brad's building and tried to open the lobby door but it was locked. A skinny blond kid that I recognized as a hustler came out of the building. I asked him if he knew a kid named Brad and I described him.

"Who wants to know?" he asked.

"Me," I answered in a nonconfrontational way. "I just want to talk to him, that's all."

"I don't know him," he said unconvincingly.

I tried to catch the lobby door before it latched, but the kid said, "No." He pushed my arm away and let the door close. Then he walked about fifty feet away and stopped.

"Don't stand there, go away."

I really didn't want to hang around here for any length of time anyway, so I went back down by the Fisherman's Wharf area. The fog was clearing and it was warming up some. In a few hours, this area would be teeming with tourists.

I figured it couldn't hurt to try to find an indoor place to sleep tonight. I gave a few seedy hotels a shot—at least the ones where I could actually figure out how to get into and where to ask. No one would rent to me. One guy directed me to Ryan's youth hostel.

I really wanted today to be a good day. I didn't want to just leave here and go back and catch a freight without seeing stuff. I was beginning to feel like I was just traveling for the sake of being in motion. But other than what I'd seen from the trains or wandering around on foot, I'd missed a lot. For instance, I went through Arizona but didn't see the Grand Canyon—stuff like that.

Some long-haired, spaced-out looking young guy with a guitar case was hanging out in front of one of the seedy hotels that weren't really hotels. I asked him if he knew a place that would rent to kids. I didn't expect much of an answer, but he was friendly in a totally stoned sort of way.

"Oh wow, man," he slurred, "you're really young to be out here. No one's gonna rent to you. They got enough problems with hookers bringing people in. Hey, can you spare a few bucks?"

I handed him two bucks.

"Thanks, man."

As I aimlessly meandered around the city, a rack of brochures in a hotel lobby caught my eye. As I perused a brochure that had a picture of the Golden Gate Bridge on the cover and a map inside that showed where all of the cool stuff was, a manager-looking guy noticed me and briskly headed my way with the obvious intention of throwing me out. I took off with the brochure.

I wandered around for at least another hour and wound up in Chinatown. The shops were opening and one had sneakers.

I'd finally gotten fed up with the loose sole on my right sneaker slapping the pavement or curling under when I walked, so I'd cut three-quarters of it off. That exposed the foam rubber insides, which wore through almost immediately. Every time I stepped in even a shallow puddle, my foot got soaked from the bottom up.

The Chinese proprietors of the shoe store, who I took to be husband and wife, watched suspiciously as I picked up a cheap sneaker and held the bottom against the bottom of mine to match up the size. I really wanted to avoid taking my shoes off, but the guy insisted that we measure my foot.

"Nine and a half," he informed me as he got up to go in back and get the sneakers.

Is he telling you your age, or your shoe size?

I smiled. 'Sad thing is, it could be either one.'

As the husband brought the sneakers over, his wife handed him a new pair of socks. He charged me for the sneakers but when I asked how much for the socks, he made a "don't worry about it" gesture. I thanked them as I donned my new footwear. I crammed the old stuff in the box and they threw it away for me.

After I bought a used grey baseball jersey with blue sleeves from a thrift shop, I went into an alley to change. Instead of pulling off the threadbare T-shirt from Virginia Beach, I grabbed the chest and tore. It was harder to tear it around the neck and sleeves, but just for the hell of it I finished the job. I just wished that I wasn't putting all of this new stuff on a filthy body. Now that I looked somewhat human, I figured I'd go to Golden Gate Park and maybe look for Brad along the way.

"Mike-o, where ya been? My little brother told me you were looking for me," Brad said after I finally found him.

"That was your brother? I thought you ran away from Florida?"

"No, *you* ran away. *I* go where I want to, when I want to. Our mom sent my brother here to be with me."

"Oh." I was totally confused. "And you both wound up—" I stopped myself from saying, "out here selling yourselves on the street?"

But Brad caught the drift of what I'd almost said and in mock anger, he said, "Hey, watch that!"

I apologized, although it didn't seem very genuine, seeing as I was laughing.

Brad didn't care though. He laughed along with me.

Just when we'd both gotten serious again and Brad was lighting a cigarette with his Zippo lighter as we walked, my inner voice said, *It's a family business.* I let out that loud snort you make when you're trying to suppress a laugh.

Without even looking at me, Brad roughly shoved me into the side of a building and I dramatically acted as though I'd been knocked out and let myself fall on the sidewalk. He ignored my antics and strolled on, ever the cool dude. I sprang up and, as I raced past him, I put my hand on his shoulder and launched myself into the air.

"Hey, nice new sneaks, man," Brad said after I landed in front of him. "You'd better scruff them up quickly or someone will steal them right off of your feet."

"Even these cheap ones?"

"Hell yeah, they'll steal—" then he broke off and suddenly yelled to someone across the street, "Hey Mark, how was it?"

Mark gave him a huge grin and a "thumbs up."

"I'm going to try to figure out what bus goes to Golden Gate Park. Wanna come?" I asked Brad.

I could see the "When's the last time I did something like that just for the hell of it?" gears turning in his head.

"Sure, man, let's go. I know how to get there. Oh, we gotta make a stop first. Did you see that guy that I went off with yesterday? He's a regular customer and he's like an aide to a—a legislator or something in Sacramento and he'll give me anything I want. You should see the apartment he got me. Wanna see it?"

"Sure."

I followed close on Brad's heels as he strode into a fairly classy apartment building as though he owned the place. A skinny old guy halfway into a maintenance room or something off to the side of the lobby took notice and was about to protest, but Brad silenced him by ignoring him. I, of course, ruined the whole thing by making eye contact with the guy, which gave him an opening to say something.

"Hey there, you two boys, where do you think you're going?"

"Just ignore him," Brad said loudly as he yanked me into the elevator and pushed the button for the ninth floor.

The guy was still bent over a mop bucket, midway through wringing the mop out—the exact position he'd been in when we arrived—as the doors closed.

Before we got out on the ninth floor, I punched all of the buttons, one through twelve, so the elevator would stop on every floor.

"Children," Brad commented and shook his head as I snickered.

"Wow, this is nice," I said as I took in the sixties-style furnishings. The place was bright and airy and really seemed to be the perfect size.

"Hey, check the view," Brad said as he opened the sliding glass door to a balcony. We stood there for a few minutes, lost in our own thoughts as the sounds of the city drifted up.

"Can I take a shower before we go?"

"Yeah, go ahead, man," Brad said, gesturing. Then he flipped on the TV, lit a cigarette and plunked down on the couch.

The bathroom was off of the bedroom, so I did as Brad suggested and just closed the bedroom door so as not to fog the tiny bathroom up so much. I came out a few minutes later, feeling more refreshed than I could describe. I had everything back on except my shoes and socks, and clean carpet on clean bare feet felt like heaven.

"You ready, man?"

"Sure," I said as I sat on the floor to put my shoes and socks on.

"You know, these days they make these things called *couches*."

I smiled. "Guess I've been living outside too long."

"Yeah, I was thinking about you riding freight trains around. How do you do that shit, man? Don't gangs and prison escapees and people like that ride those things? And what happens if you get caught? Or suppose you wind up in the worst part of some fucked-up city?"

"It *is* pretty dangerous," I admitted.

"Yeah, I guess so, man. I'll stick to busses or hitchhiking."

"Leave that thing here," he said as I reached for my backpack. "It makes you look too suspicious."

Back on the first floor, Brad smacked my hand away before I could push all of the buttons again.

We took a very long bus ride. The thing stopped, like, every block. There was a cord along the ceiling that people pulled when they wanted to get off. It rang a bell up by the driver. Brad caught me glancing at it mischievously and warned, "No. . ."

"Is that the park?" I asked Brad after a while.

"Yeah, but we don't want to go to this end. It's all bullshit stuff. We want the cool end of the park."

After we'd gotten off of the bus and were walking in the park, I told Brad about how I was going to "touch off" at the Pacific Ocean.

"We're going to get to walk the bridge, aren't we?"

Brad was looking at me with an amused frown. "What bridge?"

"The Golden Gate," I answered.

'Uh-oh—it does exist back now, doesn't it?' I asked my inner voice in a sudden panic.

It was on the brochure, Mike.

"No man," said Brad. "The Golden Gate Bridge is miles away. Oh, I see," he said, putting two and two together and trying not to laugh at me, "you thought because this was called Golden Gate Park that. . ." He looked at me and laughed. His laugh was infectious and I couldn't help but laugh along with him.

"I think you'll like this place though," Brad said, a little mysteriously.

I suddenly inhaled in surprise. "Is that . . . Is that the—the *Pacific Ocean?*"

We ran down a trail through beautiful plants and trees, all of which were strange and unfamiliar to me. Suddenly we popped out onto a rocky beach. The day had been warmish and sunny, but now it was cloudy, chilly and clammy. Not at all the way I pictured "touching off" at the Pacific Ocean. I pictured some typical California beach at sunset.

"I've gotta go do something," I said thickly.

Brad sat on a boulder, lit up a cigarette and nodded his head towards the water in a "go for it" fashion.

Scenes from the journey flashed through my mind as I headed for the surf. Soaking my foot that first night as I searched for something to keep the boxcar door from closing. Watching the bobbing light of a brakeman's lantern as he switched freight cars in a railroad yard in the wee hours of the morning. Being briefly held captive by the robbers in St. Louis, wondering what their intentions were. Peacefully watching the world go by from the trains—knowing that the danger would begin when we stopped somewhere. Staring in wonder at }the countless stars in a midnight desert sky. Sitting in the park outside of

Washington, D.C. with the low-flying airliners roaring over my head. People helping me out at every turn. Countless memories.

I bent down and touched the water.

My salty tears mixed with the salt water of the ocean. I wanted to extend the moment, but moments like these just can't be extended or repeated, can they?

Well, that's that. Back to the bridge in New Jersey with you, young man. Come on, chop-chop, no time to lose, off you go, on your way, run along.

My inner voice's wisecracks had been so much a part of this journey that even that brought tears to my eyes.

29

We went back to Brad's new crash pad. Actually, he admitted that it was "Mr. X's" place when he was in town. Speaking of "Mr. X," in he walked with his slicked-back black hair and his business suit while we were watching TV. I'd say he was about forty-five years old.

When he saw me, he didn't even say hi to either one of us. Uh-oh.

"Who is this *child*, Bradley?"

"Hi Rob. This is my friend Mike."

"You know I don't like children. I thought we agreed that we weren't going to have your street friends over? Didn't we agree on that, Bradley?"

Brad gave me a "don't worry about it" wink and got up and, with one look, made Rob melt with—well, I was going to say emotion, but I guess it would really be lust or infatuation. Whatever it was, he sweet-talked Rob into letting me spend the night on the couch.

"Well he can't stay here while we go eat and he's not invited," Rob stated, referring to me as though I wasn't in the room. "I would very much like to spend the evening with you alone, Bradley."

But Brad talked him into letting me stay there while they ate.

"I'm going to go get cleaned up," Rob said. And then, still without looking at me at all, he said, "Michael, if that really is your name, I would suggest that if you are going to eat tonight, you run out now and get yourself something because once we leave you won't be allowed back in. They lock the lobby at night. Bradley, I'm trusting you on this." He closed the bedroom door behind himself.

"Hey Brad, maybe I should just—"

"No!" Brad said while grabbing my arm. "You're my friend and I take care of my friends. He's just an asshole, throwing a little kid out on the streets. Go on, hurry up—and bring me back a Coke. Don't worry about ol' Rob," he said as he grabbed his crotch and smiled. "I have exactly what he needs."

I went and got Chinese food and a few Cokes and ran back. I got off of the elevator and knocked on a door that I hoped was the correct one. elderly lady carrying a little, white poodle came out of an apartment down the hall and headed towards me.

"Hello, young man," she greeted. "Waiting for your tip?"

I was baffled by the question.

Chinese food? Delivery boy? Do I have to spell it out for you?

'Oh yeah, good thinking.'

"Well," I replied, "I'm hoping they answer the door before their food gets cold."

"Oh, dear." She smiled and shuffled around the corner to the elevators.

I smiled as well. I'd pushed every button again.

Rob yanked open the door, stuck his head out and looked side to side. "Who were you talking to?"

"The old lady down the hall."

"Oh, for Pete's sake. Bradley!"

"She just thought that I was delivering Chinese food," I whined.

He calmed down with that information. "Why would she think that? Usually the people delivering Chinese food are Chinese."

"She started talking to me and she just assumed that's what I was doing, so I embellished on it."

His eyebrows shot up. "*Embellished* on it, huh?"

I shrugged. "Well, I didn't want her to think I was here—I mean—"

Shut up, Mike.

Rob caught the implication of what I'd almost said and he turned cold and unfriendly again.

"In or out?"

"In," I said quietly.

"Then get in and stay in. Do not go out in the hallway. Do not even open this fucking door. Can you understand that?"

Brad was coming out of the bathroom to protest, but I gave him a desperate, wide-eyed "please don't" look and he stayed put.

"Yes, sir," I said submissively to Rob.

"OK then, you're not such a bad kid, are you," Rob said as he ruffled my hair. Then he subconsciously rubbed his hand clean on his pants.

'Jeez,' I thought. 'I just washed it four hours ago. It can't be oily already.'

"Are you ready, Bradley?" Rob asked before striding out.

As Brad passed me on his way out, he made a fist and out of the corner of his mouth he quietly said "If he calls me *Bradley* one more time. . ."

We both smiled.

I should have just told Rob that I didn't see anyone in the hallway. The old adult me would have just lied to keep the peace. This kid me was too . . . I don't want to say 'stupid' but . . . too *something* to think of lying to a grown-up so quickly.

I sat out on the balcony for hours, just watching the night fall and the city lights come on.

Brad and Rob got home around midnight, I would say. I was on the couch under a blanket that Brad had commandeered from Rob's linen closet. I was awake, but I pretended to be asleep. Rob and Brad were joking around and sort of sexually playing around while they were taking off their clothing.

Brad quietly said, "Hey," and although I couldn't see, I sensed that he nodded toward my fake-sleeping form on the sofa. They said no more, but thankfully they went into the bedroom and closed the door. Shortly thereafter, I drifted off.

I think I was the first one awake, but after a few minutes I heard someone stirring in the bedroom. Rob rubbed his head as he stumbled out in a bathrobe and picked up his clothes, which were scattered about on the floor.

"I know you're awake," he said. "Did you touch my wallet?"

"No, of course not," I replied through a yawn as I sat up. I had my baseball jersey on, but had taken my pants off for the luxury of only sleeping in underwear. Now I was too shy to put my pants on. I sat with the blanket covering the lower portion of my body and watched Rob open his wallet to confirm the money was still in there.

"Huh," he grunted. And then, "Where's my watch?" He rushed into the bedroom and bathroom and came back out and stalked quickly over to me before I even had time to react. He yanked the blanket off and grabbed me by the front of my shirt.

"Where's my watch, you little tramp. If you took it and pawned it, I swear to God I'll—"

"No, I swear I didn't!" Suddenly, I remembered where I'd seen it last night. "It's over by the kitchen sink! You left it there last night before you went out."

He tossed me onto the couch and stepped into the kitchen.

Holding the watch, he looked up at the ceiling and sighed. "You're right. I went to look at the time last night and didn't have it on."

"Check my pockets, check my backpack if you want. I wouldn't steal anything from you. Especially after you were nice enough to let me stay here. Besides, I hate thieves."

I think that for the first time since meeting me, Rob thought of me as a real person. His expression softened as he seemed to realize how harmless and vulnerable I was, sitting there in my underwear, trying to wrestle my pants on while defending myself. I neatly folded his blanket and laid it on the arm of the couch.

"I'm sorry, kid. Maybe we had a little too much to drink last night. Do you need to go to the bathroom before I shower?"

"Yes, please. Then I'll get out of here."

He made a "don't worry about it" hand gesture. "Bradley and I will be going to Sacramento for a while, so you should really wait for your friend to wake up so you can say goodbye."

I went to the bathroom and did my morning stuff. Brad was still asleep in the bed.

Rob changed into his clothes and then went to the kitchenette and poured orange juice and made toast. I felt extremely uncomfortable as I perched on the edge of the couch. I wanted to take off, but Rob had said to wait.

"Here, Michael, I poured you some juice."

I sat on one of the high chairs that were at the dividing counter between the living room and the kitchenette.

"Mm," said Rob with a full mouth, indicating the toast. "Eat. Jam and jelly here, butter's in the fridge."

I wanted butter, but I was too shy to just open the guy's refrigerator.

"Don't you want something on it?" Rob asked after I bit into it dry.

"I don't like jam or jelly."

"Who doesn't like jam or jelly? Do you like butter?"

I nodded yes.

He dramatically gestured towards the refrigerator.

I buttered a slice and ate. He gave me another slice and I made that one disappear as well.

"So what's your story, Michael? Ran away from home, parents threw you out, orphan, what?"

"I don't know. I just wound up out here I guess. I don't mean this to sound like I'm feeling sorry for myself or anything, but no one's looking for me, no one cares."

He shook his head in sympathy. "That's got to be tough, especially at your age."

"I never really did fit in anywhere anyway, so. . ." I shrugged. "Traveling the country has been . . . good for me, I think."

"Where did you. . ."

"Originate from?" I asked with a smile.

"For lack of a better phrase, yes."

"New Jersey."

"Really? I grew up in Hackensack."

I smiled to myself. Many years ago, after looking at a road map, I convinced myself that the location where we switched lives was in Hackensack where a few city streets crossed the Susquehanna Railroad on overhead bridges. Truth be told, I knew that the adjacent highway was missing. But I was in the height of my obsessive search (1980s). I didn't have a car then, so I talked my friend Howard into driving me there so I could check it out. It was a dud.

"How do you make money for food?" he asked.

"A guy hired me for painting, I worked at a gas station, stuff like that. But to tell you the truth, mostly I rely on the kindness of strangers."

His eyebrows shot up in a "really?" fashion. "You're the kid who was with Bradley the last time I picked him up, aren't you?"

I nodded.

"You weren't . . . ?" he frowned.

I smiled and shook my head no.

"I wouldn't have thought so—especially now that I've gotten to know you."

"By the way, Brad hates to be called Bradley."

"Does he?"

I nodded.

"But 'Bradley' is such a nice name," he said wistfully.

I held up my hands in a "what can I tell you?" gesture.

"Bradl—Brad's a good kid. Well, he's not actually a kid."

"How old is he?" I asked.

"Twenty-two."

"Twenty-two! I thought he was about sixteen, maybe seventeen."

"Now Michael, I'm not a cradle-robber. Give me a little credit. He does look young for his age, though. I almost didn't pick him up the first time because of that. Speak of the devil, look—it's awake!"

"Peace," said Brad thickly as he sat on the couch. He looked like he was hung over from last night.

"Michael and I were just talking about you, Brad."

Brad shot me a look because Rob had called him "Brad" but I looked innocently away.

"Don't be alarmed, my friend. It was all good stuff," Rob told him as he walked over and massaged his shoulders. Brad rocked his head slowly back and forth, enjoying the massage.

"All right, we have to get ready to go to Sacramento. I have a one o'clock meeting."

"I'm all set," Brad said.

Rob glanced my way.

"Well," I said, taking my cue, "It was nice meeting you, Rob. Thank you so much for letting me stay here last night."

"Michael, it has been my pleasure. You are welcome here any time I'm in town. We'll be in Sacramento for a few weeks, but may sneak back into 'Frisco now and then."

Brad was glaring at me with a "What the hell did you do to turn this guy into such a sweetheart?" look, but I ignored it.

"Come on, Mike, I'll walk you to the elevator," Brad said.

"Rob really likes you," Brad said as we walked down the hall. "There aren't many people that he likes."

We waited there in silence a few moments at the elevator. The elevator doors opened and I got on.

"Well. . ."

"Yeah."

"Hey, it's been really nice hanging ou—around with you, Brad."

"Yeah, man. See you around?"

I averted my eyes. "I, ah . . . I don't know where I'll be when you get back." I looked up and we briefly met eyes.

"Yeah, 'Mike the Wanderer.' Well, you know where to find me. Peace."

"Peace," I said as the elevator doors closed.

30

According to my brochure, Golden Gate Park was nowhere near the Golden Gate Bridge. Had I bothered to give the enclosed map more than a passing glance, I would have seen that the other day.

The bridge didn't look to me as though it was in a location where someone who wasn't going there on a bus tour or in a car could get to. Anyway, I had to admit that it wouldn't be as much fun alone as it would have been with Brad.

What's this? "Mike the Loner" doesn't want to go somewhere alone?

I shrugged.

I think you have a little crush on him.

'I don't have a crush on him, asshole! I just like him, that's all.'

Hmmmm…

'You know, you're an instigator. You tell me to get my act together and then you throw little things out there to undermine my self-confidence.'

Michael, Michael, it's not unusual for a young boy to—

'Shut up! You're such a jerk! Is there any aspect of my—my being that you don't dissect and criticize?'

Nobody's criticizing you. Only you know how you feel abou—

'Just shut up, okay?'

Did I have a "little crush on him?" I suppose, but not in a sexual way. I think this would be impossible for a grown-up, but in a "young boy worships and wants to emulate older boy" way, I guess I felt something for him. A ratty-looking white utility van broke up my inner battle when it pulled up alongside me.

A stranger in a van is a classic, picture-book threat to a kid alone, so I tensed to run in the opposite direction than he was traveling.

The white, middle-aged heavyset driver asked what I was doing, making it sound more like a statement than a question.

"Um. . ."

"You're a runaway," stated/questioned the man in his odd way.

"I'm . . . I don't know what I am."

"Huh. You looked like you just lost your last friend in the world. You wanna make some money?"

"Doing what?"

"I'm restoring a house. What do you know how to do?"

"Well, I can spackle, paint, do tile work if I have the right tools, stuff like that."

He pulled his head back and gave me a skeptical frown.

"I worked maintenance in a hotel once," I explained.

Mike, the only "once" you would have had at your age now would have been as a kindergartener.

'Whatever,' I silently answered, 'I don't even care anymore. This guy's probably a whacko anyways.'

"You worked maintenance in a hotel?" the guy asked, perplexed. "How old *are* you?"

"A hell of a lot older than I look," I mumbled, mostly to myself.

The guy's eyebrows shot up as he gave his head a shake.

"You're not crazy, are you?" he asked as his hand drifted up to the shift lever, ready to put the van in drive.

"A crazy person would answer 'no'. But yeah, I'm sort of crazy—in a nice way."

He smiled for the first time. "I'm Ned."

"Mike. Nice to meet you."

"Yeah. You interested?"

Getting into this van could be the last thing you ever do.

'No, pleading for my life would probably be the last thing. . .'

I did some quick calculating. I desperately needed not only some money, but some off-the-street time where I was occupied. Aside from the "boy gets killed by the serial killer" movie-script setup, the guy himself didn't give me bad vibes. I figured if his intentions were bad, he would have been OK with anything I said and talked me into getting into the van. As it was, he was wary of me and ready to drive off.

Unless it's because you're just too flat-out ugly to bother abducting.

I hid my smile from the guy as I got into the van while silently saying, 'The hits just keep on coming,' to my inner voice.

Just to keep the horror movie theme complete, our destination was a partially boarded-up house in a mediocre neighborhood. He parked the van and said, "This was my mom's house, but she passed away," as he unlocked the door.

"I'm sorry."

He shrugged. "It was a few years ago. Come on, I'll show you around."

"Did you grow up in this house?" I asked.

He shook his head but didn't explain.

'If this body got killed,' I wondered as we entered, 'would I just pop back into 2015, or …?'

He briefed me on his intentions for cleaning up and repairing the house. He said he'd pay me seventy-five cents an hour, but I asked for a dollar.

"Seventy-five cents an hour for a few days. Then, if you threaten to strike but I feel that you're worth keeping, we'll talk."

"Um, the only thing is that I have no place to live. . ."

"Well, I really don't want you staying here. I can't have the neighbors seeing some strange kid coming and going from this house during the week. And you're sure as hell not staying with me and my dogs out in Marin County. No offense."

"No. When are you going to start working here?"

"Oh, I only have time to do it on the weekends. I work for the water company during the week. The only reason I'm in the city at all right now is because I have the day off so I can plan how I'm going to tackle this. I keep putting it off, but houses have a way of deteriorating when they sit empty."

"What day is today?" I asked him.

"Tuesday."

Damn. This was a perfect opportunity to make some money and have somewhere safe and dry to sleep if he would just let me stay here.

"I don't know," I said. "I want the work, but I have nowhere to live. I wouldn't even have any way of cleaning up at the end of the day."

"Well, the water will be turned on by then. Aren't there youth shelters or something for you kids?"

"I'm too young. All they want to do is turn me over to the cops."

"You can't get a room in a cheap hotel?"

I shook my head. "Too young."

"You *are* really young," he commented as though noticing it for the first time. "What'll the cops do? Send you home? Is that so bad?"

"I don't have a family or a home. I don't know what they'd do."

We stood there in silence.

"Could you just drop me back off?" I asked Ned. "I don't know where I am or how to walk out of this neighborhood or if it's safe."

"Yeah. I thought I'd be helping you out by offering, but you're in kind of deep. And it seems as though you—yeah, let's go."

He brought me back to the area where he picked me up.

"Here," he said as he wrote down his phone number. "If you change your mind, call me."

"Oh, it's not a matter of changing my mind—I want the job. I just need to find somewhere to stay, that's all."

"Well, good luck, kid," he said as he put the van in drive. "Call me if you change your mind."

I rolled my eyes as he drove off. 'I already *told* him that it's not a matter of changing my mind. People just don't understand. Oh, son of a bitch! Oh, man, *double* son of a bitch!'

Yes, there were two reasons to get upset. One was that there was a cop car sitting across the intersection from where I was walking, and it was in the middle of the day on a school day and I was the only one out here walking at the moment. It was too late to do anything about it but keep walking because I was already in his field of vision. There was not one single store or lobby or anything to just duck into and get off of the street. The second problem (which actually made the first one a little less of a threat, I suppose) was that my backpack was still in Ned's van. At least I wouldn't look as suspicious to the cop.

'Damn it—why the hell did I have that guy drop me here anyway? It's not like I live around here. Man, I am such a total fuck-up.'

Calm down, Michael. Just calm down.

'I can't. But I have to *look* calm walking past the cop, don't I? Oh yeah, of course I do.' I screwed my face up and, in an exaggeratedly sarcastic voice, uttered, "Because Mike's too *young* to be walking around on his own!"

I was really getting myself worked up at this point; 'Mike's too young to do anything! All right, you know what? I'm not even going to bother to run. I'm at the point where—'

MICHAEL! It's not even a cop car any more. Look at it. It's an old cop car that someone bought at auction. And it's empty. Calm. Down.

I'd been sneaking quick peeks at it out of the corner of my eye and now I could see that there was no one in it. I looked right at it and it was obviously not still an active cop car.

I cooled down and worked myself back up in one paragraph.

'Whew. OK. The backpack is no big deal. I mean, it was falling apart anyway. And there's nothing in there that's really important. You know what? I don't even care, man. Whatever. I'll blow the rest of my money on a new backpack, new blanket, new sweatshirt, because God forbid I should be able to find work and some place indoors to sleep tonight.'

The backpack *had* been falling apart. The shock to the shoulder straps from jumping out of boxcars had ripped one of them off where it attached at the bottom. I didn't have any way to sew it back on, so I did a "field repair" by cutting a small hole in the backpack with my scissors, inserting the end of the strap through the hole and tying it to a stick inside the backpack. The stick was too big to pass back through the hole, so it held. When the second strap broke loose, I loosened the strap adjustments, made another hole and tied the ends together inside the backpack.

Now I had less than when I started this adventure. It seemed that my good luck was running out.

Oh, would you stop with the drama already? Call Ned later and he'll come back with your stupid, piece of junk backpack—that you got for free, I might add.

"I'm just gonna go steal clothes and a blanket off of someone's clothesline, that's what I'm gonna do," I said in a snotty voice. "I'm not going to blow the rest of my money on—"

Ned rolled up in his van. I met eyes with him and nodded thanks as I opened the door and grabbed my backpack.

"Call me," he said.

I nodded and watched him drive off again.

Yeah Mike, call him if you change your mind.

I did a half-laugh, half-cry. 'You never pass up a chance to push my buttons, do you?'

Well, someone *has to keep you levelheaded. Most of the things that you freak out over are disaster scenarios that you make up in your own mind.*

I was embarrassed by my inability to control my emotions. I'd just gone from adult-style disappointment to a little kid tantrum to adult-style reasoning to little kid manic humor all in the space of five minutes.

Hey, Mr. Negative.

I rolled my eyes and sighed. 'What.'

Remember your vow under the truck trailer the night before last?

I figured my inner voice was going to hold me to some self-improvement pledge I made under duress in the wee hours, so I answered sarcastically, 'No. Refresh my memory.'

You vowed you'd get a shower and sleep in a bed last night.

My eyes widened and I smiled in wonder. 'Wow, that's right!' Once again, I'd wished for something I really needed and it happened.

Then I laughed and taunted, 'Yeah, but it wasn't a bed; it was a couch.'

Oh, you ungrateful little vermin!

I figured it was time to shake the dust of San Francisco off of my heels and move on. Yet I really hated the thought of leaving in defeat, like a dog with his tail tucked between his legs.

Right, you wouldn't want to set a precedent. I mean, it's not like you've ever been run out of Sacramento by a sheriff or chased out of Barstow by a thirteen-year-old.

'Yeah, but this would be admitting personal defeat, and it really *would* be setting a precedent. What comes next? Using my situation as a crutch to just be lazy and make no effort?'

Haven't you been doing that all along?

I tried to think of a comeback, but couldn't.

:31

"No," replied Ryan's tinny voice through the pay phone where I'd waited on hold for about five minutes. "One *can* get a work release as a kid to have a job, but one would have to go through the proper procedures to do it. For instance, it couldn't interfere with school. But you're too young to register for that program in the first place. And then there is the matter of parental permission. You claim to have no family or adult supervision. But I don't know how that could be possible because you won't open up to me. I'm not trying to lecture you or discourage you from seeking my help, but you have to go through the proper channels. Mike, I—please don't hang up on me again, but I really need to be frank with you here."

"I won't hang up. I told you—I'm sorry I did that. Besides, it cost me ninety cents in dimes just getting you on the phone again."

"I spend almost every waking hour here, so I don't know how you managed to call every time I stepped out for a few minutes."

"I was beginning to think you were avoiding me."

Ryan ignored my comment and continued. "Anyway, this would all be a 'step' process. Step one would be—and I'm not implying that you are some type of criminal or outlaw here, so please don't get all upset—but step one would be for you to turn yourself in. I would strongly urge you to do this through me."

"But. . ." I interjected.

"Just hear me out, OK? You promised to listen and not get distracted."

"Yes, I *am* listening to you. It's just that—"

"Mike, you asked for my advice and I'm giving it to you, but you have be open-minded and pay attention for a few minutes."

I sighed. "OK, go on."

Ryan said nothing. I pumped another nickel into the pay phone before the operator had the chance to obnoxiously break in and ask for more money. It made little clicking noises as the nickel passed through.

"Hello?" said Ryan flatly, thinking that I'd hung up on him again.

"No, that was just me, putting another nickel in the phone."

"Oh, OK. The reason that I didn't continue was your tone of voice. I don't think you have any intention of—hold on, Mike." I could hear mumbling as Ryan covered the phone to discuss something with someone.

Meanwhile, a businessman who'd shown up outside of the phone booth paced back and forth impatiently as he waited for me to finish.

When Ryan came back on the line, I said, "Ryan, please don't get mad at me. I wasn't saying it sarcastically—it's just that I can't turn myself in. You don't know the situation that I'm in."

"No, I don't and until you decide to open up and tell me, I can't really help you. You have to meet me halfway here. You can't just write your own rules, Mike. I don't even know where you *got* that crazy idea. You present a unique case because you are an extremely grown-up and intelligent young man, yet you expect to be able to play the system as though no one else has any intelligence. Now I realize that you have used this to your advantage as a survival mechanism. Don't quote me on this, but I applaud you for it. But you're not as old and wise as you seem to think you are, so please don't try to play me as an idiot."

"No, I'm really not. I called *you*, remember?"

More mumbling as he talked to someone else in the room with him. "Mike, you can call me any time, and if I'm not too busy I'll be glad to help you. But I have many kids that I help, and the first step in the process is to get to the root of the problem. Now I'll be glad to guide you through the *process*, but as I said, you would have to meet me halfway. Listen, I have to go. I have other pressing issues here that I must attend to. You have my number. I assume you have a few more dimes left. When you are *really* ready for help, give me a call, OK?"

"OK, Ryan. Thanks for your time. God bless you."

"God bless you too, Mike. Be careful out there."

"I will. Bye."

Ryan was already discussing something with someone else in the room before his phone hung up.

You had your shot at Ryan the "reverend slash psychologist" and you blew it.

'Yeah, yeah, yeah. Well, I didn't actually blow it, it's just that I can't tell him my story.'

Once again, you pushed someone who was trying to get close to you away. And as usual, you're blaming the outcome on something else. By not showing up for lunch, you made him look like an idiot in front of whoever he'd called to help you that day. Then you insulted him and hung up on him. Now you just wasted his time, acting as though he's not trustworthy. What're you going to do next, burn his hostel down? You blew it. Mike, you can't blast "don't even try *to get close to me" vibes at everyone you meet and then be disappointed by their reactions.*

I did a "what can you do?" gesture. 'Oh well, nothing gained, nothing lost.'

Actually, ninety-five cents lost.

I waved that off with my hand. 'I'm going broke anyway, so what's another ninety-five cents?'

What the hell was I thinking, calling Ryan and asking him to help me get a job. Even if measured by the limits of my ten-year-old brain, it was an embarrassingly dumb thing to do. Ryan and my inner voice had essentially both told me the same thing; I was trying to write my own rules and have the best of both worlds.

"You know," I said quietly, "if I didn't know any better, or I guess I *should* say that if I believed that everyone's life had some grand purpose to it, then I'd say that the only reason I was successful in this switching thing at the bridge in New Jersey was to teach me a lesson."

When the guy outside noticed that I was no longer on the phone, he rapped his knuckles on the glass. I debated pretending to make another phone call so I could stay safe and secure in here a little longer, but I decided not to push my luck. I pushed open the folding glass doors of the phone booth and let him pass. I countered his stern glance with my most charming smile and he angrily turned away and slammed the phone booth door shut. I watched people on the street, all of whom seemed to have somewhere to go and something to do.

So, have *you learned anything from this?*

'Yeah, but probably not the right thing. I learned to always believe in yourself and to follow your dreams, no matter what happens.'

Even if those dreams aren't really the best course of action to take?

I smiled and answered, 'You never know until you try.'

I caught my reflection in a window. Even after all of this time in 1967 and even as adjusted to being a kid as I was, I was always surprised by how very young and little I was.

'Besides, as I've said, it's a little late to worry about that *now*, isn't it?'

It was indeed a little late to worry about whether or not I should have dabbled

in reality. If I applied my inner voice's convoluted logic to explain the situation—
some complicated bullshit about how I'd made this "me" up and it was inevitable
that I'd step into the dream, or Saturn was aligned with Venus or who the hell
knows what-all—then I'd had no choice but to drive to the bridge and switch to
"this me" anyway. I couldn't even keep track of all of the whys and hows of this
life-switching crap any more. At this point, I didn't even care enough to try.

I reflected on how exciting, how new and fresh the concept of switching lives
with another "me" at the bridge had been before I actually did it. The tiny, clear,
clean light of a long-lost dream somewhere deep in the recesses of my mind
had sustained me through everything from the mundane routine of a stable life
to depression so deep that only the knowledge that I could pull the plug on the
whole situation and kill myself any time I wanted to was what kept me from a
total breakdown.

I came close to ending it a few times. But my incessant inner voice kept stress-
ing that I'd have nothing to lose by at least finding the bridge and seeing if the
dream was real before dying. It's strange that when I finally did find the bridge, I
was in a more stable, content frame of mind.

'Oh, if only I hadn't wasted all of those years. If only I'd tried to switch sooner.'

I wandered down the street, a poor, homeless, run-down, shaggy-haired, lost
little boy in a big city. No identity, thousands of miles and forty-eight years away
from home.

"I never should have come to California," I bitched to the seals that were
lounging at Fisherman's Wharf.

It wasn't California's fault, though; it was mine. This trip—indeed, this whole
adventure—was, in a way that's difficult to explain, "done." I wasn't committed
to living a genuine kid's life and that was really what was needed if I was going to stay here in this body and 1967. I couldn't even say that I was committed
to anything, because trying to reason things out in a not-fully-developed child's
brain created constant conflict. This kid brain could absorb seemingly unlimited
information and process it in supersonic speed, yet emotions and external stimuli
played a much bigger role in my decision-making processes than they do for a
grown-up. My adult decisions were boring to a kid and my kid decisions seemed
reckless to an adult. It's no wonder I had so many meltdowns.

And although ten-years-old feels timeless when you originally *are* ten, step into it from an adult's perspective and that age seems as just a snapshot in a body that's rapidly transforming. Sure, adults change constantly as well; they gain a few extra stubborn pounds, get the first and then a few more grey hairs, a few more wrinkles, a little less energy. But in five years, an adult is still basically the same person. For kids, the rate of change is so rapid that it's almost as though you'd expect them to be blurry in pictures, as though they're racing along at ten times the speed of a grown-up. In a very real sense, they are. This body I was in should be maturing, but I was never quite sure if it was or it wasn't and it existed independent of time, or what.

It occurred to me for the first time that we humans, as sentient, living creatures, actually *need* change in our bodies and lives. That the slow wind-down towards old age and death is something that—although we fight it tooth and nail—is essential to our mental well-being. Who would have ever believed *that*?

I drew in a deep breath and sighed. "I never thought I'd say this, but . . . maybe it's time to go home."

I'm not saying a word.

I arrived in the Los Angeles area via a railroad yard in a town which was apparently named City of Industry. From there, I caught a local bus into L.A. I didn't care for L.A., but I was amazed at how the downtown was a real "big city downtown" back now. There were stores and shoppers and hotels and just lots of people out walking around.

I passed a highway interchange while wandering around, and I struck up a conversation with an AWOL (Absent Without Official Leave) marine named Jeremy. He was hitchhiking, but he was worried that he'd get caught, dragged back to the marine base and severely punished. He didn't like being exposed out there on the ramp, so I told him about how I hop freight trains and that I was heading back to New Jersey. He decided that my idea was a better option and came with me.

At my insistence, we waited for nightfall before sneaking into the rail yard. It was in a very high-crime area and the security was stricter than what I was used to. We entered via an industrial street that dead-ended at the tracks. As we were walking between a warehouse and the tracks, an inbound train approached on the track closest to us. We hid from the bright engine headlight behind some small, mostly dead evergreen trees that were planted along the edge of a humming, fenced-in electrical substation. After the engines passed us, we stood back out in the open.

Much to our surprise, there were cops with flashlights on an empty auto rack on the slowly moving inbound train. The cops spotlighted us as they rolled past and they yelled, "Get out of the yards!" Jeremy thought we'd just walk back to the dead-end street.

"No, they've already radioed someone and if we go back that way, we'll get arrested before we make it to the end of the block," I told him.

"How do you know?" he asked.

"Because I've been doing this stuff a long time," I answered as I scrutinized the area for the best escape. "Just trust me on this."

"Well, I'm staying put right here," he declared, indicating our hiding spot behind the bushes.

I knew that seconds counted here. "Jeremy, that's the first place they'll look." 'And you were a marine?' I wanted to add, but didn't.

"Well you said we couldn't walk down the street, so. . ."

"I know, I know, I know what I said. OK, here's what we're gonna. . ."

The sound of a canvas backpack scraping and small branches snapping cut me short as Jeremy squeezed himself and his duffel bag between the evergreens and the fence.

"Jeremy, I don't even have a flashlight and I can see you."

I waited a few precious seconds.

"You coming with me or not?"

He didn't answer, so I left him there. I hopped over the moving train that the cops had been on and ran back towards the dead-end street to see what was happening.

I had some steadfast rules while living on the road: one was to escape immediately when trouble arose instead of hoping that it would turn out OK. Another was to avoid running so far away that you lose track of what your pursuers are doing.

Exactly what I said was going to happen, happened: empty cop car at the end of the dead-end street and an AWOL marine getting arrested behind the warehouse. I always felt guilty about that.

That was enough of L.A. for me and I caught a bus back to City of Industry and hopped an eastbound train.

'Do me a favor,' I addressed my inner voice. 'If I ever mention coming back to California, make me smack myself in the head!'

I didn't know if "time" wanted me home or not, but it sure wasn't making things easy. Here are just a few examples:

I got on an eastbound train in Pueblo, Colorado at sunrise, rode all day in a boxcar and arrived in Kansas City at what I naturally assumed was dusk on the same day. But as I walked into town, the activity seemed more like *morning* activity. I asked someone the time and he said it was seven o'clock.

"Um . . . a.m. or p.m.?"

"A.m.," he answered doubtfully, as though trying to discern if I was crazy or a smart-ass.

How could I have been in the same boxcar for over twenty-four hours and not noticed? Didn't I even get out to go to the bathroom?

I wandered around Kansas City for the day, doing whatever it was that I did to kill time. In late afternoon I decided to see if a crappy old hotel would rent to me. It had been a while since I'd even tried to rent a room, so I wasn't real optimistic. Much to my surprise, the friendly, jocular old man behind the desk rented me a room.

This guy was a piece of work. He looked like an old prospector who'd just come down from the hills. I half-expected to glance out front and see his pack mule hitched to a streetlight pole. He handed me a hotel registration card and a pen and pointed to the spot where you were supposed to write in your auto information. He waited a few seconds and then smiled squinty-eyed at the blank expression on my face. He was obviously amused by this road-weary, dirty kid who walked in like any tired adult traveler and asked for a room.

The room itself was a classic boarding house room that would have made a great black and white poster-sized photo. A tired, sagging bed was complemented by a chair that looked like someone had garbage-picked it and dragged it up here. A bare light bulb hung from wires in the ceiling that came from an ornate ring where there obviously had once been a nice light fixture. There was a sink in the corner, complete with working faucets and a mirror. The sink smelled as though it was regularly used as a urinal (I confess, I used it as one as well). Opposite the door was a shade and a curtain-less, floor-to-ceiling window.

I wanted some privacy, so I took the top sheet off of the bed to hang it over the window. Although the curtain rod was missing, the brackets were still there. After dragging the chair under the window and climbing all of the way atop the back, I still couldn't reach. While making the attempt, I noticed that there were already holes in the sheet where someone else had once rammed it over the brackets.

You'd think they would have just slit the sheet down the middle and left it up there. It would perfectly complement the rest of the décor.

I laughed as I tossed the sheet onto the bed and headed down the hall to the communal bathroom to take a shower. Before venturing into the shower stall, I bent in for a closer look. Like a forensics expert looking for DNA evidence, I studied the slimy, blackened floor in horrified fascination.

"I'm gonna need some forceps over here," I said and laughed.

For what, harvesting the mushrooms?

"Ewwww!"

That one did it, and I passed on using the shower.

Just then, someone tried the bathroom door that I'd latched behind me. I gathered my stuff and let in a very stern-looking, bearded man. He ignored my hello—quite possibly because he'd heard me in there talking to myself and laughing.

I returned to my room, lay on the bed fully clothed and closed my eyes.

I awoke at dusk, so I assumed that I'd only slept a few hours. I was famished, so I headed out for something to eat.

As I was passing the front desk, the friendly old guy said, "Hey kid, are you going to pay for tonight?"

I thought he was just messing with me, so I smiled, waved and kept going.

"Hey," he said and held out his hand for money.

I cocked my head and frowned in confusion. "Didn't I just pay you a couple of hours ago?"

"That was last night."

"*Last* night? No, it was . . . What time is it?"

"Six thirty."

"A.m. or p.m.?"

"P.m. Son, you done slept twenty-four hours! I didn't want to bother you because you looked like you were really wiped out."

So now I'd somehow managed to lose two days out of the past—what—four? Or maybe a week or a month had passed. I was losing all concept of time and it wouldn't have surprised me to step from the hotel into a foot of snow. Maybe I had a bad fever or something? Was there such a thing as a symptomless bad fever?

I had no answers, except to say that I'd been having way too many blackouts and was losing way too much time lately. Or was I gaining time?

I dawdled in Kansas City—simply because I didn't have the drive to move on and I was a little scared of when and where I might wake up next. I somehow hit it off with some potheads that I met in a park and they let me crash at their place for a few nights. For some odd reason, I decided to change my name to Sean.

Why would someone who doesn't even know their real name make up a phony name? my inner voice had asked me.

I guess I'd always liked that name.

Anyway, we were out driving around, and the driver ran a red light and we got pulled over. The two cops separated the three of us. The cop with me asked me my name and I automatically answered "Mike." Meanwhile, the guys I was with told their cop my name was Sean. I was facing away from them and I didn't react when their cop called me over because I wasn't used to reacting to the name Sean.

"I believe he's talking to *you*," said my cop.

Oops, of course he was. What a mess. I thought I was done for. The guys I was with had enough pot stashed in the car to stuff your couch cushions with. The amazing thing is that the cops never searched the car, never gave the driver a ticket, *had* to have concluded that I was a runaway (with two names), but let us all get back in the car and leave! Ah, the wonderful sixties! Peace and love and cops who just want you the hell out of their town so they don't have to go through the hassle of arresting you. Ya gotta love it.

I randomly hopped a train that brought me to Iowa just at dusk, where it felt autumn-cold. I walked up to the engines to ask if they had any water. The guys were off of the engine, standing with their duffle bags.

"Where were you riding?" one of them asked me in an amused fashion.

"About fifty cars back. Where are we?"

"Iowa. Running away from home?"

I shook my head. "Heading home."

They of course offered help, asked why I didn't just call home, etc. I don't even remember what story I told them.

"What you want to do, although I shouldn't be helping you," said another of the railroad guys, "is catch an empty boxcar that has a name from back east—say, 'Jersey Central'—and stick with it. Usually, we send the empties back to their home railroads."

'Well, I'll be damned. You learn something new every day.'

Warned that I should make myself scarce before the next train crew arrived, I left the tracks and headed down the road into the medium-sized town. Some teenagers in a souped-up car took off out of an eatery, screeching and smoking their tires as they raced down the main street. They attracted the attention of a cop, who put his red light on and gave chase.

I got something to eat and then hunkered down in a cemetery for the chilly night. I slept in a lot of cemeteries during my time on the road. It's not as morbid as it sounds. There's usually well groomed grass to camp out on, and cemeteries are peaceful and deserted at night. I wound up giving up on sleep in the wee hours of the morning and had a cold, wet, miserable ride from Iowa to the Chicago area. I never went into the city. The surrounding urban blight was so scary that I never left the railroad yard area.

The next four trains that I hopped only traveled a short distance from one railroad yard to another. I got completely disorientated as to which direction anything was going and I was starting to wonder if I'd ever get out of the Chicago area without hopping on a bus. I wanted to take the railroader in Iowa's advice and find a car with "New Jersey" in its railroad name, but I never did see one. There were "Pennsylvania" and "New York Central" cars; but there were about ten thousand of them going in every direction.

At one point I had a kind of dreadful mental movie, starting at ground level and going ever higher while showing an endless landscape of factories and railroad yards. And here I was, tiny little Mike, lost forever in this industrial quagmire.

I did finally find an empty boxcar that said "Boston and Maine" and I figured that was close enough so I rode it out to Cleveland, Ohio before giving up on it in the railroad yards there. I went back to random train hopping and wound up in Buffalo. One of my wrong decisions there took me damn near to Canada: Niagara Falls, New York. From there, after a short ride back to yards in Buffalo, I continued south.

I bounced and swayed my way through the beautiful river valleys of upstate New York and didn't take a break from riding until I got to Binghamton. Early the next morning, after a frigid night camping by the river, I hopped a freight out of the east end of the Binghamton rail yards that I assumed would take me to New Jersey. Instead, I wound up in Scranton, Pennsylvania. Although I hated riding them, I hopped a slow, eastbound coal train out of Scranton that I hoped was heading to the Port of New York. Unfortunately, my ride terminated in the Delaware Water Gap area amongst numerous other coal cars at a power plant. My normal practice was to walk to the other end of the yards and catch another train. But the tracks at the other end didn't look as though they got much use. Across the river from New Jersey, I'd reached a dead end.

33

I aimlessly wandered back towards the Delaware Water Gap along the tracks that I'd ridden in on. A train passed on a different line that traversed the river on a cool old arched bridge.

"*That's* the train I should have been on," I mumbled. No chance of hopping it, though—it was going way too fast. "If only I'd been a little more patient in Scranton." I sighed.

I stopped walking and stared out over river. Although New Jersey was on the other side, I was still quite a ways from my switching spot. I had no idea if the switch back needed to be on August 24. If that was the case, I was over eleven months ahead of schedule. So, why the hell had I returned here? I'd been riding along with where fate seemed to be leading me, but I somehow lost my connection to it.

The scene before me was heartbreakingly beautiful. The golden late afternoon sunshine slanted between the mountains in huge, well-defined shafts, leaving my side of the river in shadow but brightly illuminating the trees and cliffs on the New Jersey side. All of this was reflecting in the river. Yet I couldn't enjoy it. Inside my head, all was dark and dreary. I felt as aimless and adrift as a leaf floating in the current.

As the twilight turned to darkness, I walked back the way I came, past the power plant. The locomotives were still there idling, but no one seemed to be around. I followed the rusty tracks across the Delaware River into New Jersey. No trains came by, although I could hear them on the other line. Shortly after crossing the river, I dropped down to a highway and headed east. I ducked out of sight as the infrequent cars passed and I walked all night. I must have gone twenty miles and at first light, I came to railroad tracks again. It was a good idea to get off of the road before dawn, so I went over to the tracks and started walking in what seemed to be the correct direction to get back to "my" bridge.

At sunrise, a freight train passed, kind of slow, but it was going a little too fast to hop onto. The woods and farm fields gave way to a town and I quietly passed through without stopping.

'You know, that is one thing I'll miss about the sixties: towns and cities with a discernible "edge" to them.'

The towns ended and then it was farms or woods until the next one—even in much of New Jersey. In 2015, suburban sprawl had not only blended populated areas with the surrounding countryside, but in many instances had connected previously separate urban areas together.

Contentedly walking by day or night—whichever suited me—was how I spent my last days in this adventure. I mostly slept in the daylight sun because it was too much of a pain in the neck to search the darkness for somewhere safe. If it was "after-school" hours and I saw a handy store, I went into towns for food and drink.

Eventually I found my way back to the bridge, arriving at mid-morning. I was too tired for the melodrama of wondering what year (or if) the other me would show up. I walked the tracks all day, reminiscing. That night, I attempted to sleep in a field of small pine trees that were probably being grown for Christmas trees. But around midnight, soaking wet from the dew—as so often happened to me while "sleeping under the stars" (which isn't nearly as romantic as it sounds—believe me)—I gave up on sleeping. In golden morning sunlight, I went under the bridge, found the most comfortable place to lie down, and fell into a deep sleep.

I awoke a few hours later and the first thing I did was to verify which me I was (still the kid.) I slid down to the track and took a piss and then I stood and took in the scene. Some of the leaves on the inner tree branches were changing to bright yellow on the black birches and orange on the maples. A maple leaf zigzagged through the dappled sunlight and dropped near me. I picked it up and admired it. Autumn: a time of winding-down, of transition, of change.

Whenever I'd imagined switching back, I pictured the exact same scenario as the previous switch, but in reverse. Typical of everything else in this adventure, it didn't happen the way I'd envisioned it would. As my inner voice would say, you don't "do" it; it happens. Somewhere, sometime as I walked for miles in a trance-like state, I switched back. I discovered that it was much easier to walk on the ATV trail where the second track had been before it occurred to me that if the second track was gone, it was 2015. I felt my face for stubble and smiled.

I let out a "Humph" laugh in my adult voice. "It was just that easy."

Out at the tracks, before I got to my truck, time was irrelevant and it felt as though I never left either era. So the elapsed time that I lived in the sixties—but that didn't register in 2015—had no meaning for me. The little pinging noises coming from under the hood shattered that illusion. I hadn't been gone long enough for the engine to cool down. The reality of the situation came over me in a dizzying wave.

I was way too worked up to just hop in and drive—especially after not having driven for so long—so I returned to the tracks for more walking. Eventually in the late afternoon, I revisited the bridge for a final goodbye. I mentally kicked myself for not burying a "time capsule" in the sixties that I could dig up in 2015 to prove to myself that it all really happened.

I climbed back up the embankment via the same route I'd taken so long and so short ago. Just for uniformity, I paused, looked back down and said, "See you around, kiddo." There was no little Mike huddled under the bridge though; we'd become one. I guess we were always one.

I returned to my truck and leaned against the grill as I watched the traffic on the highway. Compared to 1967, the 2015 cars seemed like oversized toys made out of plastic. And even though I tried to reason myself out of it, I was still surprised that my truck started "after sitting all that time."

From the front of the CVS, everything had been modernized. But when I drove around to the back of the building, I could still see the old "A&P" brick where it hadn't been covered up.

"There's where those kids were bouncing the ball. They'd be grown-up with kids of their own by now."

As I swung the truck around: "Ha, I'll be damned," I laughed. "The dumpster!"

Obviously, it wasn't the very same one that I'd raided on my first night as a kid in 1967, but it was still in the same general spot.

Don't tell me you're hungry already?

I smiled and headed for the highway.

I got stopped at the traffic light by "my" bridge and I glanced around at the other drivers. 'Wow, there're actually *people* in these cars.'

In some kid way, I'd come to view cars as just these moving metal things that you dodged when crossing streets.

Then my eyes drifted forlornly to the bridge.

It'll always be there in some form if you need it, Mike.

I smiled and nodded. The blare of the car horn behind me got me moving through the green light.

My adjustment process after switching back went completely the opposite way that I thought it would. I thought I'd immediately have a difficult time of it. But the night I switched back, I went out to a diner with my two closest friends as though I'd only made the plans a week ago. In a strange sort of way, I had.

Of course, they noticed a change in me immediately. But as for me, aside from my apartment and everything familiar having that strange "seeing it as though for the first time" sensation that you get after a long trip away from home, I felt completely readjusted. I felt just fine being back in my adult body. I'd always kept it in "kid" shape anyway. And I was very pleased—sometimes downright giddy—over once again having adult privilege and the comfy, secure life that can come with it.

It took a few months for me to start unraveling. As the novelty of being back in 2015 wore off, I found myself longing for the open road and I felt trapped in a car, anywhere indoors and in my life. In the fall and early winter, I visited the bridge every chance I got—rain or shine. Sometimes, I'd do a "live reenactment" of my switching experience: "This is where I first saw the other Mike, this is where I had my meltdown as I walked the tracks in the rain," etc. But gradually, my visits to the bridge have slackened. I was going to try to find the old farmer's house, but I never got around to it. I figured that by now, someone had probably torn it down and crammed a couple of McMansions in its place anyway.

I'm still single and I still don't let most people—sadly, even my closest friends—get too close. I still live very much in my own little world, but I try to cut myself some slack. I mean, how could you do what I did and still relate to people?

But I *am* a lot more emotionally stable now. Things that used to bother me no longer bother me as much. I joke that I used up my lifetime quota of mental meltdowns before and during my time as the kid wandering the country.

In some ways, I never completely switched back.

My eyes, brown my whole life before I switched (even says so on my driver's license) are green now.

I have the faint scar on my hip from injuring the other body on the fence in

Virginia; my little memento and proof that it really did happen. I love that scar. Occasionally, I'll reach back to feel it and panic if I don't find it right away. Technically, the scar should be on the other Mike's body, seeing as I was in it when I got injured. Why it's on this body I guess I'll never know.

Would I do it again? I don't know. I don't think I have the . . . the *passion* to switch again. As I write this, it's less than a month to my one-year anniversary. Now it really *is* a holiday—for me at least.

Because on August 24, 2015, I took a risk, threw it all away and became a kid again for a time. I put that poor kid through hell, but I somehow grew up, faced my fears, found peace and stopped hating myself in the process.

Every now and then—say, while brushing my teeth before bed or washing my hands in a restaurant bathroom—I unexpectedly catch my image in the mirror. With my too-long, shaggy hair (hair more befitting a ten-year-old, to be sure) falling into my now green eyes and the curious expression on my face, sometimes I don't see the fifty-three-year-old man that I am. I see the kid from under the bridge and the memories and emotions of this story come flooding back.

"I really did it, didn't I?"

Yup. Hey, have I ever asked you if it was worth it?

I smile through my tears. "Once or twice. It's always worth following your dreams."